HAVOC

HAVOC

By E. PHILLIPS OPPENHEIM

Author of "The Illustrious Prince," "The Lost
Ambassador." "A Prince of Sinners,"
"The Missioner," etc.

WITH FOUR ILLUSTRATIONS
By HOWARD CHANDLER CHRISTY

A L. BURT COMPANY

PUBLISHERS   NEW YORK

CONTENTS

CONTENTS

ILLUSTRATIONS

HAVOC

CHAPTER I

CROWNED HEADS MEET

BELLAMY, King's Spy, and Dorward, journalist, known
to fame in every English-speaking country, stood before
the double window of their spacious sitting-room, looking down upon the thoroughfare beneath. Both men
were laboring under a bitter sense of failure. Bellamy's
face was dark with forebodings; Dorward was irritated
and nervous. Failure was a new thing to him — a thing
which those behind the great journals which he represented understood less, even, than he. Bellamy loved
his country, and fear was gnawing at his heart.

Below, the crowds which had been waiting patiently
for many hours broke into a tumult of welcoming voices.
Down their thickly-packed lines the volume of sound
arose and grew, a faint murmur at first, swelling and
growing to a thunderous roar. Myriads of hats were suddenly torn from the heads of the excited multitude, hand-
kerchiefs waved from every window. It was a wonderful
greeting, this.

"The Czar on his way to the railway station," Bellamy
remarked.

The broad avenue was suddenly thronged with a mass
of soldiery — guardsmen of the most famous of Austrian
regiments, brilliant in their white uniforms, their flashing
helmets. The small brougham with its great black

horses was almost hidden within a ring of naked steel. Dorward, an American to the backbone and a bitter democrat, thrust out his under-lip.

"The Anointed of the Lord!" he muttered.

Far away from some other quarter came the same roar of voices, muffled yet insistent, charged with that faint, exciting timbre which seems always to live in the cry of the multitude.

"The Emperor," declared Bellamy. "He goes to the West station."

The commotion had passed. The crowds in the street below were on the move, melting away now with a muffled trampling of feet and a murmur of voices. The two men turned from their window back into the room. Dorward commenced to roll a cigarette with yellow-stained, nervous fingers, while Bellamy threw himself into an easy-chair with a gesture of depression.

"So it is over, this long-talked-of meeting," he said, half to himself, half to Dorward. "It is over, and Europe is left to wonder."

"They were together for scarcely more than an hour," Dorward murmured.

"Long enough," Bellamy answered. "That little room in the Palace, my friend, may yet become famous."

"If you and I could buy its secrets," Dorward remarked, finally shaping a cigarette and lighting it, "we should be big bidders, I think. I'd give fifty thousand dollars myself to be able to cable even a hundred words of their conversation."

"For the truth," Bellamy said, "the whole truth, there could be no price sufficient. We made our effort in different directions, both of us. With infinite pains I planted — I may tell you this now that the thing is over — seven spies in the Palace. They have been of as much use as rabbits. I don't believe that a single one of them got any further than the kitchens."

Dorward nodded gloomily.

"I guess they were n't taking any chances up there," he remarked. "There was n't a secretary in the room. Carstairs was nearly thrown out, and he had a permit to enter the Palace. The great staircase was held with soldiers, and Dick swore that there were Maxims in the corridors."

Bellamy sighed.

"We shall hear the roar of bigger guns before we are many months older, Dorward," he declared.

The journalist glanced at his friend keenly.

"You believe that?"

Bellamy shrugged his shoulders.

"Do you suppose that this meeting is for nothing?" he asked. "When Austria, Germany and Russia stand whispering in a corner, can't you believe it is across the North Sea that they point? Things have been shaping that way for years, and the time is almost ripe."

"You English are too nervous to live, nowadays," Dorward declared impatiently. "I'd just like to know what they said about America."

Bellamy smiled with faint but delicate irony.

"Without a doubt, the Prince will tell you," he said. "He can scarcely do more to show his regard for your country. He is giving you a special interview — you alone out of about two hundred journalists. Very likely he will give you an exact account of everything that transpired. First of all, he will assure you that this meeting has been brought about in the interests of peace. He will tell you that the welfare of your dear country is

foremost in the thoughts of his master. He will assure
you —"

"Say, you're jealous, my friend," Dorward interrupted calmly. "I wonder what you'd give me for my
ten minutes alone with the Chancellor, eh?"

"If he told me the truth," Bellamy asserted, "I'd give
my life for it. For the sort of stuff you're going to hear,
I'd give nothing. Can't you realize that for yourself,
Dorward? You know the man — false as Hell but with
the tongue of a serpent. He will grasp your hand; he
will declare himself glad to speak through you to the great
Anglo-Saxon races — to England and to his dear friends
the Americans. He is only too pleased to have the opportunity of expressing himself candidly and openly. Peace
is to be the watchword of the future. The white doves
have hovered over the Palace. The rulers of the earth
have met that the crash of arms may be stilled and that
this terrible unrest which broods over Europe shall finally
be broken up. They have pledged themselves hand in
hand to work together for this object, — Russia, broken
and humiliated, but with an immense army still available,
whose only chance of holding her place among the
nations is another and a successful war; Austria, on fire
for the seaboard — Austria, to whom war would give the
desire of her existence; Germany, with Bismarck's last
but secret words written in letters of fire on the walls of
her palaces, in the hearts of her rulers, in the brain of her
great Emperor. Colonies! Expansion! Empire! Whose
colonies, I wonder? Whose empire? Will he tell you
that, my friend Dorward?"

The journalist shrugged his shoulders and glanced at
the clock.

"I guess he'll tell me what he chooses and I shall

print it," he answered indifferently. "It's all part of the game, of course. I am not exactly chicken enough to expect the truth. All the same, my message will come from the lips of the Chancellor immediately after this wonderful meeting."

"He makes use of you," Bellamy declared, "to throw dust into our eyes and yours."

"Even so," Dorward admitted, "I don't care so long as I get the copy. It's good-bye, I suppose?"

Bellamy nodded.

"I shall go on to Berlin, perhaps, to-morrow," he said. "I can do no more good here. And you?"

"After I've sent my cable I'm off to Belgrade for a week, at any rate," Dorward answered. "I hear the women are forming rifle clubs all through Servia."

Bellamy smiled thoughtfully.

"I know one who'll want a place among the leaders," he murmured.

"Mademoiselle Idiale, I suppose?"

Bellamy assented.

"It's a queer position hers, if you like," he said. "All Vienna raves about her. They throng the Opera House every night to hear her sing, and they pay her the biggest salary which has ever been known here. Three parts of it she sends to Belgrade to the Chief of the Committee for National Defence. The jewels that are sent her anonymously go to the same place, all to buy arms to fight these people who worship her. I tell you, Dorward," he added, rising to his feet and walking to the window, "the patriotism of these people is something we colder races scarcely understand. Perhaps it is because we have never dwelt under the shadow of a conqueror. If ever Austria is given a free hand, it will be no mere war upon which she enters, — it will be a carnage, an extermination!"

Dorward looked once more at the clock and rose slowly to his feet.

"Well," he said, "I must n't keep His Excellency waiting. Good-bye, and cheer up, Bellamy! Your old country is n't going to turn up her heels yet."

Out he went — long, lank, uncouth, with yellow-stained fingers and hatchet-shaped, gray face — a strange figure but yet a power. Bellamy remained. For a while he seemed doubtful how to pass the time. He stood in front of the window, watching the dispersal of the crowds and the marching by of a regiment of soldiers, whose movements he followed with critical interest, for he, too, had been in the service. He had still a military bearing, — tall, and with complexion inclined to be dusky, a small black moustache, dark eyes, a silent mouth, — a man of many reserves. Even his intimates knew little of him. Nevertheless, his was the reticence which befitted well his profession.

After a time he sat down and wrote some letters. He had just finished when there came a sharp tap at the door. Before he could open his lips some one had entered. He heard the soft swirl of draperies and turned sharply round, then sprang to his feet and held out both his hands. There was expression in his face now — as much as he ever suffered to appear there.

"Louise!" he exclaimed. "What good fortune!"

She held his fingers for a moment in a manner which betokened a more than common intimacy. Then she threw herself into an easy-chair and raised her thick veil. Bellamy looked at her for a moment in sorrowful silence. There were violet lines underneath her beautiful eyes, her cheeks were destitute of any color. There was an abandonment of grief about her attitude which moved him. She sat as one broken-spirited, in whom the power of resistance was dead.

"It is over, then," she said softly, "this meeting. The word has been spoken."

He came and stood by her side.

"As yet," he reminded her, "we do not know what that word may be."

She shook her head mournfully.

"Who can doubt?" she exclaimed. "For myself, I feel it in the air! I can see it in the faces of the people who throng the city! I can hear it in the peals of those awful bells! You know nothing? You have heard nothing?"

Bellamy shook his head.

"I did all that was humanly possible," he said, dropping his voice. "An Englishman in Vienna to-day has very little opportunity. I filled the Palace with spies, but they had n't a dog's chance. There was n't even a secretary present. The Czar, the two Emperors and the Chancellor, — not another soul was in the room."

"If only Von Behrling had been taken!" she exclaimed. "He was there in reserve, I know, as stenographer. I have but to lift my hand and it is enough. I would have had the truth from him, whatever it cost me."

Bellamy looked at her thoughtfully. It was not for nothing that the Press of every European nation had called her the most beautiful woman in the world. He frowned slightly at her last words, for he loved her.

"Von Behrling was not even allowed to cross the threshold," he said sharply.

She moved her head and looked up at him. She was

leaning a little forward now, her chin resting upon her hands. Something about the lines of her long, supple body suggested to him the savage animal crouching for a spring. She was quiet, but her bosom was heaving, and he could guess at the passion within. With purpose he spoke to set it loose.

"You sing to-night?" he asked.

"Before God, no!" she answered, the anger blazing out of her eyes, shaking in her voice. "I sing no more in this accursed city!"

"There will be a revolution," Bellamy remarked. "I see that the whole city is placarded with notices. It is to be a gala night at the Opera. The royal party is to be present."

Her body seemed to quiver like a tree shaken by the wind.

"What do I care — I — I — for their gala night! If I were like Samson, if I could pull down the pillars of their Opera House and bury them all in its ruins, I would do it!"

He took her hand and smoothed it in his.

"Dear Louise, it is useless, this. You do everything that can be done for your country."

Her eyes were streaming and her fingers sought his.

"My friend David," she said, "you do not understand. None of you English yet can understand what it is to crouch in the shadow of this black fear, to feel a tyrant's hand come creeping out, to know that your life-blood and the life-blood of all your people must be shed, and shed in vain. To rob a nation of their liberty, ah! it is worse, this, than murder, — a worse crime than his who stains the soul of a poor innocent girl! It is a sin against nature herself!"

She was sobbing now, and she clutched his hands passionately.

"Forgive me," she murmured, "I am overwrought. I have borne up against this thing so long. I can do no more good here. I come to tell you that I go away till the time comes. I go to your London. They want me to sing for them there. I shall do it."

"You will break your engagement?"

She laughed at him scornfully.

"I am Idiale," she declared. "I keep no engagement if I do not choose. I will sing no more to this people whom I hate. My friend David, I have suffered enough. Their applause I loathe — their covetous eyes as they watch me move about the stage — oh, I could strike them all dead! They come to me, these young Austrian noblemen, as though I were already one of a conquered race. I keep their diamonds but I destroy their messages. Their jewels go to my chorus girls or to arm my people. But no one of them has had a kind word from me save where there has been something to be gained. Even Von Behrling I have fooled with promises. No Austrian shall ever touch my lips — I have sworn it!"

Bellamy nodded.

"Yes," he assented, "they call you cold here in the capital! Even in the Palace —"

She held out her hand.

"It is finished!" she declared. "I sing no more. I have sent word to the Opera House. I came here to be in hiding for a while. They will search for me everywhere. To-night or to-morrow I leave for England."

Bellamy stood thoughtfully silent.

"I am not sure that you are wise," he said. "You take it too much for granted that the end has come."

"And do you not yourself believe it ?" she demanded.
He hesitated.

"As yet there is no proof," he reminded her.

"Proof !"

She sat upright in her chair. Her hands thrust him
from her, her bosom heaved, a spot of color flared in her
cheeks.

"Proof !" she cried. "What do you suppose, then,
that these wolves have plotted for ? What else do you
suppose could be Austria's share of the feast ? Could n't
you hear our fate in the thunder of their voices when that
miserable monarch rode back to his captivity ? We are
doomed — betrayed ! You remember the Massacre of
St. Bartholomew, a blood-stained page of history for all
time. The world would tell you that we have outlived
the age of such barbarous doings. It is not true. My
friend David, it is not true. It is a more terrible thing,
this which is coming. Body and soul we are to perish."

He came over to her side once more and laid his hand
soothingly on hers. It was heart-rending to witness the
agony of the woman he loved.

"Dear Louise," he said, "after all, this is profitless.
There may yet be compromises."

She suffered her hand to remain in his, but the bitter-
ness did not pass out of her face or tone.

"Compromises !" she repeated. "Do you believe,
then, that we are like those ancient races who felt the
presence of a conqueror because their hosts were scattered in battle, and who suffered themselves passively to
be led into captivity ? My country can be conquered in
one way, and one way only, — not until her sons, ay,
and her daughters too, have perished, can these people
rule. They will come to an empty and a stricken country

— a country red with blood, desolate, with blackened houses and empty cities. The horror of it! Think, my friend David, the horror of it!"

Bellamy threw his head back with a sudden gesture of impatience.

"You take too much for granted," he declared. "England, at any rate, is not yet a conquered race. And there is France — Italy, too, if she is wise, will never suffer this thing from her ancient enemy."

"It is the might of the world which threatens," she murmured. "Your country may defend herself, but here she is powerless. Already it has been proved. Last year you declared yourself our friend — you and even Russia. Of what avail was it? Word came from Berlin and you were powerless."

Then tragedy broke into the room, tragedy in the shape of a man demented. For fifteen years Bellamy had known Arthur Dorward, but this man was surely a stranger! He was hatless, dishevelled, wild. A dull streak of color had mounted almost to his forehead, his eyes were on fire.

"Bellamy!" he cried. "Bellamy!"

Words failed him suddenly. He leaned against the table, breathless, panting heavily.

"For God's sake, man," Bellamy began, —

"Alone!" Dorward interrupted. "I must see you alone! I have news!"

Mademoiselle Idiale rose. She touched Bellamy on the shoulder.

"You will come to me, or telephone," she whispered. "So?"

Bellamy opened the door and she passed out, with a farewell pressure of his fingers. Then he closed it firmly and came back.

CHAPTER II

"WHAT'S wrong, old man?" Bellamy asked quickly.

Dorward from a side table had seized the bottle of whiskey and a siphon, and was mixing himself a drink with trembling fingers. He tossed it off before he spoke a word. Then he turned around and faced his companion.

"Bellamy," he ordered, "lock the door."

Bellamy obeyed. He had no doubt now but that Dorward had lost his head in the Chancellor's presence — had made some absurd attempt to gain the knowledge which they both craved, and had failed.

"Bellamy," Dorward exclaimed, speaking hoarsely and still a little out of breath, "I guess I've had the biggest slice of luck that was ever dealt out to a human being. If only I can get safe out of this city, I tell you I've got the greatest scoop that living man ever handled."

"You don't mean that —"

Dorward wiped his forehead and interrupted.

"It's the most amazing thing that ever happened," he declared, "but I've got it here in my pocket, got it in black and white, in the Chancellor's own handwriting."

"Got what?"

"Why, what you and I, an hour ago, would have given a million for," Dorward replied.

Bellamy's expression was one of blank but wondering incredulity.

"You can't mean this, Dorward!" he exclaimed. "You may have something — just what the Chancellor wants you to print. You're not supposing for an instant that you've got the whole truth?"

Dorward's smile was the smile of certainty, his face that of a conqueror.

"Here in my pocket," he declared, striking his chest, "in the Chancellor's own handwriting. I tell you I've got the original verbatim copy of everything that passed and was resolved upon this afternoon between the Czar of Russia, the Emperor of Austria and the Emperor of Germany. I've got it word for word as the Chancellor took it down. I've got their decision. I've got their several undertakings."

Bellamy for a moment was stricken dumb. He looked toward the door and back into his friend's face aglow with triumph. Then his power of speech returned.

"Do you mean to say that you stole it?"

Dorward struck the table with his fist.

"Not I! I tell you that the Chancellor gave it to me, gave it to me with his own hands, willingly, — pressed it upon me. No, don't scoff!" he went on quickly. "Listen! This is a genuine thing. The Chancellor's mad. He was lying in a fit when I left the Palace. It will be in all the evening papers. You will hear the boys shouting it in the streets within a few minutes. Don't interrupt and I'll tell you the whole truth. You can believe me or not, as you like. It makes no odds. I arrived punctually and was shown up into the anteroom. Even from there I could hear loud voices in the inner chamber and I knew that something was up. Presently a little fellow came out to me — a dark-bearded chap with gold-rimmed glasses. He was very polite, introduced himself

as the Chancellor's physician, regretted exceedingly that
the Chancellor was unwell and could see no one, — the
excitement and hard work of the last few days had knocked
him out. Well, I stood there arguing as pleasantly as I
could about it, and then all of a sudden the door of the
inner room was thrown open. The Chancellor himself
stood on the threshold. There was no doubt about his
being ill; his face was as pale as parchment, his eyes were
simply wild, and his hair was all ruffled as though he had
been standing upon his head. He began to talk to the
physician in German. I did n't understand him until
he began to swear, — then it was wonderful! In the end
he brushed them all away and, taking me by the arm, led
me right into the inner room. For a long time he went
on jabbering away half to himself, and I was wondering
how on earth to bring the conversation round to the
things I wanted to know about. Then, all of a sudden, he
turned to me and seemed to remember who I was and
what I wanted. 'Ah!' he said, 'you are Dorward, the
American journalist. I remember you now. Lock the
door.' I obeyed him pretty quick, for I had noticed they
were mighty uneasy outside, and I was afraid they'd be
disturbing us every moment. 'Come and sit down,' he
ordered. I did so at once. 'You're a sensible fellow,'
he declared. 'To-day every one is worrying me. They
think that I am not well. It is foolish. I am quite well.
Who would not be well on such a day as this?' I told
him that I had never seen him looking better in my life,
and he nodded and seemed pleased. 'You have come to
hear the truth about the meeting of my master with the
Czar and the Emperor of Germany?' he asked. 'That's
so,' I told him. 'America's more than a little interested
in these things, and I want to know what to tell her.'

Then he leaned across the table. 'My young friend,' he said, 'I like you. You are straightforward. You speak plainly and you do not worry me. It is good. You shall tell your country what it is that we have planned, what the things are that are coming. Yours is a great and wise country. When they know the truth, they will remember that Europe is a long way off and that the things which happen there are really no concern of theirs.' 'You are right,' I assured him, — 'dead right. Treat us openly, — that's all we ask.' 'Shall I not do that, my young friend?' he answered. 'Now look, I give you this.' He fumbled through all his pockets and at last he drew out a long envelope, sealed at both ends with black sealing wax on which was printed a coat of arms with two tigers facing each other. He looked toward the door cautiously, and there was just that gleam in his eyes which madmen always have. 'Here it is,' he whispered, 'written with my own hand. This will tell you exactly what passed this afternoon. It will tell you our plans. It will tell you of the share which my master and the other two are taking. Button it up safely,' he said, 'and, whatever you do, do not let them know outside that you have got it. Between you and me,' he went on, leaning across the table, 'something seems to have happened to them all to-day. There's my old doctor there. He is worrying all the time, but he himself is not well. I can see it whenever he comes near me.' I nodded as though I understood and the Chancellor tapped his forehead and grinned. Then I got up as casually as I could, for I was terribly afraid that he would n't let me go. We shook hands, and I tell you his fingers were like pieces of burning coal. Just as I was moving, some one knocked at the door. Then he began to storm again, kicked his chair over, threw a paperweight at the window, and talked such nonsense that I could n't follow him. I unlocked the door myself and found the doctor there. I contrived to look as frightened as possible. 'His Highness is not well enough to talk to me,' I whispered. 'You had better look after him.' I heard a shout behind and a heavy fall. Then I closed the door and slipped away as quietly as I could — and here I am."

Bellamy drew a long breath.

"My God, but this is wonderful!" he muttered. "How long is it since you left the Palace?"

"About ten minutes or a quarter of an hour," Dorward answered.

"They'll find it out at once," declared the other. "They'll miss the paper. Perhaps he'll tell them himself that he has given it to you. Don't let us run any risks, Dorward. Tear it open. Let us know the truth, at any rate. If you have to part with the document, we can remember its contents. Out with it, man, quick! They may be here at any moment."

Dorward drew a few steps back. Then he shook his head.

"I guess not," he said firmly.

Bellamy regarded his friend in blank and uncomprehending amazement.

"What do you mean?" he exclaimed. "You're not going to keep it to yourself? You know what it means to me — to England?"

"Your old country can look after herself pretty well," Dorward declared. "Anyhow, she'll have to take her chance. I am not here as a philanthropist. I am an American journalist, and I'll part to nobody with the biggest thing that's ever come into any man's hands."

Bellamy, with a tremendous effort, maintained his self-control.

"What are you going to do with it?" he asked quickly.

"I tell you I'm off out of the country to-night," Dorward declared. "I shall head for England. Pearce is there himself, and I tell you it will be just the greatest day of my life when I put this packet in his hand. We'll make New York hum, I can promise you, and Europe too."

Bellamy's manner was perfectly quiet — too quiet to be altogether natural. His hand was straying towards his pocket.

"Dorward," he said, speaking rapidly, and keeping his back to the door, "you don't realize what you're up against. This sort of thing is new to you. You haven't a dog's chance of leaving Vienna alive with that in your pocket. If you trust yourself in the Orient Express to-night, you'll never be allowed to cross the frontier. By this time they know that the packet is missing; they know, too, that you are the only man who could have it, whether the Chancellor has told them the truth or not. Open it at once so that we get some good out of it. Then we'll go round to the Embassy. We can slip out by the back way, perhaps. Remember I have spent my life in the service, and I tell you that there's no other place in the city where your life is worth a snap of the fingers but at your Embassy or mine. Open the packet, man."

"I think not," Dorward answered firmly. "I am an American citizen. I have broken no laws and done no one any harm. If there's any slaughtering about, I guess they'll hesitate before they begin with Arthur Dorward. . . . Don't be a fool, man!"

2

He took a quick step backward, — he was looking into the muzzle of Bellamy's revolver.

"Dorward," the latter exclaimed, "I can't help it! Yours is only a personal ambition — I stand for my country. Share the knowledge of that packet with me or I shall shoot."

"Then shoot and be d—d to you!" Dorward declared fiercely. "This is my show, not yours. You and your country can go to —"

He broke off without finishing his sentence. There was a thunderous knocking at the door. The two men looked at one another for a moment, speechless. Then Bellamy, with a smothered oath, replaced the revolver in his pocket.

"You've thrown away our chance," he said bitterly.

The knocking was repeated. When Bellamy with a shrug of the shoulders answered the summons, three men in plain clothes entered. They saluted Bellamy, but their eyes were traveling around the room.

"We are seeking Herr Dorward, the American journalist!" one exclaimed. "He was here but a moment ago."

Bellamy pointed to the inner door. He had had too much experience in such matters to attempt any prevarication. The three men crossed the room quickly and Bellamy followed in the rear. He heard a cry of disappointment from the foremost as he opened the door. The inner room was empty!

CHAPTER III

LOUISE looked up eagerly as he entered.

"There is news!" she exclaimed. "I can see it in your face."

"Yes," Bellamy answered, "there is news! That is why I have come. Where can we talk?"

She rose to her feet. Before them the open French windows led on to a smooth green lawn. She took his arm.

"Come outside with me," she said. "I am shut up here because I will not see the doctors whom they send, or any one from the Opera House. An envoy from the Palace has been and I have sent him away."

"You mean to keep your word, then?"

"Have I ever broken it? Never again will I sing in this city. It is so."

Bellamy looked around. The garden of the villa was enclosed by high gray stone walls. They were secure here, at least, from eavesdroppers. She rested her fingers lightly upon his arm, holding up the skirts of her loose gown with her other hand.

"I have spoken to you," he said, "of Dorward, the American journalist."

She nodded.

"Of course," she assented. "You told me that the Chancellor had promised him an interview for to-day."

"Well, he went to the Palace and the Chancellor saw him."

She looked at him with upraised eyebrows.

"The newspapers are full of lies as usual, then, I suppose. The latest telegrams say that the Chancellor is dangerously ill."

"It is quite true," Bellamy declared. "What I am going to tell you is surprising, but I had it from Dorward himself. When he reached the Palace, the Chancellor was practically insane. His doctors were trying to persuade him to go to his room and lie down, but he heard Dorward's voice and insisted upon seeing him. The man was mad — on the verge of a collapse — and he handed over to Dorward his notes, and a verbatim report of all that passed at the Palace this morning."

She looked at him incredulously.

"My dear David!" she exclaimed.

"It is amazing," he admitted, "but it is the truth. I know it for a fact. The man was absolutely beside himself, he had no idea what he was doing."

"Where is it?" she asked quickly. "You have seen it?"

"Dorward would not give it up," he said bitterly. "While we argued in our sitting-room at the hotel the police arrived. Dorward escaped through the bedroom and down the service stairs. He spoke of trying to catch the Orient Express to-night, but I doubt if they will ever let him leave the city."

"It is wonderful, this," she murmured softly. "What are you going to do?"

"Louise, you and I have few secrets from each other. I would have killed Dorward to obtain that sealed envelope, because I believe that the knowledge of its contents in London to-day would save us from disaster. To know how far each is pledged, and from which direction the first blow is to come, would be our salvation."

"I cannot understand," she said, "why he should have refused to share his knowledge with you. He is an American — it is almost the same thing as being an Englishman. And you are friends, — I am sure that you have helped him often."

"It was a matter of vanity — simply cursed vanity," Bellamy answered. "It would have been the greatest journalistic success of modern times for him to have printed that document, word for word, in his paper. He fights for his own hand alone."

"And you?" she whispered.

"He will have to reckon with me," Bellamy declared. "I know that he is going to try and leave Vienna to-night, and if he does I shall be at his heels."

She nodded her head thoughtfully.

"I, too," she announced. "I come with you, my friend. I do no more good here, and they worry my life out all the time. I come to sing in London at Covent Garden. I have agreements there which only await my signature. We will go together; is it not so?"

"Very well," he answered, "only remember that my movements must depend very largely upon Dorward's. The train leaves at eight o'clock, station time. I have already a coupé reserved."

"I come with you," she murmured. "I am very weary of this city."

They walked on for a few paces in silence. Bellamy looked around the gardens, brilliant with flowering shrubs and rose trees, with here and there some delicate piece of statuary half-hidden amongst the wealth of foliage. The villa had once belonged to a royal favorite, and the grounds had been its chief glory. They reached a sheltered seat and sat down. A few yards away a tiny waterfall came tumbling over the rocks into a deep pool. They were hidden from the windows of the villa by the boughs of a drooping chestnut tree. Bellamy stooped and kissed her upon the lips.

"Ours is a strange courtship, Louise," he whispered softly.

She took his hand in hers and smoothed it. She had returned his kiss, but she drew a little further away from him.

"Ah! my dear friend," looking at him with sorrow in her eyes, "courtship is scarcely the word, is it? For you and me there is nothing to hope for, nothing beyond."

He leaned towards her.

"Never believe that," he begged. "These days are dark enough, Heaven knows, yet the work of every one has its goal. Even our turn may come."

Something flickered for a moment in her face, something which seemed to make a different woman of her. Bellamy saw it, and hardened though he was he felt the slow stirring of his own pulses. He kissed her hand passionately and she shivered.

"We must not talk of these things," she said. "We must not think of them. At least our friendship has been wonderful. Now I must go in. I must tell my maid and arrange to steal away to-night."

They stood up, and he held her in his arms for a moment. Though her lips met his freely enough, he was very conscious of the reserve with which she yielded herself to him, conscious of it and thankful, too. They walked up the path together, and as they went she plucked a red rose and thrust it through his buttonhole.

"If we had no dreams," she said softly, "life would not be possible. Perhaps some day even we may pluck roses together."

He raised her fingers to his lips. It was not often that they lapsed into sentiment. When she spoke again it was finished.

"You had better leave," she told him, "by the garden gate. There are the usual crowd in my anteroom, and it is well that you and I are not seen too much together."

"Till this evening," he whispered, as he turned away. "I shall be at the station early. If Dorward is taken, I shall still leave Vienna. If he goes, it may be an eventful journey."

CHAPTER IV

DORWARD, whistling softly to himself, sat in a corner of his coupé rolling innumerable cigarettes. He was a man of unbounded courage and wonderful resource, but with a slightly exaggerated idea as to the sanctity of an American citizen. He had served his apprenticeship in his own country, and his name had become a household word owing to his brilliant success as war correspondent in the Russo-Japanese War. His experience of European countries, however, was limited. After the more obvious dangers with which he had grappled and which he had overcome during his adventurous career, he was disposed to be a little contemptuous of the subtler perils at which his friend Bellamy had plainly hinted. He had made his escape from the hotel without any very serious difficulty, and since that time, although he had taken no particular precautions, he had remained unmolested. From his own point of view, therefore, it was perhaps only reasonable that he should no longer have any misgiving as to his personal safety. Arrest as a thief was the worst which he had feared. Even that he seemed now to have evaded.

The coupé was exceedingly comfortable and, after all, he had had a somewhat exciting day. He lit a cigarette and stretched himself out with a murmur of immense satisfaction. He was close upon the great triumph of his life. He was perfectly content to lie there and look out upon the flying landscape, upon which the shadows were now fast descending. He was safe, absolutely safe, he assured himself. Nevertheless, when the door of his coupé was opened, he started almost like a guilty man. The relief in his face as he recognized his visitor was obvious. It was Bellamy who entered and dropped into a seat by his side.

"Wasting your time, are n't you?" the latter remarked, pointing to the growing heap of cigarettes.

"Well, I guess not," Dorward answered. "I can smoke this lot before we reach London."

Bellamy smiled enigmatically.

"I don't think that you will," he said.

"Why not?"

"You are such a sanguine person," Bellamy sighed. "Personally, I do not think that there is the slightest chance of your reaching London at all."

Dorward laughed scornfully.

"And why not?" he asked.

Bellamy merely shrugged his shoulders. Dorward seemed to find the gesture irritating.

"You've got espionage on the brain, my dear friend," he declared dryly. "I suppose it's the result of your profession. I may not know so much about Europe as you do, but I am inclined to think that an American citizen traveling with his passport on a train like this is moderately safe, especially when he's not above a scrap by way of taking care of himself."

"You're a plucky fellow," remarked Bellamy.

"I don't see any pluck about it. In Vienna, I must admit, I should n't have been surprised if they'd tried to fake up some sort of charge against me, but anyhow they

·did n't. Guess they'd find it a pretty tall order trying to interfere with an American citizen."

Bellamy looked at his friend curiously.

"I suppose you're not bluffing, by any chance, Dorward?" he said. "You really believe what you say?"

"Why in thunder should n't I?" Dorward asked.

Bellamy sighed.

"My dear Dorward," he said, "it is amazing to me that a man of your experience should talk and behave like a baby. You've taken some notice of your fellow-passengers, I suppose?"

"I've seen a few of them," Dorward answered carelessly. "What about them?"

"Nothing much," Bellamy declared, "except that there are, to my certain knowledge, three high officials of the Secret Police of Austria in the next coupé but one, and at least four or five of their subordinates somewhere on board the train."

Dorward withdrew his cigarette from his mouth and looked at his friend keenly.

"I guess you're trying to scare me, Bellamy," he remarked.

But Bellamy was suddenly grave. There had come into his face an utterly altered expression. His tone, when he spoke, was almost solemn.

"Dorward," he said, "upon my honor, I assure you that what I have told you is the truth. I cannot seem to make you realize the seriousness of your position. When you left the Palace with that paper in your pocket, you were, to all intents and purposes, a doomed man. Your passport and your American citizenship count for absolutely nothing. I have come in to warn you that if you have any last messages to leave, you had better give them to me now."

"This is a pretty good bluff you're putting up!" Dorward exclaimed contemptuously. "The long and short of it is, I suppose, that you want me to break the seal of this document and let you read it."

Bellamy shook his head.

"It is too late for that, Dorward," he said. "If the seal were broken, they'd very soon guess where I came in, and it would n't help the work I have in hand for me to be picked up with a bullet in my forehead on the railway track."

Dorward frowned uneasily.

"What are you here for, anyway, then?" he asked.

"Well, frankly, not to argue with you," Bellamy answered. "As a matter of fact, you are of no use to me any longer. I am sorry, old man. You can't say that I did n't give you good advice. I am bound to play for my own hand, though, in this matter, and if I get any benefit at all out of my journey, it will be after some regrettable accident has happened to you."

"Say, ring the bell for drinks and chuck this!" Dorward exclaimed. "I've had about enough of it. I am not denying anything you say, but if these fellows really are on board, they'll think twice before they meddle with me."

"On the contrary," Bellamy assured him, "they will not take the trouble to think at all. Their minds are perfectly made up as to what they are going to do. However, that's finished. I have nothing more to say."

Dorward gazed for a minute or two fixedly out of the window.

"Look here, Bellamy," he said, turning abruptly round,

"supposing I change my mind, supposing I open this precious document and let you read it over with me?"

Bellamy rose hastily to his feet.

"You must not think of it!" he exclaimed. "You would simply write my death-warrant. Don't allude to that matter again. I have risked enough in coming in here to sit with you."

"Then, for Heaven's sake, don't stop any longer!" Dorward said irritably. "You get on my nerves with all this foolish talk. In an hour's time I am going to bolt my door and go to sleep. We'll breakfast together in the morning, if you like."

Bellamy said nothing. The steward had brought them the whiskies and sodas which Dorward had ordered. Bellamy raised his tumbler to his lips and set it down again.

"Forgive me," he said, "I do not think that I am thirsty."

Dorward drank his off at a gulp. Almost immediately he closed his eyes. Bellamy, with a little shrug of the shoulders, left him alone. As he passed along to his own coupé, he met Louise in the corridor.

"You have seen Von Behrling?" he whispered.

She nodded.

"He is in that coupé, number 7, alone," she said. "I invited him to come in with me but he seemed embarrassed. It is his companions who watch him all the time. He has promised to talk with me later."

In the middle of the night, Louise opened her eyes to find Bellamy bending over her.

"Louise," he whispered, "it is Von Behrling who will take possession of the packet. They have been discussing whether it will not be safer to go on to London instead of doubling back. See Von Behrling again. Do all you can to persuade him to come to London, — all you can, Louise, remember."

"So!" she whispered. "I shall put on my dressing-gown and sit in the corridor. It is hot here."

Bellamy glided out, closing the door softly behind him. The train was rushing on now through the blackness of an unusually dark night. For some time he sat in his own compartment, listening. The voices whose muttered conversation he had overheard were silent now, but once he fancied that he heard shuffling footsteps and a little cry. In his heart he knew well that before morning Dorward would have disappeared. The man within him was hard to subdue. He longed to make his way to Dorward's side, to interfere in this terribly unequal struggle, yet he made no movement. Dorward was a man and a friend, but what was a life more or less? It was to a greater cause that he was pledged. Towards three o'clock he lay down on his bed and slept. . . .

The train attendant brought him his coffee soon after daylight. The man's hands were trembling.

"Where are we?" Bellamy asked sleepily.

"Near Munich, Monsieur," the man answered. "Monsieur noticed, perhaps, that we stopped for some time in the night?"

Bellamy shook his head.

"I sleep soundly," he said. "I heard nothing."

"There has been an accident," the man declared. "An American gentleman who got in at Vienna was drinking whiskey all night and became very drunk. In a tunnel he threw himself out upon the line."

Bellamy shuddered a little. He had been prepared, but none the less it was an awful thing, this.

"You are sure that he is dead?" he asked.

The man was very sure indeed.

"There is a doctor from Vienna upon the train, sir," he said. "He examined him at once, but death must have been instantaneous."

Bellamy drew a long breath and commenced to put on his clothes. The next move was for him.

CHAPTER V

BELLAMY stole along the half-lit corridors of the train until he came to the coupé which had been reserved for Mademoiselle Idiale. Assured that he was not watched, he softly turned the handle of the door and entered. Louise was sitting up in her dressing-gown, drinking her coffee. He held up his finger and she greeted him only with a nod.

"Forgive me, Louise," he whispered, "I dared not knock, and I was obliged to see you at once."

She smiled.

"It is of no consequence," she said. "One is always prepared here. The porter, the ticket-man, and at the customs — they all enter. Is anything wrong?"

"It has happened," he answered.

She shivered a little and her face became grave.

"Poor fellow!" she murmured.

"He simply sat still and asked for it," Bellamy declared, still speaking in a cautious undertone. "He would not be warned. I could have saved him, if any one could, but he would not hear reason."

"He was what you call pig-headed," she remarked.

"He has paid the penalty," Bellamy continued. "Now listen to me, Louise. I got into that small coupé next to Von Behrling's, and I feel sure, from what I overheard, that they will go on to London, all three of them."

"Who is there on the train?" she demanded.

"Baron Streuss, who is head of the Secret Police, Von Behrling and Adolf Kahn," Bellamy answered. "Then there are four or five Secret Service men of the rank and file, but they are all traveling separately. Von Behrling has the packet. The others form a sort of cordon around him."

"But why," she asked, "does he go on to London? Why not return to Vienna?"

"For one thing," Bellamy replied, with a grim smile, "they are afraid of me. Then you must remember that this affair of Dorward will be talked about. They do not want to seem in any way implicated. To return from any one of these stations down the line would create suspicion."

She nodded.

"Well?"

"I am going to leave the train at the next stop," he continued. "I find that I shall just catch the Northern Express to Berlin. From there I shall come on to London as quickly as I can. You know the address of my rooms?"

She nodded.

"15, Fitzroy Street."

"When I get there, let me have a line waiting to tell me where I can see you. While I am on the train you will find Von Behrling almost inaccessible. Directly I have gone it will be different. Play with him carefully. He should not be difficult. To tell you the truth, I am rather surprised that he has been trusted upon a mission like this. He was in disgrace with the Chancellor a short while ago, and I know that he was hurt at not being allowed to attend the conference. The others will watch him closely, but they cannot overhear everything that passes between you two. Von Behrling is a poor man. You will know how to make him wish he were rich."

Very slowly her eyebrows rose up. She looked at him doubtfully.

"It is a slender chance, David," she remarked. "Von Behrling is a little wild, I know, and he pretends to be very much in love with me, but I do not think that he would sell his country. Then, too, see how he will be watched. I do not suppose that they will leave us alone for a moment."

Bellamy took her hands in his, gripping them with almost unnatural force.

"Louise," he declared earnestly, "you don't quite realize Von Behrling's special weakness and your extraordinary strength. You know that you are beautiful, I suppose, but you do not quite know what that means. I have heard men talk about you till one would think that they were children. You have something of that art or guile — call it what you will — which passes from you through a man's blood to his brain, and carries him indeed to Heaven — but carries him there mad. Louise, don't be angry with me for what I say. Remember that I know my sex. I know you, too, and I trust you, but you can turn Von Behrling from a sane, honorable man into what you will, without suffering even his lips to touch your fingers. Von Behrling has that packet in his possession. When I come to see you in London, I will bring you twenty thousand pounds in Bank of England notes. With that Von Behrling might fancy himself on his way to America — with you."

She closed her eyes for a moment. Perhaps she wished to keep hidden from him the thoughts which chased one another through her brain. He wished to make use of her — of her, the woman whom he loved. Then she remembered that it was for her country and his, and the anger passed.

"But I am afraid," she said softly, "that the moment they reach London this document will be taken to the Austrian Embassy."

"Before then," Bellamy declared, "Von Behrling must not know whether he is in heaven or upon earth. It will not be opened in London. He can make up another packet to resemble precisely the one of which he robbed Dorward. Oh! it is a difficult game, I know, but it is worth playing. Remember, Louise, that we are not petty conspirators. It is your country's very existence that is threatened. It is for her sake as well as for England."

"I shall do my best," she murmured, looking into his face. "Oh, you may be sure that I shall do my best!"

Bellamy raised her fingers to his lips and stole away. The electric lamps had been turned out, but the morning was cloudy and the light dim. Back in his own berth, he put his things together, ready to leave at Munich. Then he rang for the porter.

"I am getting out at the next stop," he announced.

"Very good, Monsieur," the man answered.

Bellamy looked at him closely.

"You are a Frenchman?"

"It is so, Monsieur!"

"I may be wrong," Bellamy continued slowly, "but I believe that if I asked you a question and it concerned some Germans and Austrians you would tell me the truth."

The man's gesture was inimitable. Englishmen to him were obviously the salt of the earth. Germans and Aus-

trians — why, they existed as the cattle in the fields —
nothing more. Bellamy gave him a sovereign.

"There were three Austrians who got in at Vienna,"
he said. "They are in numbers ten and eleven."

"But yes, Monsieur!" the man assented. "As yet I
think they are fast asleep. Not one of them has rung for
his coffee."

"Where are they booked for?"

"For London, Monsieur."

"You do not happen," Bellamy continued, "to have
heard them say anything about leaving the train before
then?"

"On the contrary, sir," the porter answered, "two of
the gentlemen have been inquiring about the boat across
to Dover. They were very anxious to travel by a turbine."

Bellamy nodded.

"Thank you very much. You will be so discreet as
to forget that I have asked you any questions concerning
them. As for me, if one would know, I am on my way
to Berlin."

The bell rang. The man looked outside and put his
head once more in Bellamy's coupé.

"It is one of the gentleman who has rung," he declared.
"If anything is said about leaving the train, I shall report
it at once to Monsieur."

"You will do well," Bellamy answered.

The porter returned in a few moments.

"Two of the gentlemen, sir," he announced, "are un-
dressed and in their pyjamas. They have ordered their
breakfast to be served after we leave Munich."

Bellamy nodded.

"Further, sir," the man continued, coming a little
closer, "one of them asked me whether the English gentle-

man — meaning you — was going through to London
or not. I told them that you were getting out at the next
station and that I thought you were going to Berlin."

"Quite right," Bellamy said. "If they ask any more
questions, let me know."

Mademoiselle Idiale, with the aid of one of the two
maids who were traveling with her, was able to make a
sufficiently effective toilette. At a few minutes before the
time for luncheon, she walked down the corridor and
recognized Von Behrling, who was sitting with his companions in one of the compartments.

"Ah, it is indeed you, then!" she exclaimed, smiling
at him.

He rose to his feet and came out. Tall, with a fair
moustache and blue eyes, he was often taken for an Englishman and was inclined to be proud of the fact.

"You have rested well, I trust, Mademoiselle?" he
asked, bowing low over her fingers.

"Excellently," replied Louise. "Will you not take me
in to luncheon? The car is full of men and I am not comfortable alone. It is not pleasant, either, to eat with one's
maids."

"I am honored," he declared. "Will you permit me
for one moment?"

He turned and spoke to his companions. Louise saw
at once that they were protesting vigorously. She saw,
too, that Von Behrling only became more obstinate and
that he was very nearly angry. She moved a few steps
on down the corridor, and stood looking out of the window. He joined her almost immediately.

"Come," he said, "they will be serving luncheon in
five minutes. We will go and take a good place."

"Your friends, I am afraid," she remarked, "did not like your leaving them. They are not very gallant."

"To me it is indifferent," he answered, fiercely twirling his moustache. "Streuss there is an old fool. He has always some fancy in his brain."

Louise raised her eyebrows slightly.

"You are your own master, I suppose," she said. "The Baron is used to command his policemen, and sometimes he forgets. There are many people who find him too autocratic."

"He means well," Von Behrling asserted. "It is his manner only which is against him."

They found a comfortable table, and she sat smiling at him across the white cloth.

"If this is not Sachers," she said, "it is at least more pleasant than lunching alone."

"I can assure you, Mademoiselle," he declared, with a vigorous twirl of his moustache, "that I find it so."

"Always gallant," she murmured. "Tell me, is it true of you — the news which I heard just before I left Vienna? Have you really resigned your post with the Chancellor?"

"You heard that?" he asked slowly.

She hesitated for a moment.

"I heard something of the sort," she admitted. "To be quite candid with you, I think it was reported that the Chancellor was making a change on his own account."

"So that is what they say, is it? What do they know about it — these gossipers?"

"You were not allowed at the conference yesterday," she remarked.

"No one was allowed there, so that goes for nothing."

"Ah! well," she said, looking meditatively out upon

the landscape, "a year ago the thought of that conference would have driven me wild. I should not have been content until I had learned somehow or other what had transpired. Lately, I am afraid, my interest in my country seems to have grown a trifle cold. Perhaps because I have lived in Vienna I have learned to look at things from your point of view. Then, too, the world is a selfish place, and our own little careers are, after all, the most important part of it."

Von Behrling eyed her curiously.

"It seems strange to hear you talk like this," he remarked.

She looked out of the window for a moment.

"Oh! I still love my country, in a way," she answered, "and I still hate all Austrians, in a way, but it is not as it used to be with me, I must admit. If we had two lives, I would give one to my country and keep one for myself. Since we have only one, I am afraid, after all, that I am human, and I want to taste some of its pleasures."

"Some of its pleasures," Von Behrling repeated, a little gloomily. "Ah, that is easy enough for you, Mademoiselle!"

"Not so easy as it may appear," she answered. "One needs many things to get the best out of life. One needs wealth and one needs love, and one needs them while one is young, while one can enjoy."

"It is true," Von Behrling admitted, — "quite true."

"If one is not careful," she continued, "one lets the years slip by. They can never come again. If one does not live while one is young, there is no other chance."

Von Behrling assented with renewed gloom. He was twenty-five years old, and his income barely paid for his uniforms. Of late, this fact had materially interfered with his enjoyments.

"It is strange," he said, "that you should talk like this. You have the world at your feet, Mademoiselle. You have only to throw the handkerchief."

Her lips parted in a dazzling smile. The bluest eyes in the world grew softer as they looked into his. Von Behrling felt his cheeks burn.

"My friend, it is not so easy," she murmured. "Tell me," she continued, "why it is that you have so little self-confidence. Is it because you are poor?"

"I am a beggar," —bitterly.

She shrugged her shoulders.

"Well," she said, glancing down the menu which the waiter had brought, "if you are poor and content to remain so, one must presume that you have compensations."

"But I have none!" he declared. "You should know that — you, Mademoiselle. Life for me means one thing and one thing only!"

She looked at him, for a moment, and down upon the tablecloth. Von Behrling shook like a man in the throes of some great passion.

"We talk too intimately," she whispered, as the people began to file in to take their places. "After luncheon we will take our coffee in my coupé. Then, if you like, we will speak of these matters. I have a headache. Will you order me some champagne? It is a terrible thing, I know, to drink wine in the morning, but when one travels, what can one do? Here come your bodyguard. They look at me as though I had stolen you away. Remember we take our coffee together afterwards. I am bored with so much traveling, and I look to you to amuse me."

Von Behrling's journey was, after all, marked with sharp contrasts. The kindness of the woman whom he adored was sufficient in itself to have transported him into a seventh heaven. On the other hand, he had trouble with his friends. Streuss drew him on one side at Ostend, and talked to him plainly.

"Von Behrling," he said, "I speak to you on behalf of Kahn and myself. Wine and women and pleasure are good things. We two, we love them, perhaps, as you do, but there is a place and a time for them, and it is not now. Our mission is too serious."

"Well, well!" Von Behrling exclaimed impatiently, "what is all this? What do I do wrong? What have you to say against me? If I talk with Mademoiselle Idiale, it is because it is the natural thing for me to do. Would you have us three — you and Kahn and myself — travel arm in arm and speak never a word to our fellow passengers? Would you have us proclaim to all the world that we are on a secret mission, carrying a secret document, to obtain which we have already committed a crime? These are old-fashioned methods, Streuss. It is better that we behave like ordinary mortals. You talk foolishly, Streuss!"

"It is you," the older man declared, "who play the fool, and we will not have it! Mademoiselle Idiale is a Servian and a patriot. She is the friend, too, of Bellamy, the Englishman. She and he were together last night."

"Bellamy is not even on the train," Von Behrling protested. "He went north to Berlin. That itself is the proof that they know nothing. If he had had the merest suspicion, do you not think that he would have stayed with us?"

"Bellamy is very clever," Streuss answered. "There

are too many of us to deal with, — he knew that. Mademoiselle Idiale is clever, too. Remember that half the trouble in life has come about through false women."

"What is it that you want?" Von Behrling demanded.

"That you travel the rest of the way with us, and speak no more with Mademoiselle."

Von Behrling drew himself up. After all, it was he who was noble; Streuss was little more than a policeman.

"I refuse!" he exclaimed. "Let me remind you, Streuss, that I am in charge of this expedition. It was I who planned it. It was I" — he dropped his voice and touched his chest — "who struck the first blow for its success. I think that we need talk no more," he went on. "I welcome your companionship. It makes for strength that we travel together. But for the rest, the enterprise has been mine, the success so far has been mine, and the termination of it shall be mine. Watch me, if you like. Stay with me and see that I am not robbed, if you fear that I am not able to take care of myself, but do not ask me to behave like an idiot."

Von Behrling stepped away quickly. The siren was already blowing from the steamer.

CHAPTER VI

VON BEHRLING IS TEMPTED

THE night was dark but fine, and the crossing smooth. Louise, wrapped in furs, abandoned her private cabin directly they had left the harbor, and had a chair placed on the upper deck. Von Behrling found her there, but not before they were nearly half-way across. She beckoned him to her side. Her eyes glowed at him through the darkness.

"You are not looking after me, my friend," she declared. "By myself I had to find this place."

Von Behrling was ruffled. He was also humbly apologetic.

"It is those idiots who are with me," he said. "All the time they worry."

She laughed and drew him down so that she could whisper in his ear.

"I know what it is," she said. "You have secrets which you are taking to London, and they are afraid of me because I am a Servian. Tell me, is it not so? Perhaps, even, they think that I am a spy."

Von Behrling hesitated. She drew him closer towards her.

"Sit down on the deck," she continued, "and lean against the rail. You are too big to talk to up there. So! Now you can come underneath my rug. Tell me, are they afraid of me, your friends?"

"Is it without reason?" he asked. "Would not any

one be afraid of you — if, indeed, they believed that you wished to know our secrets? I wonder if there is a man alive whom you could not turn round your little finger."

She laughed at him softly.

"Ah, no!" she said. "Men are not like that, nowadays. They talk and they talk, but it is not much they would do for a woman's sake."

"You believe that?" he asked, in a low tone.

"I do, indeed. One reads love-stories — no, I do not mean romances, but memoirs — memoirs of the French and Austrian Courts — memoirs, even, written by Englishmen. Men were different a generation ago. Honor was dear to them then, honor and position and wealth, and yet there were many, very many then who were willing to give all these things for the love of a woman."

"And do you think there are none now?" he whispered hoarsely

"My friend," she answered, looking down at him, "I think that there are very few."

She heard his breath come fast between his teeth, and she realized his state of excitement.

"Mademoiselle Louise," he said, "my love for you has made me a laughing-stock in the clubs of Vienna. I — the poverty-stricken, who have nothing but a noble name, nothing to offer you — have dared to show others what I think, have dared to place you in my heart above all the women on earth."

"It is very nice of you," she murmured. "Why do you tell me this now?"

"Why, indeed?" he answered. "What have I to hope for?"

She looked along the deck. Not a dozen yards away, two cigar ends burned red through the gloom. She knew very well that those cigar ends belonged to Streuss and his friend. She laughed softly and once more she bent her head.

"How they watch you, those men!" she said. "Listen, my friend Rudolph. Supposing their fears were true, supposing I were really a spy, supposing I offered you wealth and with it whatever else you might claim from me, for the secret which you carry to England!"

"How do you know that I am carrying a secret?" he asked hoarsely.

She laughed.

"My friend," she said, "with your two absurd companions shadowing you all the time and glowering at me, how could one possibly doubt it? The Baron Streuss is, I believe, the Chief of your Secret Service Department, is he not? To me he seems the most obvious policeman I ever saw dressed as a gentleman."

"You don't mean it!" he muttered. "You can't mean what you said just now!"

She was silent for a few moments. Some one passing struck a match, and she caught a glimpse of the white face of the man who sat by her side — strained now and curiously intense.

"Supposing I did!"

"You must be mad!" he declared. "You must not talk to me like this, Mademoiselle. I have no secret. It is your humor, I know, but it is dangerous."

"There is no danger," she murmured, "for we are alone. I say again, Rudolph, supposing this were true?"

His hand passed across his forehead. She fancied that he made a motion as though to rise to his feet, but she laid her hand upon his.

"Stay here," she whispered. "No, I do not wish to drive you away. Now you are here you shall listen to me."

"But you are not in earnest!" he faltered. "Don't tell me that you are in earnest. It is treason. I am Rudolph Von Behrling, Secretary to the Chancellor."

Again she leaned towards him so that he could see into her eyes.

"Rudolph," she said, "you are indeed Rudolph Von Behrling, you are indeed the Chancellor's secretary. What do you gain from it? A pittance! Many hours work a day and a pittance. What have you to look forward to? A little official life, a stupid official position. Rudolph, here am I, and there is the world. Do I not represent other things?"

"God knows you do!" he muttered.

"I, too, am weary of singing. I want a long rest — a long rest and a better name than my own. Don't shrink away from me. It is n't so wonderful, after all. Bellamy, the Englishman, came to me a few hours ago. He was Dorward's friend. He knew well what Dorward carried. It was not his affair, he told me, and interposition from him was hopeless, but he knew that you and I were friends."

"You must stop!" Von Behrling declared. "You must stop! I must not listen to this!"

"He offered me twenty thousand pounds," she went on, "for the packet in your pocket. Think of that, my friend. It would be a start in life, would it not? I am an extravagant woman. Even if I would, I dared not think of a poor man. But twenty thousand pounds is sufficient. When I reach London, I am going to a flat which has been waiting for me for weeks — 15, Dover Street. If you bring that packet to me instead of taking it to the Austrian Embassy, there will be twenty thousand pounds and —"

Her fingers suddenly held his. She could almost hear his heart beating. Her eyes, by now accustomed to the gloom, could see the tumult which was passing within the man, reflected in his face. She whispered a warning under her breath. The two cigar ends had moved nearer. The forms of the two men were now distinct. One was leaning over the side of the ship by Von Behrling's side. The other stood a few feet away, gazing at the lights of Dover. Von Behrling staggered to his feet. He said something in an angry undertone to Streuss. Louise rose and shook out her furs.

"My friend," she said, turning to Von Behrling, "if your friends can spare you so long, will you fetch one of my maids? You will find them both in my cabin, number three. I wish to walk for a few moments before we arrive.'

Von Behrling turned away like a man in a dream. Mademoiselle Idiale followed him slowly, and behind her came Von Behrling's companions.

The details of the great singer's journey had been most carefully planned by an excited manager who had received the telegram announcing her journey to London. There was an engaged carriage at Dover, into which she was duly escorted by a representative of the Opera Syndicate, who had been sent down from London to receive her. Von Behrling seemed to be missing. She had seen nothing of him since he had descended to summon her maids. But just as the train was starting, she heard the sound of angry voices, and a moment later his white face was pressed through the open window of the carriage.

"Louise," he muttered, "I am on fire! I cannot talk to you! I fear that they suspect something. They have told me that if I travel with you they will force their way in. Even now, Streuss comes. Listen for your telephone to-night or whenever I can. I must think — I must think!"

He passed on, and Louise, leaning back in her seat, closed her eyes.

CHAPTER VII

"WE PLAY FOR GREAT STAKES"

BELLAMY, travel-stained and weary, arrived at his rooms at two o'clock on the following afternoon to find amongst a pile of correspondence a penciled message awaiting him in a handwriting he knew well. He tore open the envelope.

DAVID DEAR, — I have just arrived and I am sending you these few lines at once. As to what progress I have made, I cannot say for certain, but there is a chance. You had better get the money ready and come to me here. If R. could only escape from Streuss and those who watch him all the time, I should be quite sure, but they are suspicious. What may happen I cannot tell. I do my best and I have hated it. Get the money ready and come to me.

LOUISE.

Bellamy drew a little breath and tore the note into pieces. Then he rang for his servant.

"A bath and some clean clothes quickly," he ordered. "While I am changing, ring up Downing Street and see if Sir James is there. If not, find out exactly where he is. I must see him within half an hour. Afterwards, get me a taxicab."

The man obeyed with the swift efficiency of the thoroughly trained servant. In rather less than the time which he had stated, Bellamy had left his rooms. Before four o'clock he had arrived at the address which Louise had given him. A commissionaire telephoned his name to the first floor, and in a very few moments a pale-faced French man-servant, in sombre black livery, descended and bowed to Bellamy.

"Monsieur will be so good as to come this way," he directed.

Bellamy followed him into the lift, which stopped at the first floor. He was ushered into a small boudoir, already smothered with roses.

"Mademoiselle will be here immediately," the man announced. "She is engaged with a gentleman from the Opera, but she will leave him to receive Monsieur."

Bellamy nodded.

"Pray let Mademoiselle understand," he said, "that I am entirely at her service. My time is of no consequence."

The man bowed and withdrew. Louise came to him almost directly from an inner chamber. She was wearing a loose gown, but the fatigue of her journey seemed already to have passed away. Her eyes were bright, and a faint color glowed in her cheeks.

"David," she exclaimed, "thank Heaven that you are here!"

She took both his hands and held them for a moment. Then she walked to the door, made sure that it was securely fastened, and stood there listening for a moment.

"I suppose I am foolish," she said, coming back to him, "and yet I cannot help fancying that I am being watched on every side since we landed in England. I detest my new manager, and I don't trust any of the servants he has engaged for me. You got my note?"

"Yes," he answered, "I had your note — and I am here."

The restraint of his manner was obvious. He was

standing a little away from her. She came suddenly up to him, her hands fell upon his shoulders, her face was upturned to his. Even then he made no motion to embrace her.

"David," she whispered softly, "what I am doing — what I have done — was at your suggestion. I do it for you, I do it for my country, I do it against every natural feeling I possess. I hate and loathe the lies I tell. Are you remembering that? Is it in your heart at this moment?"

He stooped and kissed her.

"Forgive me," he said, "it is I who am to blame, but I am only human. We play for great stakes, Louise, but sometimes one forgets."

"As I live," she murmured, "the kiss you gave me last is still upon my lips. What I have promised goes for nothing. What he has promised is this — the papers to-night."

"Unopened?"

"Unopened," she repeated, softly.

"But how is it to be done?" Bellamy asked. "He must have arrived in London when you did last night. How is it they are not already at the Embassy?"

"The Ambassador was commanded to Cowes," she explained. "He cannot be back until late to-night. No one else has a key to the treaty safe, and Von Behrling declined to give up the document to any one save the Ambassador himself."

Bellamy nodded.

"What about Streuss?"

"Streuss and the others are all furious," Louise said. "Yet, after all, Behrling has a certain measure of right on his side. His orders were to see with his own eyes this envelope deposited in the safe by the Ambassador himself."

"He returns to-night!" Bellamy exclaimed quickly. She nodded.

"Before he comes," she declared, "I think that the document will be in your hands."

"How is it to be done?"

"The report is written," she explained, "on five pages of foolscap. They are contained in a long envelope, sealed with the Chancellor's crest. Von Behrling, being one of the family, has the same crest. He has prepared another envelope, the same size and weight, and signed it with his seal. It is this which he will hand over to the Ambassador if he should return unexpectedly. The real one he has concealed."

"Is he here?" Bellamy inquired.

"Thank Heavens, no!" she answered. "My dear David, what are you thinking of? He is not here and he dare not come here. You are to go to your rooms," she added, glancing at the clock, "and between five and six o'clock this evening you will be rung up on the telephone. A rendezvous will be given you for later on to-night. You must take the money there and receive the packet. Von Behrling will be disguised and prepared for flight."

Bellamy's eyes glowed.

"You believe this?" he exclaimed.

"I believe it," she replied. "He is going to do it. After he has seen you, he will make his way to Plymouth. I have promised — don't look at me, David — I have promised to join him there."

Bellamy was grave.

"There will be trouble," he said. "He will come back.

He will want to shoot you. He may be slow-witted in some things, but he is passionate."

"Am I a coward?" she asked, with a scornful laugh. "Have I ever shown fear of my life? No, David! It is not that of which I am afraid. It is the memory of the man's touch, it is the look which was in your face when you came into the room. These are the things I fear — not death."

Bellamy drew her into his arms and kissed her.

"Forgive me," he begged. "At such times a man is a weak thing — a weak and selfish thing. I am ashamed of myself. I should have known better than to have doubted you for a moment. I know you so well, Louise. I know what you are."

She smiled.

"Dear," she said, "you have made me happy. And now you must go away. Remember that these few minutes are only an interlude. Over here I am Mademoiselle Idiale who sings to-night at Covent Garden. See my roses. There are two rooms full of reporters and photographers in the place now. The leader of the orchestra is in my bedroom, and two of the directors are drinking whiskies and sodas with this new manager of mine in the dining-room. Between five and six o'clock this afternoon you will get the message. It is somewhere, I think, in the city that you will have to go. There will be no trouble about the money? Nothing but notes or gold will be of any use."

"I have it in my pocket," he answered. "I have it in notes, but he need never fear that they will be traced. The numbers of notes given for Secret Service purposes are expunged from every one's memory."

She drew a little sigh.

"It is a great sum," she said. "After all, he should be grateful to me. If only he would be sensible and get away to the United States or to South America! He could live there like a prince, poor fellow. He would be far happier."

"I only hope that he will go," Bellamy agreed. "There is one thing to be remembered. If he does not go, if he stays for twenty-four hours in this country, I do not believe that he will live to do you harm. The men who are with him are not the sort to stop short at trifles. Besides Streuss and Kahn, they have a regular army of spies at their bidding here. If they find out that he has tricked them, they will hunt him down, and before long."

Louise shivered.

"Oh, I hope," she exclaimed, "that he gets away! He is a traitor, of course, but he is a traitor to a hateful cause, and, after all, I think it is less for the money than for my sake that he does it. That sounds very conceited, I suppose," she added, with a faint smile. "Ah! well, you see, for five years so many have been trying to turn my head. No wonder if I begin to believe some of their stories. David, I must go. I must not keep Dr. Henschell waiting any longer."

"To-morrow," he said, "to-morrow early I shall come. I am afraid I shall miss your first appearance in England, Louise."

The sound of a violin came floating out from the inner room.

"That is my signal," she declared smiling. "Dr. Henschell was almost beside himself that I came away. I come, Doctor," she called out. "David, good fortune!" she added, giving him her hands. "Now go, dear."

CHAPTER VIII

THE HAND OF MISFORTUNE

BETWEEN the two men, seated opposite each other in the large but somewhat barely furnished office, the radical differences, both in appearance and mannerisms, perhaps, also, in disposition, had never been more strongly evident. They were partners in business and face to face with ruin. Stephen Laverick, senior member of the firm, although an air of steadfast gloom had settled upon his clean-cut, powerful countenance, retained even in despair something of that dogged composure, temperamental and wholly British, which had served him well along the road to fortune. Arthur Morrison, the man who sat on the other side of the table, a Jew to his finger-tips notwithstanding his altered name, sat like a broken thing, with tears in his terrified eyes, disordered hair, and parchment-pale face. Words had flown from his lips in a continual stream. He floundered in his misery, sobbed about it like a child. The hand of misfortune had stripped him naked, and one man, at least, saw him as he really was.

"I can't stand it, Laverick, — I could n't face them all. It's too cruel — too horrible! Eighteen thousand pounds gone in one week, forty thousand in a month! Forty thousand pounds! Oh, my God!"

He writhed in agony. The man on the other side of the table said nothing.

"If we could only have held on a little longer! 'Unions' must turn! They will turn! Laverick, have you tried all

your friends? Think! Have you tried them all? Twenty
thousand pounds would see us through it. We should get
our own money back — I am sure of it. There's Rendell,
Laverick. He'd do anything for you. You're always
shooting or playing cricket with him. Have you asked
him, Laverick? He'd never miss the money."

"You and I see things differently, Morrison," Laverick
answered. "Nothing would induce me to borrow money
from a friend."

"But at a time like this," Morrison pleaded passionately.
"Every one does it sometimes. He'd be glad to help you.
I know he would. Have you ever thought what it will be
like, Laverick, to be hammered?"

"I have," Laverick admitted wearily. "God knows
it seems as terrible a thing to me as it can to you! But
if we go down, we must go down with clean hands. I've
no faith in your infernal market, and not one penny will
I borrow from a friend."

The Jew's face was almost piteous. He stretched himself across the table. There were genuine tears in his
eyes.

"Laverick," he said, "old man, you're wrong. I know
you think I've been led away. I've taken you out of our
depth, but the only trouble has been that we haven't had
enough capital, and no backing. Those who stand up
will win. They will make money."

"Unfortunately," Laverick remarked, "we cannot
stand up. Please understand that I will not discuss this
matter with you in any way. I will not borrow money
from Rendell or any friend. I have asked the bank
and I have asked Pages, who will be our largest creditors.
To help us would simply be a business proposition, so
far as they are concerned. As you know, they have re-

fused. If you see any hope in that direction, why don't you try some of your own friends? For every one man I know in the House, you have seemed to be bosom friends with at least twenty."

Morrison groaned.

"Those I know are not that sort of friend," he answered. "They will drink with you and spend a night out or a week-end at Brighton, but they do not lend money. If they would, do you think I would mind asking? Why, I would go on my knees to any man who would lend us the money. I would even kiss his feet. I cannot bear it, Laverick! I cannot! I cannot!"

Laverick said nothing. Words were useless things, wasted upon such a creature. He eyed his partner with a contempt which he took no pains to conceal. This, then, was the smart young fellow recommended to him on all sides, a few years ago, as one of the shrewdest young men in his own particular department, a person bound to succeed, a money-maker if ever there was one! Laverick thought of him as he appeared at the office day by day, glossy and immaculately dressed, with a flower in his buttonhole, boots that were a trifle too shiny, hat and coat, gloves and manner, all imitation but all very near the real thing. What a collapse!

"You're going to stay and see it through?" he whined across the table.

"Certainly," Laverick answered.

The young man buried his face in his hands.

"I can't! I can't!" he moaned. "I could n't bear seeing all the fellows, hearing them whisper things — oh, Lord! Oh, Lord! . . . Laverick, we've a few hundreds left. Give me something and let me out of it. You're a stronger sort of man than I am. You can face it, — I

can't! Give me enough to get abroad with, and if ever I
do any good I'll remember it, I will indeed."

Laverick was silent for a moment. His companion
watched his face eagerly. After all, why not let him go?
He was no help, no comfort. The very sight of him was
contemptible.

"I have paid no money into the bank for several days,"
Laverick said slowly. "When they refused to help us,
it was, of course, obvious that they guessed how things
were."

"Quite right, quite right!" the young man interrupted
feverishly. "They would have stuck to it against the overdraft. How much have we got in the safe?"

"This afternoon," Laverick continued, "I changed all
our cheques. You can count the proceeds for yourself.
There are, I think, eleven hundred pounds. You can
take two hundred and fifty, and you can take them with
you — to any place you like."

The young man was already at the safe. The notes
were between them, on the table. He counted quickly
with the fingers of a born manipulator of money. When
he had gathered up two hundred and fifty pounds, Laverick's hand fell upon his.

"No more," he ordered sternly.

"But, my dear fellow," Morrison protested, "half of
eleven hundred is five hundred and fifty. Why should
we not go halves? That is only fair, Laverick. It is little
enough. We ought to have had a great deal more."

Laverick pushed him contemptuously away and locked
up the remainder of the notes.

"I am letting you take two hundred and fifty pounds
of this money," he said, "for various reasons. For one, I
can bear this thing better alone. As for the rest of the

money, it remains there for the accountant who liquidates our affairs. I do not propose to touch a penny of it."

The young man buttoned up his coat with an hysterical little laugh. Such ways were not his ways. They were not, indeed, within the limit of his understanding. But of his partner he had learned one thing, at least. The word of Stephen Laverick was the word of truth. He shambled toward the door. On the whole, he was lucky to have got the two hundred and fifty pounds.

"So long, Laverick," he said from the door. "I'm —I'm sorry."

It was characteristic of him that he did not venture to offer his hand. Laverick nodded, not unkindly. After all, this young man was as he had been made.

"I wish you good luck, Morrison," he said. "Try South Africa."

CHAPTER IX

THE roar of the day was long since over. The rattle of vehicles, the tinkling of hansom bells, the tooting of horns from motor-cars and cabs, the ceaseless tramp of footsteps, all had died away. Outside, the streets were almost deserted. An occasional wayfarer passed along the flagged pavement with speedy footsteps. Here and there a few lights glimmered at the windows of some of the larger blocks of offices. The bustle of the day was finished. There is no place in London so strangely quiet as the narrow thoroughfares of the city proper when the hour approaches midnight.

Laverick, who since his partner's departure had been studying with infinite care his private ledger, closed it at last with a little snap and leaned back in his chair. After all, save that he had got rid of Morrison, it had been a wasted evening. Not even he, whose financial astuteness no man had ever questioned, could raise from those piles of figures any other answer save the one inevitable one, the knowledge of which had been like a black nightmare stalking by his side for the last thirty-six hours. One by one during the evening his clerks had left him, and it was a proof not only of his wonderful self-control but also of the confidence which he invariably inspired, that not a single one of them had the slightest idea how things were. Not a soul knew that the firm of Laverick & Morrison was already practically derelict, that they had on the morrow twenty-five thousand pounds to find, neither credit nor balance at their bankers, and eight hundred and fifty pounds in the safe.

Laverick, haggard from his long vigil, locked up his books at last, turned out the lights, and locking the doors behind him walked into the silent street. Instinctively he turned his steps westwards. This might well be the last night on which he would care to show himself in his accustomed haunts, the last night on which he could mix with his fellows freely, and without that terrible sense of consciousness which follows upon disaster. Already there was little enough left of it. It was too late to change and go to his club. The places of amusement were already closed. To-morrow night, both club and theatres would lie outside his world. He walked slowly, yet he had scarcely taken, in fact, a dozen steps when, with a purely mechanical impulse, he paused by a stone-flagged entry to light a cigarette. It was a passage, almost a tunnel for a few yards, leading to an open space, on one side of which was an old churchyard — strange survival in such a part — and on the other the offices of several firms of stockbrokers, a Russian banker, an actuary. It was the barest of impulses which led him to glance up the entry before he blew out the match. Then he gave a quick start and became for a moment paralyzed. Within a few feet of him something was lying on the ground — a dark mass, black and soft — the body of a man, perhaps. Just above it, a pair of eyes gleamed at him through the semi-darkness.

Laverick at first had no thought of tragedy. It might be a tramp or a drunkard, perhaps, — a fight, or a man taken ill. Then something sinister about the light of those burning eyes set his heart beating faster. He struck another match with firm fingers, and bent forward. What he saw upon the ground made him feel a little sick. What he saw racing away down the passage prompted him to swift pursuit. Down the arched court into the open space he ran, himself an athlete, but mocked by the swiftness of the shadowlike form which he pursued. At the end was another street — empty. He looked up and down, seeking in vain for any signs of life. There was nothing to tell him which way to turn. Opposite was a very labyrinth of courts and turnings. There was not even the sound of a footfall to guide him. Slowly he retraced his steps, lit another match, and leaned over the prostrate figure. Then he knew that it was a tragedy indeed upon which he had stumbled.

The man was dead, and he had met with his death by unusual means. These were the first two things of which Laverick assured himself. Without any doubt, a savage and a terrible crime had been committed. A horn-handled knife of unusual length had been driven up to the hilt through the heart of the murdered man. There had been other blows, notably about the head. There was not much blood, but the position of the knife alone told its ugly story. Laverick, though his nerves were of the strongest, felt his head swim as he looked. He rose to his feet and walked to the opening of the passage, gasping. The street was no longer empty.

About thirty yards away, looking westwards, a man was standing in the middle of the road. The light from the lamp-post escaped his face. Laverick could only see that he was slim, of medium height, dressed in dark clothes, with his hands in the pockets of his overcoat. To all appearance, he was watching the entry. Laverick took a step towards him — the man as deliberately took a step further away. Laverick held up his hand.

"Hullo!" he called out, and beckoned.

The person addressed took no notice. Laverick advanced another two or three steps — the man retreated a similar distance. Laverick changed his tactics and made a sudden spring forward. The man hesitated no longer — he turned and ran as though for his life. In a few minutes he was round the corner of the street and out of sight. Laverick returned slowly to the entry.

A distant clock struck midnight. A couple of clerks came along the pavement on the other side, their hands and arms full of letters. Laverick hesitated. He was never afterwards able to account for the impulse which prevented his calling out to them. Instead he lurked in the shadows and watched them go by. When he was sure that they had disappeared, he bent once more over the body of the murdered man. Already that huddled-up heap was beginning to exercise a nameless and terrible fascination for him. His first feelings of horror were mingled now with an insatiable curiosity. What manner of man was he? He was tall and strongly built; fair — of almost florid complexion. His clothes were very shabby and apparently ready-made. His moustache was upturned, and his hair was trimmed closer than is the custom amongst Englishmen. Laverick stooped lower and lower until he found himself almost on his knees. There was something projecting from the man's pocket as though it had been half snatched out — a large portfolio of brown leather, almost the size of a satchel. Laverick drew it out, holding it in one hand whilst with firm fingers he struck another match. Then, for the first time, a little cry broke from his lips. Both sides of the pocket-book were filled with bank-notes. As his match flickered out, he caught a glimpse of the figures in the left-hand corner — £500! — great rolls of them! Laverick rose gasping to his feet. It was a new Arabian Nights, this! — a dream! — a continuation of the nightmare which had threatened him all day! Or was it, perhaps, the madness coming — the madness which he had begun only an hour or so ago to fear!

He walked into the gaslit streets and looked up and down. The mysterious stranger had vanished. There was not a soul in sight. He clutched the rough stone wall with his hands, he kicked the pavement with his heels. There was no doubt about it — everything around him was real. Most real of all was the fact that within a few feet of him lay a murdered man, and that in his hands was that brown leather pocket-book with its miraculous contents. For the last time Laverick retraced his steps and bent over that huddled-up shape. One by one he went through the other pockets. There was a packet of Russian cigarettes; an empty card-case of chased silver, and obviously of foreign workmanship; a cigarette holder stained with much use, but of the finest amber, with rich gold mountings. There was nothing else upon the dead man, no means of identification of any sort. Laverick stood up, giddy, half terrified with the thoughts that went tearing through his brain. The pocket-book began to burn his hand; he felt the perspiration breaking out anew upon his forehead. Yet he never hesitated. He walked like a man in a dream, but his footsteps were steady and short. Deliberately, and without any sign of hurry, he made his way towards his offices. If a policeman had come in sight up or down the street, he had decided to call him and to acquaint him with what had happened. It was the one chance he held against himself, — the gambler's method of decision, perhaps, unconsciously arrived at. As it turned out, there was still not a soul in sight. Laverick opened the outer door with his latchkey, let himself in and closed it. Then he groped his way through the clerk's office into his own room, switched on the electric light and once more sat down before his desk.

He drew his shaded writing lamp towards him and looked around with a nervousness wholly unfamiliar. Then he opened the pocket-book, drew out the roll of bank-notes and counted them. It was curious that he felt no surprise at their value. Bank-notes for five hundred pounds are not exactly common, and yet he proceeded with his task without the slightest instinct of surprise. Then he leaned back in his chair. Twenty thousand pounds in Bank of England notes! There they lay on the table before him. A man had died for their sake, — another must go through all the days with the price of blood upon his head — a murderer — a haunted creature for the rest of his life. And there on the table were the spoils. Laverick tried to think the matter out dispassionately. He was a man of average moral fibre — that is to say, he was honest in his dealings with other men because his father and his grandfather before him had been honest, and because the penalty for dishonesty was shameful. Here, however, he was face to face with an altogether unusual problem. These notes belonged, without a doubt, to the dead man. Save for his own interference, they would have been in the hands of his murderer. The use of them for a few days could do no one any harm. Such risk as there was he took himself. That it was a risk he knew and fully realized. Laverick had sat in his place unmoved when his partner had poured out his wail of fear and misery. Yet of the two men it was probable that Laverick himself had felt their position the more keenly. He was a man of some social standing, with a large circle of friends; a sportsman, and with many interests outside the daily routine of his city life. To him failure meant more than the loss of money; it would rob him of everything in life worth having. The days to come had been emptied of all promise. He had held himself stubbornly because he was a man, because he had strength enough to refuse to let his mind dwell upon the indignities and humiliation to come. And here before him was possible salvation. There was a price to be paid, of course, a risk to be run in making use even for an hour of this money. Yet from the first he had known that he meant to do it.

Quite cool now, he opened his private safe, thrust the pocket-book into one of the drawers, and locked it up. Then he lit a cigarette, finally shut up the office and walked down the street. As he passed the entry he turned his head slowly. Apparently no one had been there, nothing had been disturbed. Straining his eyes through the darkness, he could even see that dark shape still lying huddled up on the ground. Then he walked on. He had burned his boats now and was prepared for all emergencies. At the corner he met a policeman, to whom he wished a cheery good-night. He told himself that the thing which he had done was for the best. He owed it to himself. He owed it to those who had trusted him. After all, it was the chief part of his life — his city career. It was here that his friends lived. It was here that his ambitions flourished. Disgrace here was eternal disgrace.

His father and his grandfather before him had been men honored and respected in this same circle. Disgrace to him, such disgrace as that with which he had stood face to face a few hours ago, would have been, in a certain sense, a reflection upon their memories. The names upon the brass plates to right and to left of him were the names of men he knew, men with whom he desired to stand well, whose friendship or contempt made life worth living or the reverse. It was worth a great risk — this effort of his to keep his place. His one mistake — this association with Morrison — had been such an unparalleled stroke of bad luck. He was rid of the fellow now. For the future there should be no more partners. He had his life to live. It was not reasonable that he should allow himself to be dragged down into the mire by such a creature.

He found an empty taxicab at the corner of Queen Victoria Street, and hailed it.

"Whitehall Court," he told the driver.

CHAPTER X

BELLAMY was a man used to all hazards, whose supreme effort of life it was to meet success and disaster with unvarying mien. But this was disaster too appalling even for his self-control. He felt his knees shake so that he caught at the edge of the table before which he was standing. There was no possible doubt about it, he had been tricked. Von Behrling, after all, — Von Behrling, whom he had looked upon merely as a stupid, infatuated Austrian, ready to sell his country for the sake of a woman, had fooled him utterly!

The man who sat at the head of the table — the only other occupant of the room — was in Court dress, with many orders upon his coat. He had just been attending a Court function, from which Bellamy's message had summoned him. Before him on the table was an envelope, hastily torn open, and several sheets of blank paper. It was upon these that Bellamy's eyes were fixed with an expression of mingled horror and amazement. The Cabinet Minister had already pushed them away with a little gesture of contempt.

"Bellamy," he said gravely, "it is not like you to make so serious an error."

"I hope not, sir," Bellamy answered. "I — yes, I have been deceived."

The Minister glanced at the clock.

"What is to be done?" he asked.

Bellamy, with an effort, pulled himself together. He caught up the envelope, looked once more inside, held up the blank sheets of paper to the lamp and laid them down. Then with clenched fists he walked to the other side of the room and returned. He was himself again.

"Sir James, I will not waste your time by saying that I am sorry. Only an hour ago I met Von Behrling in a little restaurant in the city, and gave him twenty thousand pounds for that envelope."

"You paid him the money," the Minister remarked slowly, "without opening the envelope."

Bellamy admitted it.

"In such transactions as these," he declared, "great risks are almost inevitable. I took what must seem to you now to be an absurd risk. To tell you the honest truth, sir, and I have had experience in these things, I thought it no risk at all when I handed over the money. Von Behrling was there in disguise. The men with whom he came to this country are furious with him. To all appearance, he seemed to have broken with them absolutely. Even now —"

"Well?"

"Even now," Bellamy said slowly, with his eyes fixed upon the wall of the room, and a dawning light growing stronger every moment in his face, "even now I believe that Von Behrling made a mistake. An envelope such as this had been arranged for him to show the others or leave at the Austrian Embassy in case of emergency. He had it with him in his pocket-book. He even told me so. God in Heaven, he gave me the wrong one!"

The Minister glanced once more at the clock.

"In that case," he said, "perhaps he would not go to the Embassy to-night, especially if he was in disguise.

You may still be able to find him and repair the .
error."

"I will try," answered Bellamy. "Thank Heaven!"
he added, with a sudden gleam of satisfaction, "my
watchers are still dogging his footsteps. I can find out
before morning where he went when he left our rendezvous.
There is another way, too. Mademoiselle — this man
Von Behrling believed that she was leaving the country
with him. She was to have had a message within the
next few hours."

The Minister nodded thoughtfully.

"Bellamy, I have been your friend and you have done
us good service often. The Secret Service estimates, as
you know, are above supervision, but twenty thousand
pounds is a great deal of money to have paid for this."

He touched the sheets of blank paper with his forefinger. Bellamy's teeth were clenched.

"The money shall be returned, sir."

"Do not misunderstand me," Sir James went on,
speaking a little more kindly. "The money, after all, in
comparison with what it was destined to purchase, is
nothing. We might even count it a fair risk if it was
lost."

"It shall not be lost," Bellamy promised. "If Von
Behrling has played the traitor to us, then he will go back
to his country. In that case, I will have the money from
him without a doubt. If, on the other hand, he was honest
to us and a traitor to his country, as I firmly believe, it
may not yet be too late."

"Let us hope not," Sir James declared. "Bellamy,"
he continued, a note of agitation trembling in his tone,
"I need not tell you, I am sure, how important this matter
is. You work like a mole in the dark, yet you have brains,

— you understand. Let me tell you how things are with us. A certain amount of confidence is due to you, if to any one. I may tell you that at the Cabinet Council to-day a very serious tone prevailed. We do not understand in the least the attitude of several of the European Powers. It can be understood only under certain assumptions. A note of ours sent through the Ambassador to Vienna has remained unanswered for two days. The German Ambassador has left unexpectedly for Berlin on urgent business. We have just heard, too, that a secret mission from Russia left St. Petersburg last night for Paris. Side by side with all this," Sir James continued, "the Czar is trying to evade his promised visit here. The note we have received speaks of his health. Well, we know all about that. We know, I may tell you, that his health has never been better than at the present moment."

"It all means one thing and one thing only," Bellamy affirmed. "In Vienna and Berlin to-day they look at an Englishman and smile. Even the man in the street seems to know what is coming."

Sir James leaned a little back in his seat. His hands were tightly clenched, and there was a fierce light in his hollow eyes. Those who were intimate with him knew that he had aged many years during the last few weeks.

"The cruel part is," he said softly, "that it should have come in my administration, when for ten years I have prayed from the Opposition benches for the one thing which would have made us safe to-day."

"An army," murmured Bellamy.

"The days are coming," Sir James continued, "when those who prated of militarism and the security of our island walls will see with their own eyes the ruin they have brought upon us. Secretly we are mobilizing all that we have to mobilize," he added, with a little sigh. "At the very best, however, our position is pitiful. Even if we are prepared to defend, I am afraid that we shall see things on the Continent in which we shall be driven to interfere, or else suffer the greatest blow which our prestige has ever known. If we could only tell what was coming!" he wound up, looking once more at those empty sheets of paper. "It is this darkness which is so alarming!"

Bellamy turned toward the door.

"You have the telephone in your bedroom, sir?" he asked.

"Yes, ring me up at any time in the night or morning, if you have news."

Bellamy drove at once to Dover Street. It was half-past one, but he had no fear of not being admitted. Louise's French maid answered the bell.

"Madame has not retired?" Bellamy inquired.

"But no, sir," the woman assured him, with a welcoming smile. "It is only a few minutes ago that she has returned."

Bellamy was ushered at once into her room. She was gorgeous in blue satin and pearls. Her other maid was taking off her jewels. She dismissed both the women abruptly.

"I absolutely could n't avoid a supper-party," she said, holding out her hands. "You expected that, of course. You were not at the Opera House?"

He shook his head, and walking to the door tried the handle. It was securely closed. He came back slowly to her side. Her eyes were questioning him fiercely.

"Well?" she exclaimed. "Well?"

"Have you heard from Von Behrling?"

"No," she answered. "He knew that I must sing to-

night. I have been expecting him to telephone every
moment since I got home. You have seen him?"

"I have seen him," Bellamy admitted. "Either he
has deceived us both, or the most unfortunate mistake
in the world has happened. Listen. I met him where
he appointed. He was there, disguised, almost unrecognizable. He was nervous and desperate; he had the air
of a man who has cut himself adrift from the world. I
gave him the money, — twenty thousand pounds in Bank
of England notes, Louise, — and he gave me the papers,
or what we thought were the papers. He told me that
he was keeping a false duplicate upon him for a little time,
in case he was seized, but that he was going to Liverpool
Street station to wait, and would telephone you from the
hotel there later on. You have not heard yet, then?"

She shook her head.

"There has been no message, but go on."

"He gave me the wrong document — the wrong envelope," continued Bellamy. "When I took it to — to
Downing Street, it was full of blank paper."

The color slowly left her cheeks. She looked at him
with horror in her face.

"Do you think that he meant to do it?" she exclaimed.

"We cannot tell," Bellamy answered. "My own impression is that he did not. We must find out at once
what has become of him. He might even, if he fancies
himself safe, destroy the envelope he has, believing it to
be the duplicate. He is sure to telephone you. The moment you hear you must let me know."

"You had better stay here," she declared. "There
are plenty of rooms. You will be on the spot then."

Bellamy shook his head.

"The joke of it is that I, too, am being watched where-

ever I go.   That fellow Streuss has spies everywhere.
That is one reason why I believe that Von Behrling was
serious."

"Oh, he was serious!" Louise repeated.

"You are sure?" Bellamy asked.   "You have never
had even any doubt about him?"

"Never," she answered firmly.   "David, I had not
meant to tell you this.   You know that I saw him for a
moment this morning.   He was in deadly earnest.   He
gave me a ring — a trifle — but it had belonged to his
mother.   He would not have done this if he had been
playing us false."

Bellamy sprang to his feet.

"You are right, Louise!" he exclaimed.   "I shall go
back to my rooms at once.   Fortunately, I had a man
shadowing Von Behrling, and there may be a report for
me.   If anything comes here, you will telephone at once?"

"Of course," she assented.

"You do not think it possible," he asked slowly, "that
he would attempt to see you here?"

Louise shuddered for a moment.

"I absolutely forbade it, so I am sure there is no chance
of that."

"Very well, then," he decided, "we will wait.   Dear,"
he added, in an altered tone, "how splendid you
look!"

Her face suddenly softened.

"Ah, David!" she murmured, "to hear you speak
naturally even for a moment — it makes everything seem
so different!"

He held out his arms and she came to him with a little
sigh of satisfaction.

"Louise," he said, "some day the time may come

when we shall be able to give up this life of anxiety and terrors.   But it cannot be yet — not for your country's sake or mine."

She kissed him fondly.

"So long as there is hope!" she whispered.

CHAPTER XI

IT seemed to Louise that she had scarcely been in bed an hour when the more confidential of her maids — Annette, the Frenchwoman — woke her with a light touch of the arm. She sat up in bed sleepily.

"What is it, Annette?" she asked. "Surely it is not mid-day yet? Why do you disturb me?"

"It is barely nine o'clock, Mademoiselle, but Monsieur Bellamy — Mademoiselle told me that she wished to receive him whenever he came. He is in the boudoir now, and very impatient."

"Did he send any message?"

"Only that his business was of the most urgent," the maid replied.

Louise sighed, — she was really very sleepy. Then, as the thoughts began to crowd into her brain, she began also to remember. Some part of the excitement of a few hours ago returned.

"My bath, Annette, and a dressing-gown," she ordered. "Tell Monsieur Bellamy that I hurry. I will be with him in twenty minutes."

To Bellamy, the twenty minutes were minutes of purgatory. She came at last, however, fresh and eager; her hair tied up with ribbon, she herself clad in a pink dressing-gown and pink slippers.

"David!" she cried, — "my dear David — !"

Then she broke off.

"What is it?" she asked, in a different tone.

He showed her the headlines of the newspaper he was carrying.

"Tragedy!" he answered hoarsely. "Von Behrling was true, after all, — at least, it seems so."

"What has happened?" she demanded.

Bellamy pointed once more to the newspaper.

"He was murdered last night, within fifty yards of the place of our rendezvous."

A little exclamation broke from Louise's lips. She sat down suddenly. The color called into her cheeks by the exercise of her bath was rapidly fading away.

"David," she murmured, "is this true?"

"It is indeed," Bellamy assured her. "Not only that, but there is no mention of his pocket-book in the account of his murder. It must have been engineered by Streuss and the others, and they have got away with the pocket-book and the money."

"What can we do?" she asked.

"There is nothing to be done," Bellamy declared calmly. "We are defeated. The thing is quite apparent. Von Behrling never succeeded, after all, in shaking off the espionage of the men who were watching him. They tracked him to our rendezvous, they waited about while I met him. Afterwards, he had to pass along a narrow passage. It was there that he was found murdered."

"But, David, I don't understand! Why did they wait until after he had seen you? How did they know that he had not parted with the paper in the restaurant? To all intents and purposes he ought to have done so."

"I cannot understand that myself," Bellamy admitted. "In fact, it is inexplicable."

She took up the newspaper and glanced at the report.

Then, "You are sure, I suppose, that this does refer to
Von Behrling? He is quite unidentified, you see."

"There is no doubt about it," Bellamy declared. "I
have been to the Mortuary. It is certainly he. All our
work has been in vain — just as I thought, too, that we
had made a splendid success of it."

She looked at him compassionately.

"It is hard lines, dear," she admitted. "You are tired,
too. You look as though you had been up all night."

"Yes, I am tired," he answered, sinking into a chair.
"I am worse than tired. This has been the grossest
failure of my career, and I am afraid that it is the end of
everything. I have lost twenty thousand pounds of
Secret Service money; I have lost the one chance which
might have saved England. They will never trust me
again."

"You did your best," she said, coming over and
sitting on the arm of his chair. "You did your best,
David."

She laid her hands upon his forehead, her cheek against
his — smooth and cold — exquisitely refreshing it seemed
to his jaded nerves.

"Ah, Louise!" he murmured, "life is getting a little
too strenuous. Perhaps we have given too much of it up
to others. What do you think?"

She shook her head.

"Dear, I have felt like that sometimes, yet what can we
do? Could we be happy, you and I, in exile, if the things
which we dread were coming to pass? Could I go away
and hide while my countrymen were being butchered
out of existence? — And you — you are not the sort of
man to be content with an ignoble peace. No, it isn't
possible. Our work may not be over yet — "

There was a knock at the door, and Annette entered with many apologies.

"Mademoiselle," she explained, "a thousand pardons, and to Monsieur also, but there is a gentleman here who says that his business is of the most urgent importance, and that he must see you at once. I have done all that I can, but he will not go away. He knows that Monsieur Bellamy is here, too," she added, turning to him, "and he says his business has to do with Monsieur as well as Mademoiselle."

Bellamy almost snatched the card from the girl's fingers. He read out the name in blank amazement.

"Baron de Streuss!"

There was a moment's silence. Louise and he exchanged wondering glances.

"What can this mean?" she asked hoarsely.

"Heaven knows!" he answered. "Let us see him together. After all — after all — "

"You can show the gentleman in, Annette," her mistress ordered.

"If he has the papers," Bellamy continued slowly, "why does he come to us? It is not like these men to be vindictive. Diplomacy to them is nothing — a game of chess. I do not understand."

The door opened. Annette announced their visitor. Streuss bowed low to Louise — he bowed, also, to Bellamy.

"I need not introduce myself," he said. "With Mr. Bellamy I have the honor to be well acquainted. Madame is known to all the world."

Louise nodded, somewhat coldly.

"We can dispense with an introduction, I think, Monsieur le Baron," she said. "At the same time, you will perhaps explain to what I owe this somewhat unexpected pleasure?"

"Mademoiselle, an explanation there must certainly be. I know that it is an impossible hour. I know, too, that to have forced my presence upon you in this manner may seem discourteous. Yet the urgency of the matter, I am convinced, justifies me."

Louise motioned him to a chair, but he declined with a little bow of thanks.

"Mademoiselle," he said, "and you, Mr. Bellamy, we need not waste words. We have played a game of chess together. You, Mademoiselle, and Mr. Bellamy on the one side — I and my friends upon the other. The honor of Rudolph Von Behrling was the pawn for which we fought. The victory remains with you."

Bellamy never moved a muscle. Louise, on the contrary, could not help a slight start.

"Under the circumstances," the Baron continued smoothly, "the struggle was uneven. I do myself the justice to remember that from the first I realized that we played a losing game. Mademoiselle," he added, "from the days of Cleopatra — ay, and throughout those shadowy days which lie beyond — the diplomats of the world have been powerless when matched against your sex. Rudolph Von Behrling was an honest fellow enough until he looked into your eyes. Mademoiselle, you have gifts which might, perhaps, have driven from his senses a stronger man."

Louise smiled, but there was no suggestion of mirth in the curl of her lips. Her eyes all the time sought his questioningly. She did not understand.

"You flatter me, Baron," she murmured.

"No, I do not flatter you, I speak the truth. This

plain talking is pleasant enough when the time comes that one may indulge in it. That time, I think, is now. Rudolph Von Behrling, against my advice, but because he was the Chancellor's nephew, was associated with me in a certain enterprise, the nature of which is no secret to you, Mademoiselle, or to Mr. Bellamy here. We followed a man who, by some strange chance, was in possession of a few sheets of foolscap, the contents of which were alike priceless to my country and priceless to yours. The subsequent history of those papers should have been automatic. The first step was fulfilled readily enough. The man disappeared — the papers were ours. Von Behrling was the man who secured them, and Von Behrling it was who retained them. If my advice had been followed, I admit frankly that we should have ignored all possible comment and returned with them at once to Vienna. The others thought differently. They ruled that we should come on to London and deposit the packet with our Ambassador here. In a weak moment I consented. It was your opportunity, Mademoiselle, — an opportunity of which you have splendidly availed yourself."

This time Louise held herself with composure. Bellamy's brain was in a whirl but he remained silent.

"I come to you both," the Baron continued, "with my hands open. I come — I make no secret of it — I come to make terms. But first of all I must know whether I am in time. There is one question which I must ask. I address it, sir, to you," he added, turning to Bellamy. "Have you yet placed in the hands of your Government the papers which you obtained from Von Behrling?"

Bellamy shook his head.

The Baron drew a long breath of relief. Though he

had maintained his *savoir faire* perfectly, the fingers which for a moment played with his tie, as though to rearrange it, were trembling.

"Well, then, I am in time. Will you see my hand?"

"Mademoiselle and I," answered Bellamy, "are at least ready to listen to anything you may have to say."

"You know quite well," the Baron continued, "what it is that I have come to say, yet I want you to remember this. I do not come to bribe you in any ordinary manner. The things which are to come will happen; they must happen, if not this year, next, — if not next year, within half a decade of years. History is an absolute science. The future as well as the past can be read by those who know the signs. The thing which has been resolved upon is certain. The knowledge of the contents of those papers by your Government might delay the final catastrophe for a short while; it could do no more. In the long run, it would be better for your country, Mr. Bellamy, in every way, that the end come soon. Therefore, I ask you to perform no traitorous deed. I ask you to do that which is simply reasonable for all of us, which is, indeed, for the advantage of all of us. Restore those papers to me instead of handing them to your Government, and I will pay you for them the sum of one hundred thousand pounds!"

"One hundred thousand pounds!" Bellamy repeated.

"One hundred thousand pounds!" murmured Louise.

There was a brief, intense pause. Louise waited, warned by the expression in Bellamy's face. Silence, she felt, was safest, and it was Bellamy who spoke.

"Baron," said he, "your visit and your proposal are both a little amazing. Forgive me if I speak alone with Mademoiselle for a moment."

"Most certainly," the Baron agreed. "I go away and leave you — out of the room, if you will."

"It is not necessary," Bellamy replied. "Louise!"

The Baron withdrew to the window, and Bellamy led Louise into the furthest corner of the room.

"What can it mean?" he whispered. "What do you suppose has happened?"

"I cannot imagine. My brain is in a whirl."

"If they have not got the pocket-book," Bellamy muttered, "it must have gone with Von Behrling to the Mortuary. If so, there is a chance. Louise, say nothing; leave this to me."

"As you will," she assented. "I have no wish to interfere. I only hope that he does not ask me any questions."

They came once more into the middle of the room, and the Baron turned to meet them.

"You must forgive Mademoiselle," said Bellamy, "if she is a little upset this morning. She knows, of course, as I know and you know, that Von Behrling was playing a desperate game, and that he carried his life in his hands. Yet his death has been a shock — has been a shock, I may say, to both of us. From your point of view," Bellamy went on, "it was doubtless deserved, but —"

"What, in God's name, is this that you say?" the Baron interrupted. "I do not understand at all! You speak of Von Behrling's death! What do you mean?"

Bellamy looked at him as one who listens to strange words.

"Baron," he said, "between us who know so much there is surely no need for you to play a part. Von Behrling knew that you were watching him. Your spies were shadowing him as they have done me. He knew that he was running terrible risks. He was not unprepared and he has paid. It is not for us —"

"Now, in God's name, tell me the truth!" Baron de Streuss interrupted once more. "What is it that you are saying about Von Behrling's death?"

Bellamy drew a little breath between his teeth. He leaned forward with his hands resting upon the table.

"Do you mean to say that you do not know?"

"Upon my soul, no!" replied the Baron.

Bellamy threw open the newspaper before him.

"Von Behrling was murdered last night, ten minutes after our interview."

CHAPTER XII

THE Baron adjusted his eyeglass with shaking fingers. His face now was waxen-white as he spread out the newspaper upon the table and read the paragraph word by word.

TERRIBLE CRIME IN THE CITY

Early this morning the body of a man was discovered in a narrow passageway leading from Crooked Friars to Royal Street, under circumstances which leave little doubt but that the man's death was owing to foul play. The deceased had apparently been stabbed, and had received several severe blows about the head. He was shabbily dressed but was well supplied with money, and he was wearing a gold watch and chain when he was found.

LATER

There appears to be no further doubt but that the man found in the entry leading from Crooked Friars had been the victim of a particularly murderous assault. Neither his clothes nor his linen bore any mark by means of which he could be identified. The body has been removed to the nearest mortuary, and an inquest will shortly be held.

Streuss looked up from the newspaper and the reality of his surprise was apparent. He had all the appearance of a man shaken with emotion. While he looked at his two companions wonderingly, strange thoughts were forming in his mind.

"Von Behrling dead!" he muttered. "But who — who could have done this?"

"Until this moment," Bellamy answered dryly, "it was not a matter concerning which we had any doubt. The only wonder to us was that it should have been done too late."

"You mean," Streuss said slowly, "that he was murdered after he had completed his bargain with you?"

"Naturally."

"I suppose," the Baron continued, "there is no question but that it was done afterwards? You smile," he exclaimed, "but what am I to think? Neither I nor my people had any hand in this deed. How about yours?"

Bellamy shook his head.

"We do not fight that way," he replied. "I had bought Von Behrling. He was of no further interest to me. I did not care whether he lived or died."

"There is something very strange about this," the Baron said. "If neither you nor I were responsible for his death, who was?"

"That I can't tell you. Perhaps later in the day we shall hear from the police. It is scarcely the sort of murder which would remain long undetected, especially as he was robbed of a large sum in bank-notes."

"Supplied by His Majesty's Government, I presume?" Streuss remarked.

"Precisely," Bellamy assented, "and paid to him by me."

"At any rate," Streuss said grimly, "we have now no more secrets from one another. I will ask you one last question. Where is that packet at the present moment ?"

Bellamy raised his eyebrows.

"It is a question," he declared, "which you could scarcely expect me to answer."

"I will put it another way," Streuss continued. "Supposing you decide to accept my offer, how long will it be before the packet can be placed in my hands ?"

"If we decide to accept," Bellamy answered, "there is no reason why there should be any delay at all."

Streuss was silent for several moments. His hands were thrust deep down into the pockets of his overcoat. With eyes fixed upon the tablecloth, he seemed to be thinking deeply, till presently he raised his head and looked steadily at Bellamy.

"You are sure that Von Behrling has not fooled you ? You are sure that you have that identical packet ?"

"I am absolutely certain that I have," Bellamy answered, without flinching.

"Then accept my price and have done with this matter," Streuss begged. "I will sign a draft for you here, and I will undertake to bring you the money, or honor it wherever you say, within twenty-four hours."

"I cannot decide so quickly," said Bellamy, shaking his head. "Mademoiselle Idiale and I must talk together first. I am not sure," he added, "whether I might not find a higher bidder."

Streuss laughed mirthlessly.

"There is little fear of that," he said. "The papers are of no use except to us and to England. To England, I will admit that the foreknowledge of what is to come would be worth much, although the eventful result would be the same. It is for that reason that I am here, for that reason that I have made you this offer."

"Mademoiselle and I must discuss it," Bellamy declared. "It is not a matter to be decided upon off-hand. Remember that it is not only the packet which you are offering to buy, but also my career and my honor."

"One hundred thousand pounds," Streuss said slowly. "From your own side you get nothing — nothing but your beggarly salary and an occasional reprimand. One hundred thousand pounds is not immense wealth, but it is something."

"Your offer is a generous one," admitted Bellamy, "there is no doubt about that. On the other hand, I cannot decide without further consideration. It is a big thing for us, remember. I have worked very hard for the contents of that packet."

Once more Streuss felt an uneasy pang of incredulity. After all, was this Englishman playing with him? So he asked: "You are quite sure that you have it?"

"There is no means of convincing you of which I care to make use. You must be content with my word. I have the packet. I paid Von Behrling for it and he gave it to me with his own hands."

"I must accept your word," Streuss declared. "I give you three days for reflection. Before I go, Mr. Bellamy, forgive me if I refer once more to this," — touching the newspaper which still lay upon the table. "Remember that Rudolph Von Behrling moved about a marked man. Your spies and mine were most of the time upon his heels. Yet in the end some third person seems to have intervened. Are you quite sure that you know nothing of this?"

"Upon my honor," Bellamy replied, "I have not the

slightest information concerning Von Behrling's death beyond what you can read there. It was as great a surprise to me as to you."

"It is incomprehensible," Streuss murmured.

"One can only conclude," Bellamy remarked thoughtfully, "that someone must have seen him with those notes. There were people moving about in the little restaurant where we met. The rustle of bank-notes has cost more than one man his life."

"For the present," Streuss said, "we must believe that it was so. Listen to me, both of you. You will be wiser if you do not delay. You are young people, and the world is before you. With money one can do everything. Without it, life is but a slavery. The world is full of beautiful dwelling-places for those who have the means to choose. Remember, too, that not a soul will ever know of this transaction, if you should decide to accept my offer."

"We shall remember all those things," Bellamy assured him.

Streuss took up his hat and gloves.

"With your permission, then, Mademoiselle," he concluded, turning to Louise, "I go. I must try and understand for myself the meaning of this thing which has happened to Von Behrling."

"Do not forget," Bellamy said, "that if you discover anything, we are equally interested." . . .

They heard him go out. Bellamy purposely held the door open until he saw the lift descend. Then he closed it firmly and came back into the room. Louise and he looked at each other, their faces full of anxious questioning.

"What does it mean?" Louise cried. "What can it mean?"

"Heaven alone knows!" Bellamy answered. "There is

not a gleam of daylight. My people are absolutely innocent of any attempt upon Von Behrling. If Streuss tells
the truth, and I believe he does, his people are in the same
position. Who, then, in the name of all that is miraculous,
can have murdered and robbed Von Behrling?"

"In London, too," Louise murmured. "It is not
Vienna, this, or Belgrade."

"You are right," Bellamy agreed. "London is one
of the most law-abiding cities in Europe. Besides, the
quarter where the murder occurred is entirely unfre-
quented by the criminal classes. It is simply a region of
great banks and the offices of merchant princes."

"Is it possible that there is some one else who knew
about that document?" Louise asked, — "some one
else who has been watching Von Behrling?"

Bellamy shook his head.

"How can that be? Besides, if any one else were
really on his track, they must have believed that he had
parted with it to me. I shall go back now to Downing
Street to ask for a letter to the Chief of Scotland Yard.
If anything comes out, I must have plenty of warning."

"And I," she said, with an approving nod, "shall go
back to bed again. These days are too strenuous for me.
Won't you stay and take your coffee with me?"

Bellamy held her hand for a moment in his.

"Dear," he said, "I would stay, but you understand,
don't you, what a maze this is into which we have wandered. Von Behrling has been murdered by some person
who seems to have dropped from the skies. Whoever
they may be, they have in their possession my twenty
thousand pounds and the packet which should have been
mine. I must trace them if I can, Louise. It is a poor
chance, but I must do my best. I myself am of the opinion

that Von Behrling was murdered for the money, and for the money only. If so, that packet may be in the hands of people who have no idea what use to make of it. They may even destroy it. If Streuss returns and you are forced to see him, be careful. Remember, we have the document — we are hesitating. So long as he believes that it is in our possession, he will not look elsewhere."

"I will be careful," Louise promised, with her arms around his neck. "And, dear, take care. When I think of poor Rudolph Von Behrling, I tremble, also, for you. It seems to me that your danger is no less than his."

"I do not go about with twenty thousand pounds in my pocket-book," with a smile.

She shook her head.

"No, but Streuss believes that you have the document which he is pledged to recover. Be careful that they do not lead you into a trap. They are not above anything, these men. I heard once of a Bulgarian in Vienna who was tortured — tortured almost to death — before he spoke. Then they thrust him into a lunatic asylum. Remember, dear, they have no consciences and no pity."

"We are in London," he reminded her.

"So was Von Behrling," she answered quickly, — "not only in London but in a safe part of London. Yet he is dead."

"It was not their doing," he declared. "In their own country, they have the whole machinery of their wonderful police system at their backs, and no fear of the law in their hearts. Here they must needs go cautiously. I don't think you need be afraid," he added, smiling, as he opened the door. "I think I can promise you that if you will do me the honor we will sup together to-night."

"You must fetch me from the Opera House," Louise

insisted. "It is a bargain. I have suffered enough neglect at your hands. One thing, David, — where do you go first from here?"

"To find the man," Bellamy answered gravely, "who was watching Von Behrling when he left me. If any man in England knows anything of the murder, it must be he. He should be at my rooms by now."

CHAPTER XIII

STEPHEN LAVERICK'S CONSCIENCE.

STEPHEN LAVERICK was a bachelor — his friends called him an incorrigible one. He had a small but pleasantly situated suite of rooms in Whitehall Court, looking out upon the river. His habits were almost monotonous in their regularity, and the morning following his late night in the city was no exception to the general rule. At eight o'clock, the valet attached to the suite knocked at his door and informed him that his bath was ready. He awoke at once from a sound sleep, sat up in bed, and remembered the events of the preceding evening.

At first he was inclined to doubt that slowly stirring effort of memory. He was a man of unromantic temperament, unimaginative, and by no means of an adventurous turn of mind. He sought naturally for the most reasonable explanation of this strange picture, which no effort of his will could dismiss from his memory. It was a dream, of course. But the dream did not fade. Slowly it spread itself out so that he could no longer doubt. He knew very well as he sat there on the edge of his bed that the thing was truth. He, Stephen Laverick, a man hitherto of upright character, with a reputation of which unconsciously he was proud, had robbed a dead man, had looked into the burning eyes of his murderer, had stolen away with twenty thousand pounds of someone else's money. Morally, at any rate, — probably legally as well, — he was a thief. A glimpse inside his safe on the part of an astute detective might very easily bring him under the grave suspicion of being a criminal of altogether deeper dye.

Stephen Laverick was, in his way, something of a philosopher. In the cold daylight, with the sound of the water running into his bath, this deed which he had done seemed to him foolish and reprehensible. Nevertheless, he realized the absolute finality of his action. The thing was done; he must make the best of it. Behaving in every way like a sensible man, he did not send for the newspapers and search hysterically for their account of last night's tragedy, but took his bath as usual, dressed with more than ordinary care, and sat down to his breakfast before he even unfolded the paper. The item for which he searched occupied by no means so prominent a position as he had expected. It appeared under one of the leading headlines, but it consisted of only a few words. He read them with interest but without emotion. Afterwards he turned to the Stock Exchange quotations and made notes of a few prices in which he was interested.

He completed in leisurely fashion an excellent breakfast and followed his usual custom of walking along the Embankment as far as the Royal Hotel, where he called a taxicab and drove to his offices. A little crowd had gathered around the end of the passage which led from Crooked Friars, and Laverick himself leaned forward and looked curiously at the spot where the body of the murdered man had lain. It seemed hard to him to reconstruct last night's scene in his mind now that the narrow street was filled with hurrying men and a stream of vehicles blocked every inch of the roadway. In his early morning mood the thing was impossible. In a moment or two he paid his driver and dismissed him.

He fancied that a certain relief was visible among his clerks when he opened the door at precisely his usual time and with a cheerful "Good-morning!" made his way into the private office. He lit his customary cigarette and dealt rapidly with the correspondence which was brought in to him by his head-clerk. Afterwards, as soon as he was alone, he opened the safe, thrust the contents of that inner drawer into his breast-pocket, and took up once more his hat and gloves.

"I am going around to the bank," he told his clerk as he passed out. "I shall be back in half-an-hour — perhaps less."

"Very good, sir," the man answered. "Will Mr. Morrison be here this morning?"

Laverick hesitated.

"No, Mr. Morrison will not be here to-day."

It was only a few steps to his bankers, and his request for an interview with the manager was immediately granted. The latter received him kindly but with a certain restraint. There are not many secrets in the city, and Morrison's big plunge on a particular mining share, notwithstanding its steady drop, had been freely commented upon.

"What can I do for you, Mr. Laverick?" the banker asked.

"I am not sure," answered Laverick. "To tell you the truth, I am in a somewhat singular position."

The banker nodded. He had not a doubt but that he understood exactly what that position was.

"You have perhaps heard," Laverick continued slowly, "that my late partner, Mr. Morrison, — "

"Late partner?" the manager interrupted.

Laverick assented.

"We had a few words last night," he explained, "and Mr. Morrison left the office with an understanding between us that he should not return. You will receive a formal intimation of that during the course of the next day or so. We will revert to the matter presently, if you wish. My immediate business with you is to discuss the fact that I have to provide something like twenty thousand pounds to-day if I decide to take up the purchases of stock which Morrison has made."

"You understand the position, of course, Mr. Laverick, if you fail to do so?" the manager remarked gravely.

"Naturally," Laverick answered. "I am quite aware of the fact that Morrison acted on behalf of the firm and that I am responsible for his transactions. He has plunged pretty deeply, though, a great deal more deeply than our capital warranted. I may add that I had not the slightest idea as to the extent of his dealings."

The bank manager adopted a sympathetic but serious attitude.

"Twenty thousand pounds," he declared, "is a great deal of money, Mr. Laverick."

"It is a great deal of money," Laverick admitted. "I am here to ask you to lend it to me."

The bank manager raised his eyebrows.

"My dear Mr. Laverick!" he exclaimed reproachfully.

"Upon unimpeachable security," Laverick continued.

The bank manager was conscious that he had allowed a little start of surprise to escape him, and bit his lip with annoyance. It was entirely contrary to his tenets to display at any time during office hours any sort of emotion.

"Unimpeachable security," he repeated. "Of course, if you have that to offer, Mr. Laverick, although the sum is a large one, it is our business to see what we can do for you."

"My security is of the best," Laverick declared grimly. "I have bank-notes here, Mr. Fenwick, for twenty thousand pounds."

The bank manager was again guilty of an unprofessional action. He whistled softly under his breath. A very respectable client he had always considered Mr. Stephen Laverick, but he had certainly never suspected him of being able to produce at a pinch such evidence of means. Laverick smoothed out the notes and laid them upon the table.

"Mr. Fenwick," he said, "I believe I am right in assuming that when one comes to one's bankers, one enters, as it were, into a confessional. I feel convinced that nothing which I say to you will be repeated outside this office, or will be allowed to dwell in your own mind except with reference to this particular transaction between you and me. I have the right, have I not, to take that for granted?"

"Most certainly," the banker agreed.

"From a strictly ethical point of view," Laverick went on, "this money is not mine. I hold it in trust for its owner, but I hold it without any conditions. I have power to make what use I wish of it, and I choose to-day to use it on my own behalf. Whether I am justified or not is scarcely a matter, I presume, which concerns this excellent banking establishment over which you preside so ably. I do not pay these bank-notes in to my account and ask you to credit me with twenty thousand pounds. I ask you to allow me to deposit them here for seven days as security against an overdraft. You can then advance me enough money to meet my engagements of to-day."

The banker took up the notes and looked them through,

one by one. They were very crisp, very new, and absolutely genuine.

"This is somewhat an extraordinary proceeding, Mr. Laverick," he said.

"I have no doubt that it must seem so to you," Laverick admitted. "At the same time, there the money is. You can run no risk. If I am exceeding my moral right in making use of these notes, it is I who will have to pay. Will you do as I ask?"

The banker hesitated. The transaction was somewhat a peculiar one, but on the face of it there could be no possible risk. At the same time, there was something about it which he could not understand.

"Your wish, Mr. Laverick," he remarked, looking at him thoughtfully, "seems to be to keep these notes out of circulation."

Laverick returned his gaze without flinching.

"In a sense, that is so," he assented.

"On the whole," the banker declared, "I should prefer to credit them to your account in the usual way."

"I am sorry," Laverick answered, "but I have a sentimental feeling about it. I prefer to keep the notes intact. If you cannot follow out my suggestion, I must remove my account at once. This is n't a threat, Mr. Fenwick, — you will understand that, I am sure. It is simply a matter of business, and owing to Morrison's speculations I have no time for arguments. I am quite satisfied to remain in your hands, but my feeling in the matter is exactly as I have stated, and I cannot change. If you are to retain my account, my engagements for to-day must be met precisely in the way I have pointed out."

The banker excused himself and left the room for a few moments. When he returned, he shrugged his shoul-

ders with the air of one who is giving in to an unreason-
able client.

"It shall be as you say, Mr. Laverick," he announced.
"The notes are placed upon deposit. Your engagements
to-day up to twenty thousand pounds shall be duly
honored."

Laverick shook hands with him, talked for a moment
or two about indifferent matters, and strolled back towards
his office. He had rather the sense of a man who moves
in a dream, who is living, somehow, in a life which does n't
belong to him. He was doing the impossible. He knew
very well that his name was in every one's mouth. People
were looking at him sympathetically, wondering how he
could have been such a fool as to become the victim of an
irresponsible speculator. No one ever imagined that he
would be able to keep his engagements. And he had
done it. The price might be a great one, but he was prepared to pay. At any moment the sensational news might
be upon the placards, and the whole world might know
that the man who had been murdered in Crooked Friars
last night had first been robbed of twenty thousand pounds.
So far he had felt himself curiously free from anything
in the shape of direct apprehensions. Already, however,
the shadow was beginning to fall. Even as he entered his
office, the sight of a stranger offering office files for sale
made him start. He half expected to feel a hand upon
his shoulder, a few words whispered in his ear. He set
his teeth tight. This was his risk and he must take it.

For several hours he remained in his office, engaged in
a scheme for the redirection of its policy. With the
absence of Morrison, too, there were other changes to be
made, — changes in the nature of the business they were
prepared to handle, limits to be fixed. It was not until

nearly luncheon time that the telephone, the simultaneous arrival of several clients, and the breathless entry of his own head-clerk rushing in from the house, told him what was going on.

" 'Unions' have taken their turn at last!" the clerk announced, in an excited tone. "They sagged a little this morning, but since eleven they have been going steadily up. Just now there seems to be a boom. Listen."

Laverick heard the roar of voices in the street, and nodded. He was prepared to be surprised at nothing.

"They were bound to go within a day or two," he remarked. "Morrison was n't an absolute idiot."

The luncheon hour passed. The excitement in the city grew. By three o'clock, ten thousand pounds would have covered all of Laverick's engagements. Just before closing-time, it was even doubtful whether he might not have borrowed every pénny without security at all. He took it all quite calmly and as a matter of course. He left the office a little earlier than usual, and every man whom he met stopped to slap him on the back and chaff him. He escaped as soon as he could, bought the evening papers, found a taxicab, and as soon as he had started spread them open. It was a remarkable proof of the man's self-restraint that at no time during the afternoon had he sent out for one of these early editions. He turned them over now with firm fingers. There was absolutely no fresh news. No one had come forward with any suggestion as to the identity of the murdered man. All day long the body had lain in the Mortuary, visited by a constant stream of the curious, but presumably unrecognized. Laverick could scarcely believe the words he read. The thing semed ludicrously impossible. The twenty thousand pounds must have come from some one. Why did they keep silence? What was the mystery about it? Could it be that they were not in a position to disclose the fact? Curiously enough, this unnatural absence of news inspired him with something which was almost fear. He had taken his risks boldly enough. Now that Fate was playing him this unexpectedly good turn, he was conscious of a growing nervousness. Who could he have been, this man? Whence could he have derived this great sum? One person at least must know that he had been robbed — the man who murdered him must know it. A cold shiver passed through Laverick's veins at the thought. Somewhere in London there must be a man thirsting for his blood, a man who had committed a murder in vain and been robbed of his spoil.

Laverick had no engagements for that evening, but instead of going to his club he drove straight to his rooms, meaning to change a little early for dinner and go to a theatre. He found there, however, a small boy waiting for him with a note in his hand. It was addressed in pencil only, and his name was printed upon it.

Laverick tore it open with a haste which he only imperfectly concealed. There was something ominous to him in those printed characters. Its contents, however, were short enough.

DEAR LAVERICK,

I must see you. Come the moment you get this. Come without fail, for your own sake and mine. A. M.

Laverick looked at the boy. His fingers were trembling, but it was with relief. The note was from Morrison.

"There is no address here," he remarked.

"The gent said as I was to take you back with me," the boy answered.

"Is it far?" Laverick asked.

"Close to Red Lion Square," the boy declared. "Not more nor five minutes in one of them taxicabs. The gent said we was to take one. He is in a great hurry to see you."

Laverick did not hesitate a moment.

"Very well," he said, "we'll start at once."

He put on his hat again and waited while the commissionaire called them a taxicab.

"What address?" he asked.

"Number 7, Theobald Square," the boy said.

Laverick nodded and repeated the address to the driver.

"What the dickens can Morrison be doing in a part like that!" he thought, as they passed up Northumberland Avenue.

CHAPTER XIV

THE Square was a small one, and in a particularly unsavory neighborhood. Laverick, who had once visited his partner's somewhat extensive suite of rooms in Jermyn Street, rang the bell doubtfully. The door was opened almost at once, not by a servant but by a young lady who was obviously expecting him. Before he could open his lips to frame an inquiry, she had closed the door behind him.

"Will you please come this way?" she said timidly.

Laverick found himself in a small sitting-room, unexpectedly neat, and with the plainness of its furniture relieved by certain undeniable traces of some cultured presence. The girl who had followed him stood with her back to the door, a little out of breath. Laverick contemplated her in surprise. She was under medium height, with small pale face and wonderful dark eyes. Her brown hair was parted in the middle and arranged low down, so that at first, taking into account her obvious nervousness, he thought that she was a child. When she spoke, however, he knew that for some reason she was afraid. Her voice was soft and low, but it was the voice of a woman.

"It is Mr. Laverick, is it not?" she asked, looking at him eagerly.

"My name is Stephen Laverick," he admitted. "I understood that I should find Mr. Arthur Morrison here."

"Yes," the girl answered, "he sent for you. The note was from him. He is here."

She made no movement to summon him. She still stood, in fact, with her back to the door. Laverick was distinctly puzzled. He felt himself unable to place this timid, childlike woman, with her terrified face and beautiful eyes. He had never heard Morrison speak of having any relations. His presence in such a locality, indeed, was hard to understand unless he had met with an accident. Morrison was one of those young men who would have chosen Hell with a " W " rather than Heaven E. C.

"I am afraid," Laverick said, "that for some reason or other you are afraid of me. I can assure you that I am quite harmless," he added smiling. "Won't you sit down and tell me what is the matter? Is Mr. Morrison in any trouble?"

"Yes," she answered, "he is. As for me, I am terrified."

She came a little away from the door. Laverick was a man who inspired trust. His tone, too, was unusually kind. He had the protective instinct of a big man toward a small woman.

"Come and tell me all about it," he suggested. "I expected to hear that he had gone abroad."

"Mr. Laverick," she said, looking up at him tremulously. "I was hoping that you could have told me what it was — that had come to him."

"Well, that rather depends," Laverick answered. "We certainly had a terribly anxious time yesterday. Our business has been most unfortunate — "

"Yes, yes!" the girl interrupted. "Please go on. There have been business troubles, then."

"Rather," Laverick continued. "Last night they reached such a pitch that I gave Morrison some money

and it was agreed that he should leave the firm and try
his luck somewhere else. I quite understood that he was
going abroad."

The girl seemed, for some reason, relieved.

"There was something, then," she said, half to herself.
"There was something. Oh, I am glad of that! You
were angry with him, perhaps, Mr. Laverick?"

Laverick stood with his back to the little fireplace and
with his hands behind him — a commanding figure in
the tiny room full of feminine trifles. He looked a great
deal more at his ease than he really was.

"Perhaps I was inclined to be short-tempered," he
admitted. "You see, to be frank with you, the department of our business that was going wrong was the one
over which Morrison has had sole control. He had
entered into certain speculations which I considered unjustifiable. To-day, however, matters took an unexpected
turn for the better."

Almost as he spoke his face clouded. Morrison, of
course, would be triumphant. Perhaps he would even
expect to be reinstated. For many reasons, this was a
thing which Laverick did not desire.

"Now tell me," he continued, "what is the matter with
Morrison, and why has he sent for me, and, if you will
pardon my saying so, why is he here instead of in his
own rooms?"

"I will explain," she began softly.

"You will please explain sitting down," he said firmly.

"And don't look so terrified," he added, with a little
laugh. "I can assure you that I am not going to eat you,
or anything of that sort. You make me feel quite uncomfortable."

She smiled for the first time, and Laverick thought

that he had never seen anything so wonderful as the change in her features. The strained rigidity passed away. An altogether softer light gleamed in her wonderful eyes. She was certainly by far the prettiest child he had ever seen. As yet he could not take her altogether seriously.

"Thank you," she said, sinking down upon the arm of an easy-chair. "First of all, then, Arthur is here because he is my brother."

"Your brother!" Laverick repeated wonderingly.

Somehow or other, he had never associated Morrison with relations. Besides, this meant that she must be of his race. There was nothing in her face to denote it except the darkness of her eyes, and that nameless charm of manner, a sort of ultra-sensitiveness, which belongs sometimes to the highest type of Jews. It was not a quality, Laverick thought, which he should have associated with Morrison's sister.

"My brother, in a way," she resumed. "Arthur's father was a widower and my mother was a widow when they were married. You are surprised?"

"There is no reason why I should be," he answered, curiously relieved at her last statement. "Your brother and I have been connected in business for some years. We have seen very little of one another outside."

"I dare say," she continued, still timidly, "that Arthur's friends would not be your friends, and that he would n't care for the same sort of things. You see, my mother is dead and also his father, and as we are n't really related at all, I cannot expect that he would come to see me very often. Last night, though, quite late — long after I had gone to bed — he rang the bell here. I was frightened, for just now I am all alone, and my servant only comes in the morning. So I looked out of the window and I saw him on the pavement, huddled up against the door. I hurried down and let him in. Mr. Laverick," she went on, with an appealing glance at him, "I have never seen any one look like it. He was terrified to death. Something seemed to have happened which had taken away from him even the power of speech. He pushed past me into this room, threw himself into that chair," she added, pointing across the room, "and he sobbed and beat his hands upon his knees as though he were a woman in a fit of hysterics. His clothes were all untidy, he was as pale as death, and his eyes looked as though they were ready to start out of his head."

"You must indeed have been frightened," Laverick said softly.

"Frightened! I shall never forget it! I did not sleep all night. He would tell me nothing — he has scarcely spoken a sensible word. Early this morning I persuaded him to go upstairs, and made him lie down. He has taken two draughts which I bought from the chemist, but he has not slept. Every now and then he tries to get up, but in a minute or two he throws himself down on the bed again and hides his face. If any one rings at the bell, he shrieks. If he hears a footfall in the street, even, he calls out for me. Mr. Laverick, I have never been so frightened in my life. I did n't know whom to send for or what to do. When he wrote that note to you I was so relieved. You can't imagine how glad I am to think you have come!"

Laverick's eyes were full of sympathy. One could see that the scene of last night had risen up again before her eyes. She was shrinking back, and the terror was upon her once more. He moved over to her side, and with an impulse which, when he thought of it afterwards, amazed him, laid his hand gently upon her shoulder.

"Don't worry yourself thinking about it," he said. "I will talk to your brother. We did have words, I'll admit, last night, but there wasn't the slightest reason why it should have upset him in this way. Things in the city were shocking yesterday, but they have improved a great deal to-day. Let me go upstairs and I'll try and pump some courage into him."

"You are so kind," she murmured, suddenly dropping her hands from before her face and looking up at him with shining eyes, "so very kind. Will you come, then?"

She rose and he followed her out of the room, up the stairs, and into a tiny bedroom. Laverick had no time to look around, but it seemed to him, notwithstanding the cheap white furniture and very ordinary appointments, that the same note of dainty femininity pervaded this little apartment as the one below.

"It is my room," she said shyly. "There is no other properly furnished, and I thought that he might sleep upon the bed."

"Perhaps he is asleep now," Laverick whispered.

Even as he spoke, the dark figure stretched upon the sheets sprang into a sitting posture. Laverick was conscious of a distinct shock. It was Morrison, still wearing the clothes in which he had left the office, his collar crushed out of all shape, his tie vanished. His black hair, usually so shiny and perfectly arranged, was all disordered. Out of his staring eyes flashed an expression which one sees seldom in life, — an expression of real and mortal terror.

"Who is it?" he cried out, and even his voice was unrecognizable. "Who is that? What do you want?"

"It is I — Laverick," Laverick answered. "What on earth is the matter with you, man?"

Morrison drew a quick breath. Some part of the terror seemed to leave his face, but he was still an alarming-looking object. Laverick quietly opened the door and laid his hand upon the girl's shoulder.

"Will you leave us alone?" he asked. "I will come and talk to you afterwards, if I may."

She nodded understandingly, and passed out. Laverick closed the door and came up to the bedside.

"What in the name of thunder has come over you, Morrison?" he said. "Are you ill, or what is it?"

Morrison opened his lips — opened them twice — without any sort of sound issuing.

"This is absurd!" Laverick exclaimed protestingly. "I have been feeling worried myself, but there's nothing so terrifying in losing one's money, after all. As a matter of fact, things are altogether better in the city to-day. You made a big mistake in taking us out of our depth, but we are going to pull through, after all. 'Unions' have been going up all day."

Laverick's presence, and the sound of his even, matter-of-fact tone, seemed to act like a tonic upon his late partner. He made no reference, however, to Laverick's words.

"You got my note?" he asked hoarsely.

"Naturally I got it," Laverick answered impatiently, "and I came at once. Try and pull yourself together. Sit up and tell me what you are doing here, frightening your sister out of her life."

Morrison groaned.

"I came here," he muttered, "because I dared not go to my own rooms. I was afraid!"

Laverick struggled with the contempt he felt.

"Man alive," he exclaimed, "what was there to be afraid of?"

"You don't know!" Morrison faltered. "You don't know!"

Then, for the first time, it occurred to Laverick that perhaps the financial crisis in their affairs was not the only thing which had reduced his late partner to this hopeless state. He looked at him narrowly.

"Where did you go last night," he asked, "when you left me?"

"Nowhere," Morrison gasped. "I came here."

Laverick made a space for himself at the end of the bed, and sat down.

"Look here," he said, "it's no use sending for me unless you mean to tell me everything. Have you been getting yourself into any trouble apart from our affairs, or is there anything in connection with them which I don't know?"

Again Morrison opened his lips, and again, for some reason or other, he remained speechless. Then a certain fear came also upon Laverick. There was something in Morrison's state which was in itself terrifying.

"You had better tell me all about it," Laverick persisted, "whatever it is. I will help you if I can."

Morrison shook his head. There was a glass of water by his side. He thrust his finger into it and passed it across his lips. They were dry, almost cracking.

"Look here," he said, "I've got a breakdown — that's what's the matter with me. My nerves were never good. I'm afraid of going mad. The anxiety of the last few weeks has been too much for me. I want to get out of the country quickly, and I don't know how to manage it. I can't think. Directly I try to think my head goes round."

"There is nothing in the world to prevent your going away," Laverick answered. "It is the simplest matter possible. Even if we had gone under to-day, no one could have stopped your going wherever you chose to go. Ruin, even if it had been ruin,— and I told you just now that business was better,— is not a crime. Pull yourself together, for Heaven's sake, man! You should be ashamed to come here and frighten that poor little girl downstairs almost to death."

Morrison gripped his partner's arm.

"You must do as I ask," he declared hoarsely. "It does n't matter about prices being better. I want to get away. You must help me."

Laverick looked at him steadily. Morrison was an ordinary young man of his type, something of a swaggerer, probably at heart a coward. But this was no ordinary fear —not even the ordinary fear of a coward. Laverick's face became graver. There was something else, then!

"I will get you out of the country if I can," said he. "There is no difficulty about it at all unless you are concealing something from me. You can catch a fast steamer to-morrow, either for South Africa or New York, but before I make any definite plans, had n't you better tell me exactly what happened last night?"

Once more Morrison's lips parted without the ability to frame words. Then a feeble moan escaped him. He threw up his hands and his head fell back. The ghastliness of his face spread almost to his lips, and he sank back among the pillows. Laverick strode across the room to the door.

"Are you anywhere about?" he called out.

The girl was by his side in a moment.

"There is nothing to be alarmed at," he said, "but

your brother has fainted. Bring me some sal volatile
if you have it, and I think that you had better run out
and get a doctor. I will stay with him. I know exactly
what to do."

She pointed to the dressing-table, where a little bottle
was standing, and ran downstairs without a word. Laverick mixed some of the spirit, and moved over to the side
of the fainting man.

CHAPTER XV

The doctor, a grave, incurious person, arrived within a few minutes to find Morrison already conscious but absolutely exhausted. He felt his patient's pulse, prescribed a draught, and followed Laverick down into the sitting-room.

"An ordinary case of nervous exhaustion," he pronounced. "The patient appears to have had a very severe shock lately. He will be all right with proper diet and treatment, and a complete rest. I will call again to-morrow."

He accepted the fee which Laverick slipped into his hand, and took his departure. Once more Laverick was alone with the girl, who had followed them downstairs.

"There is nothing to be alarmed at, you see," he remarked.

"It is not his health which frightens me. I am sure — I am quite sure that he has something upon his mind. Did he tell you nothing?"

"Nothing at all," Laverick answered, with an inward sense of thankfulness. "To tell you the truth, though, I am afraid you are right and that he did get into some sort of trouble last night. He was just about to tell me something when he fainted."

Upstairs they could hear him moaning. The girl listened with pitiful face.

"What am I to do?" she asked. "I cannot leave him like this, and if I am not at the theatre in twenty minutes, I shall be fined."

"The theatre?" Laverick repeated.

She nodded.

"I am on the stage," she said, — "only a chorus girl at the Universal, worse luck. Still, they don't allow us to stay away, and I can't afford to lose my place."

"Do you mean to say that you have been keeping yourself here, then?" Laverick asked bluntly.

"Of course," she answered. "I do not like to be a burden on any one, and after all, you see, Arthur and I are really not related at all. He has always told me, too, that times have been so bad lately."

Laverick was on the point of telling her that bad though they had been Arthur Morrison had never drawn less than fifteen hundred a year, but he checked himself. It was not his business to interfere.

"I think," he said, "that your brother ought to have provided for you. He could have done so with very little effort."

"But what am I to do now?" she asked him. "If I am absent, I shall lose my place."

Laverick thought for a moment.

"If you went round there and told them," he suggested, "would that make any difference? I could stay until you came back."

"Do you mind?" she asked eagerly. "It would be so kind of you."

"Not at all," he answered. "Perhaps you would be good enough to bring a taxicab back, and I could take it on to my rooms. Take one from here, if you can find it. There are always some at the corner."

"I'd love to," she answered. "I must run upstairs and get my hat and coat."

He watched her go up on tiptoe for fear of disturbing her brother. Her feet seemed almost unearthly in the lightness of their pressure. Not a board creaked. She seemed to float down to him in a most becoming little hat but a shockingly shabby jacket, of whose deficiencies she seemed wholly unaware. Her lips were parted once more in a smile.

"He is fast asleep and breathing quite regularly," she announced. "It is nice of you to stay."

He looked at her almost jealously.

"Do you know," he said, "you ought not to go about alone?"

She laughed, softly but heartily.

"Have you any idea how old I am?"

"I took you for fourteen when I came inside," he answered. "Afterwards I thought you might be sixteen. Later on, it seemed to me possible that you were eighteen. I am absolutely certain that you are not more than nineteen."

"That shows how little you know about it. I am twenty, and I am quite used to going about alone. Will you sit upstairs or here? I am so sorry that I have nothing to offer you."

"Thanks, I need nothing. I think I will sit upstairs in case he wakes."

She nodded and stole out, closing the door behind her noiselessly. Laverick watched her from the window until she was out of sight, moving without any appearance of haste, yet with an incredible swiftness. When she had turned the corner, he went slowly upstairs and into the room where Morrison still lay asleep. He drew a chair to the bedside and leaning forward opened out the evening paper. The events of the last hour or so had completely blotted out from his mind, for the time being, his own expedition into the world of tragical happenings. He glanced at the sleeping man, then opened his paper. There was very little fresh news except that this time the fact was mentioned that upon the body of the murdered man was discovered a sum larger than was at first supposed. It seemed doubtful, therefore, whether robbery, after all, was the motive of the crime, especially as it took place in a neighborhood which was by no means infested with criminals. There was a suggestion of political motive, a reference to the " Black Hand," concerning whose doings the papers had been full since the murder of a well-known detective a few weeks ago. But apart from this there was nothing fresh.

Laverick folded up the paper and leaned back in his chair. The strain of the last twenty-four hours was beginning to tell even upon his robust constitution. The atmosphere of the room, too, was close. He leaned back in his chair and was suddenly weary. Perhaps he dozed. At any rate, the whisper which called him back to realization of where he was, came to him so unexpectedly that he sat up with a sudden start.

Morrison's eyes were open, he had raised himself on his elbow, his lips were parted. His manner was quieter, but there were black lines deep engraven under his eyes, in which there still shone something of that haunting fear.

"Laverick !" he repeated hoarsely.

Laverick, fully awakened now, leaned towards him.

"Hullo," he said, "are you feeling more like yourself ?"

Morrison nodded.

"Yes," he admitted, "I am feeling — better. How did you come here? I can't remember anything."

"You sent for me," Laverick answered. "I arrived to find you pretty well in a state of collapse. Your sister has gone round to the theatre to ask them to excuse her this evening."

"I remember now that I sent for you," Morrison continued. "Tell me, has any one been around at the office asking after me?"

"No one particular," Laverick answered, — "no one at all that I can think of. There were one or two inquiries through the telephone, but they were all ordinary business matters."

The man on the bed drew a little breath which sounded like a sigh of relief.

"I have made a fool of myself, Laverick," he said hoarsely.

"You are making a worse one of yourself by lying here and giving way," Laverick declared, "besides frightening your sister half to death.

Morrison passed his hand across his forehead.

"We talked — some time ago, " he went on, "about my getting away. You promised that you would help me. You said that I could get off to Africa or America to-morrow."

"Not the slightest difficulty about that," Laverick answered. "There are half-a-dozen steamers sailing, at least. At the same time, I suppose I ought to remind you that the firm is going to pull through. Mind — don't take this unkindly but the truth is best — I will not have you back again. There may have to be a more definite readjustment of our affairs now, but the old business is finished with."

"I don't want to come back," Morrison murmured. "I have had enough of the city for the rest of my life. I'd rather get away somewhere and make a fresh start. You'll help me, Laverick, won't you?"

"Yes, I will help you," Laverick promised.

"You were always a good sort," Morrison continued, "much too good for me. It was a rotten partnership for you. We could never have pulled together."

"Let that go," Laverick interrupted. "If you really mean getting away, that simplifies matters, of course. Have you made any plans at all? Where do you want to go?"

"To New York," answered Morrison; "New York would suit me best. There is money to be made there if one has something to make a start with."

"There will be some more money to come to you," Laverick answered, "probably a great deal more. I shall place our affairs in the hands of an accountant, and shall have an estimate drawn up to yesterday. You shall have every penny that is due to you. You have quite enough, however, to get there with. I will see to your ticket to-night, if possible. When you've arrived you can cable me your address, or you can decide where you will stay before you leave, and I will send you a further remittance."

"You're a good sort, Laverick," Morrison mumbled.

"You'd better give me the key of your rooms," Laverick continued, "and I will go back and put together some of your things. I suppose you will not want much to go away with. The rest can be sent on afterwards. And what about your letters?"

Morrison, with a sudden movement, threw himself almost out of the bed. He clutched at Laverick's shoulder frantically.

"Don't go near my rooms, Laverick!" he begged.

"Promise me that you won't! I don't want any letters! I don't want any of my things!"

Laverick was dumfounded.

"You mean you want to go away without — "

"I mean just what I have said," Morrison continued hysterically. "If you go there they will watch you, they will follow you, they will find out where I am. I should be there now but for that."

Laverick was silent for a moment. The matter was becoming serious.

"Very well," he said, "I will do as you say. I will not go near your rooms. I will get you a few things somewhere to start with."

Morrison sank back upon his pillow.

"Thank you, Laverick," he said; "thank you. I wish — I wish — "

His voice seemed to die away. Laverick glanced towards him, wondering at the unfinished sentence. Once again the man's face seemed to be convulsed with horror. He flung himself face downward upon the bed and tore at the sheets with both his hands.

"Don't be a fool," Laverick said sternly. "If you've anything on your mind apart from business, tell me about it and I'll do what I can to help you."

Morrison made no reply. He was sobbing now like a child. Laverick rose to his feet and went to the window. What was to be done with such a creature! When he got back, Morrison had raised himself once more into a sitting posture. His appearance was absolutely spectral.

"Laverick," he said feebly, "there is something else, but I cannot tell you — I cannot tell any one."

"Just as you please, of course," Laverick answered. "I am simply anxious to help you."

"You can do that as it is!" Morrison exclaimed
feverishly. "You must promise me something — promise
that if any one asks for me to-morrow before I get away,
you will not tell them where I am. Say you suppose that
I am at my rooms, or that I have gone into the country
for a few days. Say that you are expecting me back.
Don't let any one know that I have gone abroad, until
I am safely away. And then don't tell a soul where I have
gone."

"Have you been up to any tricks with your friends?"
Laverick asked sternly.

"I have n't — I swear that I have n't," Morrison declared. "It's something quite outside business — quite
outside business altogether."

"Very well," answered Laverick, "I will promise what
you have asked, then. Listen — here is your sister back
again," he added, as he heard the taxicab stop outside.
"Pull yourself together and don't frighten her so much.
I am going down to meet her. I shall tell her that you are
better. Try and buck up when she comes in to see you."

"I'll do my best," Morrison said humbly. "If you
knew! If you only knew!"

He began to sob again. Laverick left the room and,
descending the stairs, met the girl in the hall. Her white
face questioned him before her lips had time to frame the
speech.

"Your brother is very much better," Laverick said. "I
am sure that you need not be anxious about him."

"I am so glad," she murmured. "They let me off but
I had to pay a fine. I had no idea before that I was so
important. Shall I go to him now?"

"One moment," Laverick answered, holding open the
door of the sitting-room. "Miss Morrison," he went on, —

"Miss Leneveu is my name," she interrupted.

"I beg your pardon. Your brother evidently has something on his mind apart from business. I am afraid that he has been getting into some sort of trouble. I don't think there is any object in bothering him about it, but the great thing is to get him away."

"You will help?" she begged.

"I will help, certainly," Laverick answered. "I have promised to. You must see that he is ready to leave here at seven o'clock to-morrow morning. He wants to go to New York, and the special to catch the German boat will leave Waterloo somewhere about eight to eight-thirty."

"But his clothes!" she cried. "How can he be ready by then?"

"Your brother does not wish me or any one to go near his rooms or to send him any of his belongings," Laverick continued quietly.

"But how strange!" the girl exclaimed. "Do you mean to say, then, that he is going without anything?"

"I am afraid," Laverick said kindly, "that we must take it for granted that your brother has got mixed up in some undesirable business or other. He is nervously anxious to keep his whereabouts an entire secret. He has been asking me whether any one has been to the office to inquire for him. Under the circumstances, I think the best thing we can do is to humor him. I shall buy him before to-morrow morning a cheap dressing-case and a ready-made suit of clothes, and a few things for the voyage. Then I shall send a cab for you both at seven o'clock and meet you at the station.

"You are very kind," she murmured. "What should I have done without you? Oh, I cannot think!"

The protective instinct in the man was suddenly strong.

Naturally unaffectionate, he was conscious of an almost overmastering desire to take her hands in his, even to lift her up and kiss away the tears which shone in her deep, childlike eyes. He reminded himself that she was a stranger, that her appearance of youth was a delusion, that she could only construe such an action as a liberty, an impertinence, offered under circumstances for which there could be no possible excuse.

He moved away towards the door.

"Naturally," he said, "I am glad to be of use to your brother. You see," he explained, a little awkwardly, "after all, we have been partners in business."

He caught a look upon her face and smiled.

"Naturally, too," he continued, "it has been a great pleasure for me to do anything to relieve your anxiety."

She gave him her hands then of her own accord. The gratitude which shone out of her swimming eyes seemed mingled with something which was almost invitation. Laverick was suddenly swept off his feet. Something had come into his life — something absurd, uncounted upon, incomprehensible. The atmosphere of the room seemed electrified. In a moment, he had done what only a second or two before he had told himself would be the action of a cad. He had taken her, unresisting, up into his arms, kissed her eyes and lips. Afterwards, he was never able to remember those few moments clearly, only it seemed to him that she had accepted his caress almost without hesitation, with the effortless serenity of a child receiving a natural consolation in a time of trouble. But Laverick was conscious of other feelings as he leaned hard back in the corner of his taxicab and was driven swiftly away.

CHAPTER XVI

THE WAITER AT THE " BLACK POST "

LAVERICK, notwithstanding that the hour was becoming late, found an outfitter's shop in the Strand still open, and made such purchases as he could on Morrison's behalf. Then, with the bag ready packed, he returned to his rooms. Time had passed quickly during the last three hours. It was nearly nine o'clock when he stepped out of the lift and opened the door of his small suite of rooms with the latchkey which hung from his chain. He began to change his clothes mechanically, and he had nearly finished when the telephone bell upon his table rang.

"Who's that?" he asked, taking up the receiver.

"Hall-porter, sir," was the answer. "Person here wishes to see you particularly."

"A person!" Laverick repeated. "Man or woman?"

"Man, sir."

"Better send him up," Laverick ordered.

"He's a seedy-looking lot, sir," the porter explained. "I told him that I scarcely thought you'd see him."

"Never mind," Laverick answered. "I can soon get rid of the fellow if he's cadging."

He went back to his room and finished fastening his tie. His own affairs had sunk a little into the background lately, but the announcement of this unusual visitor brought them back into his mind with a rush. Notwithstanding his iron nerves, his fingers shook as he drew on his dinner-jacket and walked out to the passageway to answer the bell which rang a few seconds later. A man stood outside, dressed in shabby black clothes, whose face somehow was familiar to him, although he could not, for the moment, place it.

"Do you want to see me?" Laverick asked.

"If you please, Mr. Laverick," the man replied, "if you could spare me just a moment."

"You had better come inside, then," Laverick said, closing the door and preceding the way into the sitting-room. At any rate, there was nothing threatening about the appearance of this visitor — nor anything official.

"I have taken the liberty of coming, sir," the man announced, "to ask you if you can tell me where I can find Mr. Arthur Morrison."

Laverick's face showed no sign of his relief. What he felt he succeeded in keeping to himself.

"You mean Morrison — my partner, I suppose?" he answered.

"If you please, sir," the man admitted. "I wanted a word or two with him most particular. I found out his address from the caretaker of your office, but he don't seem to have been home to his rooms at all last night, and they know nothing about him there."

"Your face seems familiar to me," Laverick remarked. "Where do you come from?"

The man hesitated.

"I am the waiter, sir, at the 'Black Post,' — little bar and restaurant, you know," he added, "just behind your offices, sir, at the end of Crooked Friars' Alley. You've been in once or twice, Mr. Laverick, I think. Mr. Morrison's a regular customer. He comes in for a drink most mornings."

Laverick nodded.

"I knew I'd seen your face somewhere," he said. "What do you want with Mr. Morrison?"

The man was silent. He twirled his hat and looked embarrassed.

"It's a matter I should n't like to mention to any one except Mr. Morrison himself, sir," he declared finally. "If you could put me in the way of seeing him, I'd be glad. I may say that it would be to his advantage, too."

Laverick was thoughtful for a moment.

"As it happens, that's a little difficult," he explained. "Mr. Morrison and I disagreed on a matter of business last night. I undertook certain responsibilities which he should have shared, and he arranged to leave the firm and the country at once. We parted — well, not exactly the best of friends. I am afraid I cannot give you any information."

"You have n't seen him since then, sir?" the man asked.

Laverick lied promptly but he lied badly. His visitor was not in the least convinced.

"I am afraid I have n't made myself quite plain, sir," he said. "It's to do him a bit o' good that I'm here. I'm not wishing him any harm at all. On the contrary, it's a great deal more to his advantage to see me than it will be mine to find him."

"I think," Laverick suggested, "that you had better be frank with me. Supposing I knew where to catch Morrison before he left the country, I could easily deal with you on his behalf."

The man looked doubtful.

"You see, sir," he replied awkwardly, "it's a matter I would n't like to breathe a word about to any one but Mr. Morrison himself. It's — it's a bit serious."

The man's face gave weight to his words. Curiously enough, the gleam of terror which Laverick caught in his white face reminded him of a similar look which he had seen in Morrison's eyes barely an hour ago. To gain time, Laverick moved across the room, took a cigarette from a box and lit it. A conviction was forming itself in his mind. There was something definite behind these hysterical paroxysms of his late partner, something of which this man had an inkling.

"Look here," he said, throwing himself into an easy-chair, "I think you had better be frank with me. I must know more than I know at present before I help you to find Morrison, even if he is to be found. We did n't part very good friends, but I'm his friend enough — for the sake of others," he added, after a moment's hesitation, "to do all that I could to help him out of any difficulty he may have stumbled into. So you see that so far as anything you may have to say to him is concerned, I think you might as well say it to me."

"You could n't see your way, then, sir," the man continued doggedly, "to tell me where I could find Mr. Morrison himself?"

"No, I could n't," Laverick decided. "Even if I knew exactly where he was — and I'm not admitting that — I could n't put you in touch with him unless I knew what your business was."

The man's eyes gleamed. He was a typical waiter — pasty-faced, unwholesome-looking — but he had small eyes of a greenish cast, and they were expressive.

"I think, sir," he said, "you've some idea yourself, then, that Mr. Morrison has been getting into a bit of trouble."

"We won't discuss that," Laverick answered. "You

must either go away — it's past nine o'clock and I have n't had my dinner yet — or you must treat me as you would Mr. Morrison."

The man looked upon the carpet for several moments.

"Very well, sir," he said, "there's no great reason why I should put myself out about this at all. The only thing is — "

He hesitated.

"Well, go on," Laverick said encouragingly.

"I think," the man continued, "that Mr. Morrison — knowing, as I will do, sir, the sort of gent he is — would be more likely ɔ talk common sense with me about this matter than you, sir."

"I'll imagine I'm Morrison, for the moment," Laverick said smiling, "especially as I'm acting for him."

The man looked around the room. The door behind had been left ajar. He stepped backward and closed it.

"You'll pardon the liberty, sir," he said, "but this is a serious matter I'm going to speak about. I'll just tell you a little thing and you can form your own conclusions. Last night we was open late at the 'Black Post.' We keep open, sir, as you know, when you gentlemen at the Stock Exchange are busy. About nine o'clock there was a strange customer came in. He had two drinks and he sat as though he were waiting. In about arf-an-hour another gent came in, and they went into a corner together and seemed to be doing some sort of business. Anyways, there was papers passed between them. I was fairly busy about then, as there were one or two more customers in the place, but I noticed these two talking together, and I noticed the dark gentleman leave. The others went out a few minutes afterwards, and the gent who had come first was alone in the place. He sat in the corner and he

had a pocket-book on the table before him. I had a sort
of casual glance at it when I brought him a drink, and it
seemed to me that it was full of bank-notes. He sat there
just like a man extra deep in thought. Just after eleven,
in came Mr. Morrison. I could see he was rare and put
out, for he was white, and shaking all over. 'Give me a
drink, Jim,' he said, — 'a big brandy and soda, big as
you make 'em.'"

The man paused for a moment as though to collect himself. Laverick was suddenly conscious of a strange thrill
creeping through his pulses.

"Go on," he said. "That was after he left me. Go on."

"He was quite close to the other gent, Mr. Morrison
was," the waiter continued, "but they did n't say nowt
to each other. All of a sudden I see Mr. Morrison set down
his glass and stare at the other chap as though he'd seen
something that had given him a turn. I leaned over the
counter and had a look, too. There he sat — this tall,
fair chap who had been in the place so long — with his
big pocket-book on the table in front of him, and even
from where I was I could see that there was a great pile
of bank-notes sticking out from it. All of a sudden he
looks up and sees Mr. Morrison a-watching him and me
from behind the counter. Back he whisks the pocket-
book into his pocket, calls me for my bill, gives me two
mouldy pennies for a tip, buttons up his coat and walks
out."

"You know who he was?" Laverick inquired.

Again the waiter paused for a moment before he
answered — paused and looked nervously around the
room. His voice shook.

"He was the man as was murdered about a hundred
yards off the 'Black Post' last night, sir," he said.

"How do you know?" Laverick asked.

"I got an hour off to-day," the waiter continued, "and went down to the Mortuary. There was no doubt about it. There he was — same chap, same clothes. I could swear to him anywhere, and I reckon I'll have to at the inquest."

Laverick's cigarette burned away between his fingers. It seemed to him that he was no longer in the room. He was listening to Big Ben striking the hour, he was back again in that tiny little bedroom with its spotless sheets and lace curtains. The man on the bed was looking at him. Laverick remembered the look and shivered.

"What has this to do with Morrison?" he demanded.

Once more the waiter looked around in that half mysterious, half terrified way.

"Mr. Morrison, sir," he said, dropping his voice to a hoarse whisper, "he followed the other chap out within thirty seconds. A sort of queer look he'd got in his face too, and he went out without paying me. I've read the papers pretty careful, sir," the man went on, "but I ain't seen no word of that pocket-book of bank-notes being found on the man as was murdered."

Laverick threw the end of his burning cigarette away. He walked to the window, keeping his back deliberately turned on his visitor. His eyes followed the glittering arc of lights which fringed the Thames Embankment, were caught by the flaring sky-sign on the other side of the river. He felt his heart beating with unaccustomed vigor. Was this, then, the secret of Morrison's terror? He wondered no longer at his collapse. The terror was upon him, too. He felt his forehead, and his hand, when he drew it away, was wet. It was not Morrison alone but he himself who might be implicated in this man's knowledge.

The thoughts flitted through his brain like parts of a nightmare. He saw Morrison arrested, he saw the whole story of the missing pocket-book in the papers, he imagined his bank manager reading it and thinking of that parcel of mysterious bank-notes deposited in his keeping on the morning after the tragedy. . . . Laverick was a strong man, and his moment of weakness, poignant though it had been, passed. This was no new thing with which he was confronted. All the time he had known that the probabilities were in favor of such a discovery. He set his teeth and turned to face his visitor.

"This is a very serious thing which you have told me," he said. "Have you spoken about it to any one else?"

"Not a soul, sir," the man answered. "I thought it best to have a word or two first with Mr. Morrison."

"You were thinking of attending the inquest," Laverick said thoughtfully. "The police would thank you for your evidence, and there, I suppose, the matter would end"

"You've hit it precisely, sir," the man admitted. "There the matter would end."

"On the other hand," Laverick continued, speaking as though he were reasoning this matter out to himself, "supposing you decided not to meddle in an affair which does not concern you, supposing you were not sure as to the identity of your customer last night, and being a little tired you could not rightly remember whether Mr. Morrison called in for a drink or not, and so, to cut the matter short, you dismissed the whole matter from your mind and let the inquest take its own course, — "

Laverick paused. His visitor scratched the side of his chin and nodded.

"You've put this matter plainly, sir," he said, "in what

I call an understandable, straightforward way. I'm a poor man — I've been a poor man all my life — and I've never seed a chance before of getting away from it. I see one now."

"You want to do the best you can for yourself?"

"So 'elp me God, sir, I do!" the man agreed.

Laverick nodded.

"You have done a remarkably wise thing," he said, "in coming to me and in telling me about this affair. The idea of connecting Mr. Morrison with the murder would, of course, be ridiculous, but, on the other hand, it would be very disagreeable to him to have his name mentioned in connection with it. You have behaved discreetly, and you have done Mr. Morrison a service in trying to find him out. You will do him a further service by adopting the second course I suggested with regard to the inquest. What do you consider that service is worth?"

"It depends, sir," the man answered quietly, "at what price Mr. Morrison values his life!"

CHAPTER XVII

THE man's manner was expressive. Laverick repeated his phrase, frowning.

"His life!"

"Yes, sir!"

Laverick shrugged his shoulders.

"Come," he declared, "you must not go too far with this thing. I have admitted, so as to clear the way for anything you have to say, that Mr. Morrison would not care to have his name mentioned in connection with this affair. But because he left your bar a few minutes after the murdered man, it is sheer folly to assume that therefore he is necessarily implicated in his death. I cannot conceive anything more unlikely."

The man smiled — a slow, uncomfortable smile which suggested mirth less than anything in the world.

"There are a few other things, sir," he remarked, — "one in especial."

"Well?" Laverick inquired. "Let's have it. You had better tell me everything that is in your mind."

"The man was stabbed with a horn-handled knife."

"I remember reading that," Laverick admitted. "Well?"

"The knife was mine," his visitor affirmed, dropping his voice once more to a whisper. "It lay on the edge of the counter, close to where Mr. Morrison was leaning, and as soon as he'd gone I missed it."

Laverick was silent. What was there to be said?

"Horn-handled knives," he muttered, "are not un-common things."

"One don't possess a knife for a matter of eight or nine years without being able to swear to it," the other remarked dryly.

"Is there anything more?"

"There don't need to be," was the quiet reply. "You know that, sir. So do I. There don't need to be any more evidence than mine to send Mr. Morrison to the gallows."

"We will waive that point," Laverick declared. "The jury sometimes are very hard to convince by circum-stantial evidence alone. However, as I have said, let us waive that point. Your position is clear enough. You go to the inquest, you tell all you know, and you get nothing. You are a poor man, you have worked hard all your life. The chance has come in your way to do yourself a little good. Now take my advice. Don't spoil it all by asking for anything ridiculous. It won't do for you to come into a fortune a few days after this affair, especially if it ever comes out that the murdered man was in your place. I am here to act for Mr. Morri-son. What is it that you want?"

"You are talking like a gent, sir," the man said, — "like a sensible gent, too. I'd have to keep it quiet, of course, that I'd come into a bit of money, — just at present, at any rate. I could easy find an excuse for changing my job — perhaps get away from London altogether. I've got a few pounds saved and I've always wanted to open a banking account. A gent like you, perhaps, could put me in the way of doing it."

"How much do you consider would be a satisfactory balance to commence with?" Laverick asked.

"I was thinking of a thousand pounds, sir."

Laverick was thoughtful for a few moments.

"By the way, what is your name?" he inquired at last.

"James Shepherd, sir," the man answered, — "generally called Jim, sir."

"Well, you see, Shepherd," Laverick continued, "the difficulty is, in your case, as in all similar ones, that one never knows where the thing will end. A thousand pounds is a considerable sum, but in four amounts, with three months interval between each, it could be arranged. This would be better for you, in any case. Two hundred and fifty pounds is not an unheard-of sum for you to have saved or got together. After that your investments would be my lookout, and they would produce, as I have said, another seven hundred and fifty pounds. But what security have I — has Mr. Morrison, let us say — that you will be content with this sum?"

"He hasn't any, sir," the man admitted at once. "He couldn't have any. I'm a modest-living man, and I've no desire to go shouting around that I'm independent all of a sudden. That wouldn't do nohow. A thousand pounds would bring me in near enough a pound a week if I invested it, or two pounds a week for an annuity, my health being none too good. I've no wife or children, sir. I was thinking of an annuity. With two pounds a week I'd have no cause to trouble any one again."

Laverick considered.

"It shall be done," he said. "To-morrow I shall buy shares for you to the extent of two hundred and fifty pounds. They will be deposited in a bank. Some day you can look in and see me, and I will take you round there. You are my client who has speculated under my instructions successfully, and you will sign your name and become a customer. After that, you will speculate again. When your thousand pounds has been made, I will show you how to buy an annuity. Keep your mouth shut, and last night will be the luckiest night of your life. Do you drink?"

"A drop or two, sir," the man admitted. "If I did n't, I guess I'd go off my chump."

"Do you talk when you're drunk?" Laverick asked.

"Never, sir," the man declared. "I've a way of getting a drop too much when I'm by myself. Then I tumbles off to sleep and that's the end of it. I've no fancy for company at such times."

"It's a good thing," Laverick remarked, thrusting his hand into his pocket. "Here's a five-pound note on account. I daresay you can manage to keep sober to-night, at any rate. That's all, is n't it?"

"That's all, sir," the man answered, "unless I might make so bold as to ask whether Mr. Morrison has really hooked it?"

"Mr. Morrison had decided to hook it, as you graphically say, before he came in for that drink to your bar, Shepherd," Laverick affirmed. "Business had been none too good with us, and we had had a disagreement."

The man nodded.

"I see, sir," he said, taking up his hat. "Good night, sir!"

"Good night!" Laverick answered. "You can find your way down?"

"Quite well, sir, and thank you," declared Mr. Shepherd, closing the door softly behind him.

Laverick sat down in his chair. He had forgotten that he was hungry. He was faced now with a new tragedy.

CHAPTER XVIII

THEY stood together upon the platform watching the receding train. The girl's eyes were filled with tears, but Laverick was conscious of a sense of immense relief. Morrison had been at the station some time before the train was due to leave, and, although a physical wreck, he seemed only too anxious to depart. He had all the appearance of a broken-spirited man. He looked about him on the platform, and even from the carriage, in the furtive way of a criminal expecting apprehension at any moment. The whistle of the train had been a relief as great to him as to Laverick.

"We'll write you to New York, care of Barclays," Laverick called out. "Good luck, Morrison! Pull yourself together and make a fresh start."

Morrison's only reply was a somewhat feeble nod. Laverick had not attempted to shake hands. He felt himself, at the last moment, stirred almost to anger by the perfunctory farewell which was all this man had offered to the girl he had treated so inconsiderately. His thoughts were engrossed upon himself and his own danger. He would not even have kissed her if she had not drawn his face down to hers and whispered a reassuring little message. Laverick turned away. For some reason or other he felt himself shuddering. Conversation during those last few moments had been increasingly difficult. The train was off at last, however, and they were alone.

The girl drew a long breath, which might very well have been one of relief. They turned silently toward the exit.

"Are you going back home?" Laverick asked.

"Yes," she answered listlessly. "There is nothing else to do."

"Is n't it rather sad for you there by yourself?"

She nodded.

"It is the first time," she said. "Another girl and her mother have lived with me always. They started off last week, touring. They are paying a little toward the house or I should have to go into rooms. As it is, I think that it would be more comfortable."

Laverick looked at her wonderingly.

"You seem such a child," he said, "to be left all alone in the world like this."

"But I am not a child actually, you see," she answered, with an effort at lightness. "Somehow, though, I do miss Arthur's going. His father was always very good to me, and made him promise that he would do what he could. I did n't see much of him, but one felt always that there was somebody. It's different now. It makes one feel very lonely."

"I, too," Laverick said, with commendable mendacity, "am rather a lonely person. You must let me see something of you now and then."

She looked up at him quickly. Her gaze was altogether disingenuous, but her eyes — those wonderful eyes — spoke volumes.

"If you really mean it," she said, "I should be so glad."

"Supposing we start to-day," he suggested, smiling. "I cannot ask you to lunch, as I have a busy day before me, but we might have dinner together quite early. Then

I would take you to the theatre and meet you afterwards, if you liked."

"If I liked!" she whispered. "Oh, how good you are!"

"I am not at all sure about that. Now I'll put you in this taxi and send you home."

She laughed.

"You must n't do anything so extravagant. I can get a 'bus just outside. I never have taxicabs."

"Just this morning," he insisted, "and I think he won't trouble you for his fare. You must let me, please. Remember that there's a large account open still between your half-brother and me, so you, need n't mind these trifles. Till this evening, then. Shall I fetch you or will you come to me?"

"Let me fetch you, if I may," she said. "It is n't nice for you to come down to where I live. It's such a horrid part."

"Just as you like," he answered. "I'd be very glad to fetch you if you prefer it, but it would give me more time if you came. Shall we say seven o'clock? I've written the address down on this card so that you can make no mistake."

She laughed gayly.

"You know, all the time," she said, "I feel that you are treating me as though I were a baby. I'll be there punctually, and I don't think I need tie the card around my neck."

The cab glided off. Laverick caught a glimpse of a wan little face with a faint smile quivering at the corner of her lips as she leaned out for a moment to say good-bye. Then he went back to his rooms, breakfasted, and made his way to his office.

The morning papers had nothing new to report concerning the murder in Crooked Friars' Alley. Evidently what information the police had obtained they were keeping for the inquest. Laverick, from the moment when he entered the office, had little or no time to think of the tragedy under whose shadow he had come. The long-predicted boom had arrived at last. Without lunch, he and all his clerks worked until after six o'clock. Even then Laverick found it hard to leave. During the day, a dozen people or so had been in to ask for Morrison. To all of them he had given the same reply, — Morrison had gone abroad on private business for the firm. Very few were deceived by Laverick's dry statement. He was quite aware that he was looked upon either as one of the luckiest men on earth, or as a financier of consummate skill. The failure of Laverick & Morrison had been looked upon as a certainty. How they had tided over that twenty-four hours had been known to no one — to no one but Laverick himself and the manager of his bank.

Just before four o'clock, the telephone rang at his elbow.

"Mr. Fenwick from the bank, sir, is wishing to speak to you for a moment," his head-clerk announced.

Laverick took up the telephone.

"Yes," he said, "I am Laverick. Good afternoon, Mr. Fenwick! Absolutely impossible to spare any time to-day. What is it? The account is all right, is n't it?"

"Quite right, Mr. Laverick," was the answer. "At the same time, if you could spare me a moment I should be glad to see you concerning the deposit you made yesterday."

"I will come in to-morrow," Laverick promised. "This

afternoon it is quite out of the question. I have a crowd
of people waiting to see me, and several important engagements for which I am late already."

The banker seemed scarcely satisfied.

"I may rely upon seeing you to-morrow?" he pressed.

"To-morrow," Laverick repeated, ringing off.

For a time this last message troubled him. As soon
as the day's work was over, however, and he stepped
into his cab, he dismissed it entirely from his thoughts.
It was curious how, notwithstanding this new seriousness
which had come into his life, notwithstanding that sensation of walking all the time on the brink of a precipice, he
set his face homeward and looked forward to his evening,
with a pleasure which he had not felt for many months.
The whirl of the day faded easily from his mind. He
lived no more in an atmosphere of wild excitement, of
changing prices, of feverish anxiety. How empty his
life must have unconsciously grown that he could find so
much pleasure in being kind to a pretty child! It was
hard to think of her otherwise — impossible. A strange
heritage, this, to have been left him by such a person as
Arthur Morrison. How in the world, he wondered, did
he happen to have such a connection.

She was a little shy when she arrived. Laverick had
left special orders downstairs, and she was brought up
into his sitting-room immediately. She was very quietly
dressed except for her hat, which was large and wavy.
He found it becoming, but he knew enough to understand
that her clothes were very simple and very inexpensive,
and he was conscious of being curiously glad of the fact.

"I am afraid," she said timidly, with a glance at his
evening attire, "that we must go somewhere very quiet.
You see, I have only one evening gown and I could n't

wear that. There would n't be time to change afterwards. Besides, one's clothes do get so knocked about
in the dressing-rooms."

"There are heaps of places we can go to," he assured
her pleasantly. "Of course you can't dress for the evening when you have to go on to work, but you must remember that there are a good many other smart young
ladies in the same position. I had to change because I
have taken a stall to see your performance. Tell me,
how are you feeling now?"

"Rather lonely," she admitted, making a pathetic little
grimace. "That is to say I have been feeling lonely," she
added softly. "I don't now, of course."

"You are a queer little person," he said kindly, as
they went down in the lift. "Have n't you any friends?"

She shrugged her shoulders.

"What sort of friends could I have?" she asked.
"The girls in the chorus with me are very nice, some of
them, but they know so many people whom I don't,
and they are always out to supper, or something of the
sort."

"And you?"

She shook her head.

"I went to one supper-party with the girl who is near
me," she said. "I liked it very much, but they did n't ask
me again."

"I wonder why?" he remarked.

"Oh, I don't know!" she went on drearily. "You
see, I think the men who take out girls who are in the
chorus, generally expect to be allowed to make love to
them. At any rate, they behaved like that. Such a
horrid man tried to say nice things to me and I did n't
like it a bit. So they left me alone afterwards. The girl

I lived with and her mother are quite nice, and they have a few friends we go to see sometimes on Sunday or holidays. It's dull, though, very dull, especially now they're away."

"What on earth made you think of going on the stage at all?" he asked.

"What could one do?" she answered. "My mother's money died with her — she had only an annuity — and my stepfather, who had promised to look after me, lost all his money and died quite suddenly. Arthur was in a stockbroker's office and he couldn't save anything. My only friend was my old music-master, and he had given up teaching and was director of the orchestra at the Universal. All he could do for me was to get me a place in the chorus. I have been there ever since. They keep on promising me a little part but I never get it. It's always like that in theatres. You have to be a favorite of the manager's, for some reason or other, or you never get your chance unless you are unusually lucky."

"I don't know much about theatres," he admitted. "I am afraid I am rather a stupid person. When I can get away from work I go into the country and play cricket or golf, or anything that's going. When I am up in town, I am generally content with looking up a few friends, or playing bridge at the club. I never have been a theatre-goer."

"I wonder," she asked, as they seated themselves at a small round table in the restaurant which he had chosen, — "I wonder why every now and then you look so serious."

"I didn't know that I did," he answered. "We've had thundering hard times lately in business, though. I suppose that makes a man look thoughtful."

"Poor Mr. Laverick," she murmured softly. "Are things any better now?"

"Much better."

"Then you have nothing really to bother you?" she persisted.

"I suppose we all have something," he replied, suddenly grave. "Why do you ask that?"

She leaned across the table. In the shaded light, her oval face with its little halo of deep brown hair seemed to him as though it might have belonged to some old miniature. She was delightful, like Watteau-work upon a piece of priceless porcelain — delightful when the lights played in her eyes and the smile quivered at the corner of her lips. Just now, however, she became very much in earnest.

"I will tell you why I ask that question," she said. "I cannot help worrying still about Arthur. You know you admitted last night that he had done something. You saw how terribly frightened he was this morning, and how he kept on looking around as though he were afraid that he would see somebody whom he wished to avoid. Oh! I don't want to worry you," she went on, "but I feel so terrified sometimes. I feel that he must have done something — bad. It was not an ordinary business trouble which took the life out of him so completely."

"It was not," Laverick admitted at once. "He has done something, I believe, quite foolish; but the matter is in my hands to arrange, and I think you can assure yourself that nothing will come of it."

"Did you tell him so this morning?" she asked eagerly.

"I did not," he answered. "I told him nothing. For many reasons it was better to keep him ignorant. He and I might not have seen things the same way, and I am sure that what I am doing is for the best. If I were you, Miss Leneveu, I think I would n't worry any more. Soon you will hear from your brother that he is safe in New York, and I think I can promise you that the trouble will never come to anything serious."

"Why have you been so kind to him?" she asked timidly. "From what he said, I do not think that he was very useful to you, and, indeed, you and he are so different."

Laverick was silent for a moment.

"To be honest," he said, "I think that I should not have taken so much trouble for his sake alone. You see," he continued, smiling, "you are rather a delightful young person, and you were very anxious, were n't you?"

Her hand came across the table — an impulsive little gesture, which he nevertheless found perfectly natural and delightfull. He took it into his, and would have raised the fingers to his lips but for the waiters who were hovering around.

"You are so kind," she said, "and I am so fortunate. I think that I wanted a friend."

"You poor child," he answered, "I should think you did. You are not drinking your wine."

She shook her head.

"Do you mind?" she asked. "A very little gets into my head because I take it so seldom, and the manager is cross if one makes the least bit of a mistake. Besides, I do not think that I like to drink wine. If one does not take it at all, there is an excuse for never having anything when the girls ask you."

He nodded sympathetically.

"I believe you are quite right," he said; "in a general way, at any rate. Well, I will drink by myself to your brother's safe arrival in New York. Are you ready?"

She glanced at the clock.

"I must be there in a quarter of an hour," she told him.

"I will drive you to the theatre," he said, "and then go round and fetch my ticket."

As he waited for her in the reception hall of the restaurant, he took an evening paper from the stall. A brief paragraph at once attracted his attention.

> *Murder in the City.* — We understand that very important information has come into the hands of the police. An arrest is expected to-night or to-morrow at the latest.

He crushed the paper in his hand and threw it on one side. It was the usual sort of thing. There was nothing they could have found out — nothing, he told himself.

CHAPTER XIX

As soon as he had gone through his letters on the following morning, Laverick, in response to a second and more urgent message, went round to his bank. Mr. Fenwick greeted him gravely. He was feeling keenly the responsibilities of his position. Just how much to say and how much to leave unsaid was a question which called for a full measure of diplomacy.

"You understand, Mr. Laverick," he began, "that I wished to see you with regard to the arrangement we came to the day before yesterday."

Laverick nodded. It suited him to remain monosyllabic.

"Well?" he asked.

"The arrangement, of course, was most unusual," the manager continued. "I agreed to it as you were an old customer and the matter was an urgent one."

"I do not quite follow you," Laverick remarked, frowning. "What is it you wish me to do? Withdraw my account?"

"Not in the least," the manager answered hastily.

"You know the position of our market, of course," Laverick went on. "Three days ago I was in a situation which might have been called desperate. I could quite understand that you needed security to go on making the necessary payments on my behalf. To-day, things are entirely different. I am twenty thousand pounds better off, and if necessary I could realize sufficient to pay off the whole of my overdraft within half-an-hour. That I do not do so is simply a matter of policy and prices."

"I quite understand that, my dear Mr. Laverick," the bank manager declared. "The position is simply this. We have had a most unusual and a strictly private inquiry, of a nature which I cannot divulge to you, asking whether any large sum in five hundred pound bank-notes has been passed through our account during the last few days."

"You have actually had this inquiry?" Laverick asked calmly.

"We have. I can tell you no more. The source of the inquiry was, in a sense, amazing."

"May I ask what your reply was?"

"My reply was," Mr. Fenwick said slowly, "that no such notes had passed through our account. We asked them, however, without giving any reasons, to repeat their question in a few days' time. Our reply was perfectly truthful. Owing to your peculiar stipulations, we are simply holding a certain packet for you in our security chamber. We know it to contain bank-notes, and there is very little doubt but that it contains the notes which have been the subject of this inquiry. I want to ask you, Mr. Laverick, to be so good as to open that packet, let me credit the notes to your account in the usual way, and leave me free to reply as I ought to have done in the first instance to this inquiry."

"The course which you suggest," replied the other, "is one which I absolutely decline to take. It is not for me to tell you the nature of the relations which should exist between a banker and his client. All that I can say is that those notes are deposited with you and must re-main on deposit, and that the transaction is one which must be treated entirely as a confidential one. If you decline to do this, I must remove my account, in which case I shall, of course, take the packet away with me. To be plain with you, Mr. Fenwick," he wound up, "I do not intend to make use of those notes, I never intended to do so. I simply deposited them as security until the turn in price of 'Unions' came."

"It is a very nice point, Mr. Laverick," the bank manager remarked. "I should consider that you had already made use of them."

"Every one to his own conscience," Laverick answered calmly.

"You place me in a very embarrassing position, Mr. Laverick."

"I cannot admit that at all," Laverick replied. "There is only one inquiry which you could have had which could justify you in insisting upon what you have suggested. It emanated, I presume, from Scotland Yard?"

"If it had," Mr. Fenwick answered, "no considerations of etiquette would have intervened at all. I should have felt it my duty to have revealed at once the fact of your deposit. At the same time, the inquiry comes from an even more important source,— a source which cannot be ignored."

Laverick thought for a moment.

"After all, the matter is a very simple one," he declared. "By four o'clock this afternoon my account shall be within its limits. You will then automatically restore to me the packet which you hold on my behalf, and the possession of which seems to embarrass you."

"If you do not mind," the banker answered, "I should be glad if you would take it with you. It means, I think,

a matter of six or seven thousand pounds added to your
overdraft, but as a temporary thing we will pass that."

"As you will," Laverick assented carelessly. "The
charge of those documents is a trust with me as well as
with yourself. I have no doubt that I can arrange for
their being held in a secure place elsewhere."

The usual formalities were gone through, and Laverick
left the bank with the brown leather pocket-book in his
breast-coat pocket. Arrived at his office, he locked it up
at once in his private safe and proceeded with the usual
business of the day. Even with an added staff of clerks,
the office was almost in an uproar. Laverick threw himself into the struggle with a whole-hearted desire to escape
from these unpleasant memories. He succeeded perfectly. It was two hours before he was able to sit down
even for a moment. His head-clerk, almost as exhausted,
followed him into his room.

"I forgot to tell you, sir," he announced, "that there's
a man outside — Mr. Shepherd was his name, I believe —
said he had a small investment to make which you promised to look after personally. He would insist on seeing
you — said he was a waiter at a restaurant which you
visited sometimes."

"That's all right," Laverick declared. "You can
show him in. We'll probably give him American
rails."

"Can't we attend to it in the office for you, sir?" the
clerk asked. "I suppose it's only a matter of a few
hundreds."

"Less than that, probably, but I promised the fellow
I'd look after it myself. Send him in, Scropes."

There was a brief delay and then Mr. Shepherd was
announced. Laverick, who was sitting with his coat off,

smoking a well-earned cigarette, looked up and nodded to his visitor as the door was closed.

"Sorry to keep you waiting," he remarked. "We're having a bit of a rush."

The man laid down his hat and came up to Laverick's side.

"I guess that, sir," he said, "from the number of people we've had in the 'Black Post' to-day, and the way they've all been shouting and talking. They don't seem to eat much these days, but there's some of them can shift the drink."

"I've got some sound stocks looked out for you," Laverick remarked, "two hundred and fifty pounds' worth. If you'll just approve that list as a matter of form," he added, pushing a piece of paper across, "you can come in to-morrow and have the certificates. I shall tell them to debit the purchase money to my private account, so that if any one asks you anything, you can say that you paid me for them."

"I'm sure I'm much obliged, sir," the man said. "To tell you the truth," he went on, "I've had a bit of a scare to-day."

Laverick looked up quickly.

"What do you mean?" he demanded.

"May I sit down, sir? I'm a bit worn out. I've been on the go since half-past ten."

Laverick nodded and pointed to a chair. Shepherd brought it up to the side of the table and leaned forward.

"There's been two men in to-day," he said, "asking questions. They wanted to know how many customers I had there on Monday night, and could I describe them. Was there any one I recognized, and so on."

"What did you say?"

"I declared I could n't remember any one. To the best of my recollection, I told them, there was no one served at all after ten o'clock. I would n't say for certain — it looked as though I might have had a reason."

"And were they satisfied?"

"I don't think they were," Shepherd admitted. "Not altogether, that is to say."

"Did they mention any names?" asked Laverick — "Morrison's, for instance? Did they want to know whether he was a regular customer?"

"They did n't mention no names at all, sir," the man answered, "but they did begin to ask questions about my regular clients. Fortunate like, the place was so crowded that I had every excuse for not paying any too much attention to them. It was all I could do to keep on getting orders attended to."

"What sort of men were they?" Laverick asked. "Do you think that they came from the police?"

"I should n't have said so," Shepherd replied, "but one can't tell, and these gentlemen from Scotland Yard do make themselves up so sometimes on purpose to deceive. I should have said that these two were foreigners, the same kidney as the poor chap as was murdered. I heard a word or two pass, and I sort of gathered that they'd a shrewd idea as to that meeting in the 'Black Post' between the man who was murdered and the little dark fellow."

Laverick nodded.

"Jim Shepherd," he declared, "you appear to me to be a very sagacious person."

"I'm sure I'm much obliged, sir; I can tell you, though," he added, "I don't half like these chaps coming round making inquiries. My nerves ain't quite what they were, and it gives me the jumps."

Laverick was thoughtful for a few moments.

"After all, there was no one else in the bar that night," he remarked,—"no one who could contradict you?"

"Not a soul," Jim Shepherd agreed.

"Then don't you bother," Laverick continued. "You see, you've been wise. You have n't given yourself away altogether. You've simply said that you don't recollect any one coming in. Why should you recollect? At the end of a day's work you are not likely to notice every stray customer. Stick to it, and, if you take my advice, don't go throwing any money about, and don't give your notice in for another week or so. Pave the way for it a bit. Ask the governor for a rise — say you're not making a living out of it."

"I'm on," Jim Shepherd remarked, nodding his head. "I'm on to it, sir. I don't want to get into no trouble, I'm sure."

"You can't," Laverick answered dryly, "unless you chuck yourself in. You're not obliged to remember anything. No one can ever prove that you remembered anything. Keep your eyes open, and let me hear if these fellows turn up again."

"I'm pretty certain they will, sir," the man declared. "They sat about waiting for me to be disengaged, but when my time off came, I hopped out the back way. They'll be there again to-night, sure enough."

Laverick nodded.

"Well, you must let me know," he said, "what happens."

Jim Shepherd leaned across the corner of the table and dropped his voice.

"It's an awful thing to think of, sir," he whispered, blinking rapidly. "I would n't be that young Mr. Morrison for all that great pocketful of notes. But my! there was a sight of money there, sir! He'll be a rich man for all his days if nothing comes out."

"We won't talk any more about it," Laverick insisted. "It is n't a pleasant thing to think about or talk about. We won't know anything, Shepherd. We shall be better off."

The man took his departure and the whirl of business recommenced. Laverick turned his back upon the city only a few minutes before eight and, tired out, he dined at a restaurant on his homeward way. When at last he reached his sitting-room he threw himself on the sofa and lit a cigar. Once more the evening papers had no particular news. This time, however, one of them had a leading article upon the English police system. The fact that an undetected murder should take place in a wealthy neighborhood, away from the slums, a murder which must have been premeditated, was in itself alarming. Until the inquest had been held, it was better to make little comment upon the facts of the case so far as they were known. At the same time, the circumstance could not fail to incite a considerable amount of alarm among those who had offices in the vicinity of the tragedy. It was rumored that some mysterious inquiries were being circulated around London banks. It was possible that robbery, after all, had been the real motive of the crime, but robbery on a scale as yet unimagined. The whole interest of the case now was centred upon the discovery of the man's identity. As soon as this was solved, some very startling developments might be expected.

Laverick threw the paper away. He tried to rest upon

the sofa, but tried in vain. He found himself continually glancing at the clock.

"To-night," he muttered to himself, — "no, I will not go to-night! It is not fair to the child. It is absurd. Why, she would think that I was —"

He stopped short.

"I'll change and go to the club," he decided.

He rose to his feet. Just then there was a ring at his bell. He opened the door and found a messenger boy standing in the vestibule.

"Note, sir, for Mr. Stephen Laverick," the boy announced, opening his wallet.

Laverick held out his hand. The boy gave him a large square envelope, and upon the back of it was "Universal Theatre." Laverick tried to assure himself that he was not so ridiculously pleased. He stepped back into the room, tore open the envelope, and read the few lines traced in rather faint but delicate handwriting.

Are you coming to fetch me to-night? Don't let me be a nuisance, but do come if you have nothing to do. I have something to tell you.   ZOE.

Laverick gave the boy a shilling for himself and suddenly forgot that he was tired. He changed his clothes, whistling softly to himself all the time. At eleven o'clock, he was at the stage-door of the Universal Theatre, waiting in a taxicab.

ONE by one the young ladies of the chorus came out from the stage-door of the Universal, in most cases to be assisted into a waiting hansom or taxicab by an attendant cavalier. Laverick stood back in the shadows as much as possible, smiling now and then to himself at this, to him, somewhat novel way of spending the evening. Zoe was among the last to appear. She came up to him with a delightful little gesture of pleasure, and took his arm as a matter of course as he led her across to the waiting cab.

"This sort of thing is making me feel absurdly young," he declared. "Luigi's for supper, I suppose?"

"Supper!" she exclaimed, clapping her hands. "Delightful! Two nights following, too! I did love last night."

"We had better engage a table at Luigi's permanently," he remarked.

"If only you meant it!" she sighed.

He laughed at her, but he was thoughtful for a few minutes. Afterwards, when they sat at a small round table in the somewhat Bohemian restaurant which was the fashionable rendezvous of the moment for ladies of the theatrical profession, he asked her a question.

"Tell me what you meant in your note," he begged. "You said that you had some information for me."

"I'm afraid it was n't anything very much," she admitted. "I found out to-day that some one had been inquiring at the stage-door about me, and whether I was connected in any way with a Mr. Arthur Morrison, the stockbroker."

"Do you know who it was?" he asked.

She shook her head.

"The man left no name at all. I tried to get the door-keeper to tell me about him, but he's such a surly old fellow, and he's so used to that sort of thing, that he pretended he didn't remember anything."

"It seems odd," he remarked thoughtfully, "that any one should have found you out. You were so seldom with Morrison. I dare say," he added, "it was just some one to whom your brother owes some small sum of money."

"Very likely," she answered. "But I was going to tell you. He came again to-night while the performance was on, and sent a note round. I have brought it for you to see."

The note — it was really little more than a message — was written on the back of a programme and enclosed in an envelope evidently borrowed from the box-office. It read as follows:

DEAR MISS LENEVEU,

I believe that Mr. Arthur Morrison is a connection of yours, and I am venturing to introduce myself to you as a friend of his. Could you spare me half-an-hour of your company after the performance of this evening? If you could honor me so much, you might perhaps allow me to give you some supper.

Sincerely,

PHILIP E. MILES.

Laverick felt an absurd pang of jealousy as he handed back the programme.

"I should say," he declared, "that this was simply some young man who was trying to scrape an acquaintance with you because he was or had been a friend of Morrison's."

"In that case," answered Zoe, "he is very soon forgotten."

She tore the programme into two pieces, and Laverick was conscious of a ridiculous feeling of pleasure at her indifference.

"If you hear anything more about him," he said, "you might let me know. You are a brave young lady to dismiss your admirers so summarily."

"Perhaps I am quite satisfied with one," laughing softly.

Laverick told himself that at his age he was behaving like an idiot, nevertheless his eyes across the table expressed his appreciation of her speech.

"Tell me something about yourself, Mr. Laverick," she begged.

"For instance?"

"First of all, then, how old are you?"

He made a grimace.

"Thirty-eight — thirty-nine my next birthday. Does n't that seem grandfatherly to you?"

"You must not be absurd!" she exclaimed. "It is not even middle-aged. Now tell me — how do you spend your time generally? Do you really mean that you go and play cards at your club most evenings?"

"I have a good many friends, and I dine out quite a great deal."

"You have no sisters?"

"I have no relatives at all in London," he explained.

"It is to be a real cross-examination," she warned him.

"I am quite content," he answered. "Go ahead, but remember, though, that I am a very dull person."

"You look so young for your years," she declared. "I wonder, have you ever been in love?"

He laughed heartily.

"About a dozen times, I suppose. Why? Do I seem to you like a misanthrope?"

"I don't know," she admitted, hesitatingly. "You don't seem to me as though you cared to make friends very easily. I just felt I wanted to ask you. Have you ever been engaged?"

"Never," he assured her.

"And when was the last time," she asked, "that you felt you cared a little for any one?"

"It dates from the day before yesterday," he declared, filling her glass.

She laughed at him.

"Of course, it is nonsense to talk to you like this!" she said. "You are quite right to make fun of me."

"On the contrary," he insisted. "I am very much in earnest."

"Very well, then," she answered, "if you are in earnest you shall be in love with me. You shall take me about, give me supper every night, send me some sweets and cigarettes to the theatre — oh, and there are heaps of things you ought to do if you really mean it!" she wound up.

"If those things mean being fond of you," he answered, "I'll prove it with pleasure. Sweets, cigarettes, suppers, taxicabs at the stage-door."

"It all sounds very terrible," she sighed. "It's a horrid little life."

"Yet I suppose you enjoy it?" he remarked tentatively.

"I hate it, but I must do something. I could not live on charity. If I knew any other way I could make money, I would rather, but there is no other way. I tried once to give music lessons. I had a few pupils, but they never paid — they never do pay."

"I wish I could think of something," Laverick said thoughtfully. "Of course, it is occupation you want. So far as regards the monetary part of it, I still owe your brother a great deal —"

She shook her head, interrupting him with a quick little gesture.

"No, no!" she declared. "I have never complained about Arthur. Sometimes he made me suffer, because I know that he was ashamed of having a relative in the chorus, but I am quite sure that I do not wish to take any of his money — or of anybody else's," she added. "I want always to earn my own living."

"For such a child," he remarked, smiling, "you are wonderfully independent."

"Why not?" she answered softly. "It is years since I had any one to do very much for me. Necessity teaches us a good many things. Oh, I was helpless enough when it began!" she added, with a little sigh. "I got over it. We all do. Tell me — who is that woman, and why does she stare so at you?"

Laverick looked across the room. Louise and Bellamy were sitting at the opposite table. The former was strikingly handsome and very wonderfully dressed. Her closely-clinging gown, cut slightly open in front, displayed her marvelous figure. She wore long pearl earrings, and a hat with white feathers which drooped over her fair hair. Laverick recognized her at once.

"It is Mademoiselle Idiale," he said, "the most wonderful soprano in the world."

"Why does she look so at you?" Zoe asked.

Laverick shook his head.

"I do not know her," he said. "I know who she is, of course, — every one does. She is a Servian, and they say that she is devoted to her country. She left Vienna at a moment's notice, only a few days ago, and they say that it was because she had sworn never to sing again before the enemies of her country. She had been engaged a long time to appear at Covent Garden, but no one believed that she would really come. She breaks her engagements just when she chooses. In fact, she is a very wonderful person altogether."

"I never saw such pearls in my life," Zoe whispered. "And how lovely she is! I do not understand, though, why she is so interested in you."

"She mistakes me for some one, perhaps."

It certainly seemed probable. Even at that moment she touched her escort upon the arm, and he distinctly looked across at Laverick. It was obvious that he was the subject of her conversation.

"I know the man," Laverick said. "He was at Harrow with me, and I have played cricket with him since. But I have certainly never met Mademoiselle Idiale. One does not forget that sort of person."

"Her figure is magnificent," Zoe murmured wistfully. "Do you like tall women very much, Mr. Laverick?"

"I adore them," he answered, smiling, "but I prefer small ones."

"We are very foolish people, you and I," she laughed. "We came together so strangely and yet we talk such frivolous nonsense."

"You are making me young again," he declared.

"Oh, you are quite young enough!" she assured him. "To tell you the truth, I am jealous. Mademoiselle Idiale looks at you all the time. Look at her now. Is she not beautiful?"

There was no doubt about her beauty, but those who were criticising her — and she was by far the most interesting person in the room — thought her a little sad. Though Bellamy was doing his utmost to be entertaining, her eyes seemed to travel every now and then over his head and out of the room. Wherever her thoughts were, one could be very sure that they were not fixed upon the subject under discussion.

"She is like that when she sings," Laverick remarked. "She has none of the vivacity of the Frenchwomen. Yet there was never anything so graceful in the world as the way she moves about the stage."

"If I were a man," Zoe sighed, "that is the sort of woman I would die for."

"If you were a man," he replied, "you would probably find some one whom you preferred to live for. Do you know, you are rather a morbid sort of person, Miss Zoe?"

"Ah, I like that!" she declared. "I will not be called Miss Leneveu any more by you. You must call me Miss Zoe, please, — Zoe, if you like."

"Zoe, by all means. Under the circumstances, I think it is only fitting."

His eyes wandered across the room again.

"Ah!" she cried softly, "you, too, are coming under the spell, then. I was reading about her only the other day. They say that so many men fall in love with her — so many men to whom she gives no encouragement at all."

Laverick looked into his companion's face.

"Come," he said, "my heart is not so easily won. I can assure you that I never aspire to so mighty a personage as a Covent Garden star. Don't you know that she gets a salary of five hundred pounds a week, and wears ropes of pearls which would represent ten times my entire income? Heaven alone knows what her gowns cost!"

"After all, though," murmured Zoe, "she is a woman. See, your friend is coming to speak to you."

Bellamy was indeed crossing the room. He nodded to Laverick and bowed to his companion.

"Forgive my intruding, Laverick," he said. "You do remember me, I hope? Bellamy, you know."

"I remember you quite well. We used to play together at Lord's, even after we left school."

Bellamy smiled.

"That is so," he answered. "I see by the papers that you have kept up your cricket. Mine, alas! has had to go. I have been too much of a rolling stone lately. Do you know that I have come to ask ·you a favor?"

"Go ahead," Laverick interposed.

"Mademoiselle Idiale has a fancy to meet you," Bellamy explained. "You know, or I dare say you have heard, what a creature of whims she is. If you won't come across and be introduced like a good fellow, she probably won't speak a word all through supper-time, go off in a huff, and my evening will be spoiled."

Laverick laughed heartily. A little smile played at the corner of Zoe's lips — nevertheless, she was looking slightly anxious.

"Under those circumstances," remarked Laverick, "perhaps I had better go. You will understand," he added, with a glance at Zoe, "that I cannot stay for more than a second."

"Naturally," Bellamy answered. "If Mademoiselle really has anything to say to you, I will, if I am permitted, return for a moment."

Laverick introduced him to Zoe.

"I am sure I have seen you at the Universal," he declared. "You're in the front row, are n't you? I have seen you in that clever little step-dance and song in the second act."

She nodded, evidently pleased.

"Does it seem clever to you?" she asked wistfully. "You see, we are all so tired of it."

"I think it is ripping," Bellamy declared. "I shall have the pleasure again directly," he added, with a bow.

The two men crossed the room.

"What the dickens does Mademoiselle Idiale want with me?" Laverick demanded. "Does she know that I am a poor stockbroker, struggling against hard times?"

Bellamy shrugged his shoulders.

"She is n't the sort to care who or what you are," he answered. "And as for the rest, I suppose she could buy any of us up if she wanted to. Her interest in you is rather a curious one. No time to explain it now. She'll tell you."

Louise smiled as he paused before her. She was certainly exquisitely beautiful. Her dress, her carriage, her delicate hands, even her voice, were all perfection. She gave him the tips of her fingers as Bellamy pronounced his name.

"It is so kind of you," she said, "to come and speak to me. And indeed you will laugh when I tell you why I thought that I would like to say one word with you."

Laverick bowed.

"I am thankful, Mademoiselle," he replied, "for anything which procures me such a pleasure."

She smiled.

"Ah! you, too, are gallant," she said. "But indeed, then, I fear you will not be flattered when I tell you why I was so interested. I read all your newspapers. I read of that terrible murder in Crooked Friars' Alley only a few days ago, — is not that how you call the place?"

Laverick was suddenly grave. What was this that was coming?

"One of the reports," she continued, "says that the man was a foreigner. The maker's name upon his clothes was Austrian. I, too, come from that part of Europe — if not from Austria, from a country very near — and I am always interested in my country-people. A few moments ago I asked my friend Mr. Bellamy, 'Where is this Crooked Friars' Alley?' Just then he bowed to you, and he answered me, 'It is in the city. It is within a yard or two of the offices of the gentleman to whom I just have said good-evening.' So I looked across at you and I thought that it was strange."

Laverick scarcely knew what to say.

"It was a terrible affair," he admitted, "and, as Mr. Bellamy has told you, it occurred within a few steps of my office. So far, too, the police seem completely at a loss."

"Ah!" she went on, shaking her head, "your police, I am afraid they are not very clever. It is too bad, but I am afraid that it is so. Tell me, Mr. Laverick, is this, then, a very lonely spot where your offices are?"

"Not at all," Laverick replied. "On the contrary, in the daytime it might be called the heart of the city — of the money-making part of the city, at any rate. Only this thing, you see, seems to have taken place very late at night."

"When all the offices were closed," she remarked.

"Most of them," Laverick answered. "Mine, as it happened, was open late that night. I passed the spot within half-an-hour or so of the time when the murder must have been committed."

"But that is terrible!" she declared, shaking her head. "Tell me, Mr. Laverick, if I drive to your office some morning you will show me this place, — yes?"

"If you are in earnest, Mademoiselle, I will certainly do so, but there is nothing there. It is just a passage."

"You give me your address," she insisted, "and I think that I will come. You are a stockbroker, Mr. Bellamy tells me. Well, sometimes I have a good deal of money to invest. I come to you and you will give me your advice. So! You have a card!"

Laverick found one and scribbled his city address upon it. She thanked him and once more held out the tips of her fingers.

"So I shall see you again some day, Mr. Laverick."

He bowed and recrossed the room. Bellamy was standing talking to Zoe.

"Well," he asked, as Laverick returned, "are you, too, going to throw yourself beneath the car?"

Laverick shook his head.

"I do not think so," he answered. "Our acquaintance promises to be a business one. Mademoiselle spoke of investing some money through me."

Bellamy laughed.

"Then you have kept your heart," he remarked. "Ah, well, you have every reason!"

He bowed to Zoe, nodded to Laverick, and returned to his place. Laverick looked after him a little compassionately.

"Poor fellow," he said.

"Who is he?"

"He has some sort of a Government appointment," Laverick answered. "They say he is hopelessly in love with Mademoiselle Idiale."

"Why not?" Zoe exclaimed. "He is nice. She must care for some one. Why do you pity him?"

"They say, too, that she has no more heart than a stone," Laverick continued, "and that never a man has had even a kind word from her. She is very patriotic, and all the thoughts and love she has to spare from herself are given to her country."

Zoe shuddered.

"Ah!" she murmured, "I do not like to think of heartless women. Perhaps she is not so cruel, after all. To me she seems only very, very sad. Tell me, Mr. Laverick, why did she send for you?"

"I imagine," said he, "that it was a whim. It must have been a whim."

CHAPTER XXI

LAVERICK, on the following morning, found many things to think about. He was accustomed to lunch always at the same restaurant, within a few yards of his office, and with the same little company of friends. Just as he was leaving, an outside broker whom he knew slightly came across the room to him.

"Tell me, Laverick," he asked, "what's become of your partner?"

"He has gone abroad for a few weeks. As a matter of fact, we shall be announcing a change in the firm shortly."

"Queer thing," the broker remarked. "I was in Liverpool yesterday, and I could have sworn that I saw him hanging around the docks. I should never have doubted it, but Morrison was always so careful about his appearance, and this fellow was such a seedy-looking individual. I called out to him and he vanished like a streak."

"It could scarcely have been Morrison," Laverick said. "He sailed several days ago for New York."

"That settles it," the man declared, passing on. "All the same, it was the most extraordinary likeness I ever saw."

Laverick, on his way back, went into a cable office and wrote out a marconigram to the *Lusitania*, —

Have you passenger Arthur Morrison on board? Reply.

He signed his name and paid for an answer. Then he went back to his office.

"Any one to see me?" he inquired.

"Mr. Shepherd is here waiting," his clerk told him, — "queer looking fellow who paid you two hundred and fifty pounds in cash for some railway stock."

Laverick nodded.

"I'll see him," he said. "Anything else?"

"A lady rang up — name sounded like a French one, but we could none of us catch what it was — to say that she was coming down to see you."

"If it is Mademoiselle Idiale," Laverick directed, "I must see her directly she arrives. How are you, Shepherd?" he added, nodding to the waiter as he passed towards his room. "Come in, will you? You've got your certificates all right?"

Mr. James Shepherd had the air of a man with whom prosperity had not wholly agreed. He was paler and pastier-looking than ever, and his little green eyes seemed even more restless. His attire — a long rough overcoat over the livery of his profession — scarcely enhanced the dignity of his appearance.

"Well, what is it?" Laverick asked, as soon as the door was closed.

"Our bar is being watched," the man declared. "I don't think it's anything to do with the police. Seems to be a sort of foreign gang. They're all round the place, morning, noon, and night. They've pumped everybody."

"There isn't very much," Laverick remarked slowly, "for them to find out except from you."

"They've found out something, anyway," Shepherd continued. "My junior waiter, unfortunately, who was asleep in the sitting-room, told them he was sure there were customers in the place between ten and twelve on

Monday night, because they woke him up twice, talking. They're beginning to look at me a bit doubtful."

"I shouldn't worry," Laverick advised. "The inquest's on now and you haven't been called. I don't fancy you're running any sort of risk. Any one may say they believe there were people in the bar between those hours, but there isn't any one who can contradict you outright. Besides, you haven't sworn to anything. You've simply said, as might be very possible, that you don't remember any one."

"It makes me a bit nervous, though," Shepherd remarked apologetically. "They're a regular keen-looking tribe, I can tell you. Their eyes seem to follow you all over the place."

"I shall come in for a drink presently myself," Laverick declared. "I should like to see them. I might get an idea as to their nationality, at any rate."

"Very good, sir. I'm sure I'm doing just as you suggested. I've said nothing about leaving, but I'm beginning to grumble a bit at the work, so as to pave the way. It's a hard job, and no mistake. I had thirty-nine chops between one and half-past, single-handed, too, with only a boy to carry the bread and that, and no one to serve the drinks unless they go to the counter for them. It's more than one man's work, Mr. Laverick."

Laverick assented.

"So much the better," he declared. "All the more excuse for your leaving."

"You'll be round sometime to-day, sir, then?" the man asked, taking up his hat.

"I shall look in for a few moments, for certain," Laverick answered. "If you get a chance you must point out to me one of those fellows."

Jim Shepherd departed. There was a shouting of newspaper boys in the street outside. Laverick sent out for a paper. The account of the inquest was brief enough, and there were no witnesses called except the men who had found the dead body. The nature of the wounds was explained to the jury, also the impossibility of their having been self-inflicted. In the absence of any police evidence or any identification, the discussion as to the manner of the death was naturally limited. The jury contented themselves by bringing in a verdict of "Wilful murder against some person or persons unknown." Laverick laid down the paper. The completion of the inquest was at least the first definite step toward safety. The question now before him was what to do with that twenty thousand pounds. He sat at his desk, looking into vacancy. After all, had he paid too great a price? The millstone was gone from around his neck, something new and incomprehensible had crept into his life. Yet for a background there was always this secret knowledge.

A clerk announcing Mademoiselle Idiale broke in upon his reflections. Laverick rose from his seat to greet his visitor. She was wonderfully dressed, as usual, yet with the utmost simplicity, — a white serge gown with a large black hat, but a gown that seemed to have been moulded on to her slim, faultless figure. She brought with her a musical rustle, a slight suggestion of subtle perfumes — a perfume so thin and ethereal that it was unrecognizable except in its faint suggestion of hothouse flowers. She held out her hand to Laverick, who placed for her at once an easy-chair.

"This is indeed an honor, Mademoiselle."

She inclined her head graciously.

"You are very kind," said she. "I know that here in the city you are very busy making money all the time, so I must not stay long. Will you buy me some stocks, — some good safe stocks, which will bring me in at least four per cent?"

"I can promise to do that," Laverick answered. "Have you any choice?"

"No, I have no choice," Louise told him. "I bring with me a cheque, — see, I give it to you, — it is for six thousand pounds. I would like to buy some stocks with this, and to know the names so that I may watch them in the paper. I like to see whether they go up or down, but I do not wish to risk their going down too much. It is something like gambling but it is no trouble."

"Your money shall be spent in a few minutes, Mademoiselle," Laverick assured her, "and I think I can promise you that for a week or two, at any rate, your stocks will go up. With regard to selling —"

"I leave everything to you," she interrupted, "only let me know what you propose."

"We will do our best," Laverick promised.

"It is good," she said. "Money is a wonderful thing. Without it one can do little. You have not forgotten, Mr. Laverick, that you were going to show me this passage?"

"Certainly not. Come with me now, if you will. It is only a yard or two away."

He took her out into the street. Every clerk in the office forgot his manners and craned his neck. Outside, Mademoiselle let fall her veil and passed unrecognized. Laverick showed her the entry.

"It was just there," he explained, "about half a dozen yards up on the left, that the body was found."

She looked at the place steadily. Then she looked along the passage.

"Where does it lead to — that?" she asked.

"Come and I will show you. On the left" — as they passed along the flagged pavement — "is St. Nicholas Church and churchyard. On the right here there are just offices. The street in front of us is Henschell Street. All of those buildings are stockbrokers' offices."

"And directly opposite," she asked, — "that is a café, is it not, — a restaurant, as you would call it?"

Laverick nodded.

"That is so," he agreed. "One goes in there sometimes for a drink."

"And a meeting place, perhaps?" she inquired. "It would probably be a meeting place. One might leave there and walk down this passage naturally enough."

Laverick inclined his head.

"As a matter of fact," he declared, "I think that the evidence went to prove that there were no visitors in the restaurant that night. You see, all these offices round here close at six or seven o'clock, and the whole neighborhood becomes deserted."

She shrugged her shoulders impatiently.

"Your English police, they do not know how to collect evidence. In the hands of Frenchmen, this mystery would have been solved long before now. The guilty person would be in the hands of the law. As it is, I suppose that he will go free."

"Well, we must give the police a chance, at any rate," answered Laverick. "They have n't had much time so far."

"No," she admitted, "they have not had much time. I wonder —" She hesitated for a moment and did not conclude her sentence. "Come," she exclaimed, with a little shiver, "let us go back to your office! This place is not cheerful. All the time I think of that poor man. It does make me frightened."

Laverick escorted his visitor back to the electric brougham which was waiting before his door.

"A list of stocks purchased on your behalf will reach you by to-night's post," he promised her. "We shall do our best in your interests."

He held out his hand, but she seemed in no hurry to let him go.

"You are very kind, Mr. Laverick. I would like to see you again very soon. You have heard me sing in *Samson and Delilah* ?"

"Not yet, but I am hoping to very shortly."

"To-night," she declared, "you must come to the Opera House. I leave a box for you at the door. Send me round a note that you are there, and it is possible that I may see you. It is against the rules, but for me there are no rules."

Laverick hesitating, she leaned forward and looked into his face.

"You are doing something else?" she protested. "You were, perhaps, thinking of taking out again the little girl with whom you were sitting last night?"

"I had half promised —"

"No, no!" she exclaimed, holding his hand tighter. "She is not for you — that child. She is too young. She knows nothing. Better to leave her alone. She is not for a man of the world like you. Soon she would cease to amuse you. You would be dull and she would still care. Oh, there is so much tragedy in these things, Mr. Laverick — so much tragedy for the woman! It is she always who suffers. You will take my advice. You will leave that little girl alone."

Laverick smiled.

"I am afraid," said he, "that I cannot promise that so quickly. You see, I have not known her long, but she has very few friends and I think that she would miss me. Perhaps," he added, after a second's pause, "I care for her too much."

"It is not for you," she answered scornfully, "to care too much. An Englishman, he cares never enough. A woman to him is something amusing, — his companion for a little of his spare time, something to be pleased about, to show off to his friends, — to share, even, the passion of the moment. But an Englishman he does not care too much. He never cares enough. He does not know what it is to care enough."

"Mademoiselle, there may be truth in what you say, and again there may not. We have the name, I know, of being cold lovers, but at least we are faithful."

She held up her hand with a little grimace.

"Oh, how I do hate that word!" she exclaimed. "Who is there, indeed, who wishes that you would be faithful? How much we poor women do suffer from that! Why can you never understand that a woman would be cared for very, very much, with all the strength and all the passion you can conceive, but let it not last for too long. It gets weary. It gets stale. It is as you say, — the Englishman he cares very little, perhaps, but he cares always; and the woman, if she be an artiste and a woman, she tires. But good afternoon, Mr Laverick! I must not keep you here on the pavement talking of these frivolous matters. You come to-night?"

"You are very kind," Laverick said. "If I may come until eleven o'clock, it would give me the greatest pleasure."

"As you will," she declared. "We shall see. I expect you, then. You ask for your box."

"If you wish it, certainly."

She smiled and waved her hand.

"You will tell him, please," she directed, "to drive to Bond Street."

Laverick re-entered his office, pausing for a minute to give his clerk instructions for the purchase of stocks for Mademoiselle Idiale. He had scarcely reached his own room when he was told that Mr. James Shepherd wished to speak to him for a moment upon the telephone. He took up the receiver.

"Who is it?" he asked.

"It is Shepherd," was the answer. "Is that Mr. Laverick?"

"Yes!"

"You were outside the restaurant here a few minutes ago," Shepherd continued. "You had with you a lady — a young, tall lady with a veil."

"That's right," Laverick admitted. "What about her?"

"One of the two men who watch always here was reading the paper in the window," Shepherd went on hoarsely. "He saw her with you and I heard him mutter something as though he had received a shock. He dropped his glass and his paper. He watched you every second of the time you were there until you had disappeared. Then he, too, put on his hat and went out."

"Anything else?"

"Nothing else," was the reply. "I thought you might

like to know this, sir. The man recognized the lady right enough."

"It seems queer," Laverick admitted. "Thank you for ringing me up, Shepherd. Good morning!"

Laverick leaned back in his chair. There was no doubt whatever now in his mind but that Mademoiselle Idiale, for some reason or other, was interested in this crime. Her wish to see the place, her introduction to him last night and her purchase of stocks, were all part of a scheme. He was suddenly and absolutely convinced of it. As friend or foe, she was very certainly about to take her place amongst the few people over whom this tragedy loomed.

CHAPTER XXII

ACTIVITY OF AUSTRIAN SPIES

LOUISE left her brougham in Piccadilly and walked across the Green Park. Bellamy, who was waiting, rose up from a seat, hat in hand. She took his arm in foreign fashion. They walked together towards Buckingham Palace — a strangely distinguished-looking couple.

"My dear David," she said, "the man perplexes me. To look at him, to hear him speak, one would swear that he was honest. He has just those clear blue eyes and the stolid face, half stupid and half splendid, of your athletic Englishman. One would imagine him doing a foolishly honorable thing, but he is not my conception of a criminal at all."

Bellamy kicked a pebble from the path. His forehead wore a perplexed frown.

"He did n't give himself away, then?"

"Not in the least."

"He took you out and showed you the spot where it happened?"

"Without an instant's hesitation."

"As a matter of curiosity," asked Bellamy, "did he try to make love to you?"

She shook her head.

"I even gave him an opening," she said. "Of flirtation he has no more idea than the average stupid Englishman one meets."

Bellamy was silent for several moments.

"I can't believe," he said, "that there is the least doubt but that he has the money and the portfolio. I have made one or two other inquiries, and I find that his firm was in very low water indeed only a week ago. They were spoken of, in fact, as being hopelessly insolvent. No one can imagine how they tided over the crisis."

"The man who was watching for you?" she inquired.

"He makes no mistakes," Bellamy assured her. "He saw Laverick enter that passage and come out. Afterwards he went back to his office, although he had closed up there and had been on his homeward way. The thing could not have been accidental."

"Why do you not go to him openly?" she suggested. "He is, after all, an Englishman, and when you tell him what you know he will be very much in your power. Tell him of the value of that document. Tell him that you must have it."

"It could be done," Bellamy admitted. "I think that one of us must talk plainly to him. Listen, Louise, — are you seeing him again?"

"I have invited him to come to the Opera House to-night."

"See what you can do," he begged. "I would rather keep away from him myself, if I can. Have you heard anything of Streuss?"

She shrugged her shoulders.

"Nothing directly," she replied, "but my rooms have been searched — even my dressing-room at the Opera House. That man's spies are simply wonderful. He seems able to plant them everywhere. And, David! —"

"Yes, dear?"

"He has got hold of Lassen," she continued. "I am perfectly certain of it."

Then the sooner you get rid of Lassen, the better,"
Bellamy declared.

"It is so difficult," she murmured, in a perplexed tone.
"The man has all my affairs in his hands. Up till now,
although he is uncomely, and a brute in many ways, he
has served me well."

"If he is Streuss's creature he must go," Bellamy
insisted.

She nodded.

"Let us sit down for a few minutes," she said. "I am
tired."

She sank on to a seat and Bellamy sat by her side.
In full view of them was Buckingham Palace with its
flag flying. She looked thoughtfully at it and across to
Westminster.

"Do they know, I wonder, your country-people?" she
asked.

"Half-a-dozen of them, perhaps," he answered gloomily,
— "no more."

"To-day," she declared, "I seem to have lost confidence. I seem to feel the sense of impending calamity,
to hear the guns as I walk, to see the terror fall upon the
faces of all these great crowds who throng your streets.
They are a stolid, unbelieving people — these. The blow,
when it comes, will be the harder."

Bellamy sighed.

"You are right," he said. "When one comes to think
of it, it is amazing. How long the prophets of woe have
preached, and how completely their teachings have been
ignored! The invasion bogey has been so long among us
that it has become nothing but a jest. Even I, in a way,
am one of the unbelievers."

"You are not serious, David!" she exclaimed.

"I am," he affirmed. "I think that if we could read that document we should see that there is no plan there for the immediate invasion of England. I think you would find that the blow would be struck simultaneously at our Colonies. We should either have to submit or send a considerable fleet away from home waters. Then, I presume, the question of invasion would come again. All the time, of course, the gage would be flung down, treaties would be defied, we should be scorned as though we were a nation of weaklings. Austria would gather in what she wanted, and there would be no one to interfere."

Louise was very pale but her eyes were flashing fire.

"It is the most terrible thing which has happened in history," she said, "this decadence of your country. Once England held the scales of justice for the world. Now she is no longer strong enough, and there is none to take her place. David, even if you know what that document contains, even then will it help very much?"

"Very much indeed. Don't you see that there is one hope left to us — one hope — and that is Russia? The Czar must be made to withdraw from that compact. We want to know his share in it. When we know that, there will be a secret mission sent to Russia. Germany and Austria are strong, but they are not all the world. With Russia behind and France and England westward, the struggle is at least an equal one. They have to face both directions, they have to face two great armies working from the east and from the west."

She nodded, and they sat there in silence for several moments. Bellamy was thinking deeply.

"You say, Louise," he asked, looking up quickly, "that your rooms have been searched. When was this?"

"Only last night," she replied.

Bellamy drew a little sigh of relief.

"At any rate," he said, "Streuss has no idea that the document is not in our possession. He knows nothing about Laverick. How are we going to deal with him, Louise, when he comes for his answer?"

"You have a plan?" she asked.

"There is only one thing to be done," Bellamy declared. "I shall say that we have already handed over the document to the English Government. It will be a bluff, pure and simple. He may believe it or he may not."

"You will break your compact then," she reminded him.

"I shall call myself justified," he continued. "He has attempted to rob us of the document. You are sure of what you say — that your rooms and dressing-room have been searched?"

"Absolutely certain," she declared.

"That will be sufficient," Bellamy decided. "If Streuss comes to me, I shall meet him frankly. I shall tell him that he has tried to play the burglar and that it must be war. I shall tell him that the compact is in the hands of the Prime Minister, and that he and his spies had better clear out."

She looked at him questioningly.

"Of course, you understand," he added, "there is one thing we can do, and one thing only. We must send a mission to Russia and another to France, and before the German fleet can pass down the North Sea we must declare war. It is the only thing left to us — a bold front. Without that packet we have no *casus belli*. With it, we can strike, and strike hard. I still believe that if we declare war within seven days, we shall save ourselves."

Streuss and Kahn looked, too, across the panorama of London, across the dingy Adelphi Gardens, the turbid Thames, the smoke-hung world beyond. They were together in Streuss's sitting-room on the seventh floor of one of the great Strand hotels.

"Our enterprise is a failure!" Kahn exclaimed gloomily. "We cannot doubt it any longer. I think, Streuss, that the best course you and I could adopt would be to realize it and to get back. We do no good here. We only run needless risks."

The face of the other man was dark with anger. His tone, when he spoke, shook with passion.

"You don't know what you say, Kahn!" he cried hoarsely. "I tell you that we must succeed. If that document reaches the hands of any one in authority here, it would be the worst disaster which has fallen upon our country since you or I were born. You don't understand, Kahn! You keep your eyes closed!"

"What men can do we have done," the other answered. "Von Behrling played us false. He has died a traitor's death, but it is very certain that he parted with his document before he received that twenty thousand pounds."

"Once and for all, I do not believe it!" Streuss declared. "At mid-day, I can swear to it that the contents of that envelope were unknown to the Ministers of the King here. Now if Von Behrling had parted with that document last Monday night, don't you suppose that everything would be known by now? He did not part with it. Bellamy and Mademoiselle lie when they say that they possess it. That document remains in the possession of Von Behrling's murderer, and it is for us to find him."

Kahn sighed.

"It is outside our sphere — that. What can we do against the police of this country working in their own land?"

Streuss struck the table before which they were standing. The veins in his temples were like whipcord.

"Adolf," he muttered, "you talk like a fool! Can't you see what it means? If that document reaches its destination, what do you suppose will happen?"

"They will know our plans, of course," Kahn answered. "They will have time to make preparation."

Streuss laughed bitterly.

"Worse than that!" he exclaimed. "They are not all fools, these English statesmen, though one would think so to read their speeches. Can't you see what the result would be if that document reaches Downing Street? War at a moment's notice, war six months too soon! Don't you know that every shipbuilding yard in Germany is working night and day? Don't you know that every nerve is being strained, that the muscles of the country are hammering the rivets into our new battleships? There is but one chance for this country, and if her statesmen read that document they will know what it is. It is open to them to destroy the German navy utterly, to render themselves secure against attack."

"They would never have the courage," Kahn declared. "They might make a show of defending themselves if they were attacked, but to take the initiative — no! I do not believe it."

"There is one man who has wit enough to do it," Streuss said. "He may not be in the Cabinet, but he commands it. Kahn, wake up, man! You and I together have never known what failure means. I tell you that that document is still to be bought or fought for, and we must find it. This morning Mademoiselle drove into the city and called at the offices of a stockbroker within a dozen yards of Crooked Friars' Alley. She was there a long time. The stockbroker himself came out with her into the street, took her to see the entry, stood with her there and returned. What was her interest in him, Kahn? His name is Laverick. Four days ago he was on the brink of ruin. To the amazement of every one, he met all his engagements. Why did Mademoiselle go to the city to see him? He was at his office late that Tuesday night. He had a partner who has disappeared."

Kahn looked at his companion with admiration.

"You have found all this out!" he exclaimed.

"And more," Streuss declared. "For twenty-four hours, this man Laverick has not moved without my spies at his heels."

"Why not approach him boldly?" Kahn suggested. "If he has the document, let us outbid Mademoiselle Louise, and do it quickly."

Streuss shook his head.

"You don't know the man. He is an Englishman, and if he had any idea what that document contained, our chances of buying it would be small indeed. This is what I think will happen. Mademoiselle will try to obtain it, and try in vain. Then Bellamy will tell him the truth, and he will part with it willingly. In the meantime, I believe that it is in his possession."

"The evidence is slender enough," objected Kahn.

"What if it is!" Streuss exclaimed. "If it is only a hundred to one chance, we have to take it. I have no fancy for disgrace, Adolf, and I know very well what will happen if we go back empty-handed."

The telephone bell rang. Streuss took off the receiver

and held it to his ear. The words which he spoke were few, but when he laid the instrument down there was a certain amount of satisfaction in his face.

"At any rate," he announced, "this man Laverick did not part with the document to-day. Mademoiselle Louise and Bellamy have been sitting in the Park for an hour. When they separated, she drove home and dropped him at his club. Up till now, then, they have not the document. We shall see what Mr. Laverick does when he leaves business this evening; if he goes straight home, either the document has never been in his possession, or else it is in the safe in his office; if he goes to Mademoiselle Idiale's — "

"Well?" Kahn asked eagerly.

"If he goes to Mademoiselle Idiale's," Streuss repeated slowly, "there is still a chance for us!"

CHAPTER XXIII

LAVERICK, in presenting his card at the box office at
Covent Garden that evening, did so without the slightest
misconception of the reasons which had prompted Mademoiselle Idiale to beg him to become her guest. It was
sheer curiosity which prompted him to pursue this adventure. He was perfectly convinced that personally he had
no interest for her. In some way or other he had become
connected in her mind with the murder which had taken
place within a few yards of his office, and in some other
equally mysterious manner that murder had become a
subject of interest to her. Either that, or this was one of
the whims of a spoiled and pleasure-surfeited woman.

He found an excellent box reserved for him, and a
measure of courtesy from the attendants not often vouch-
safed to an ordinary visitor. The opera was *Samson and
Delilah*, and even before her wonderful voice thrilled the
house, it seemed to Laverick that no person more lovely
than the woman he had come to see had ever moved upon
any stage. It appeared impossible that movement so
graceful and passionate should remain so absolutely
effortless. There seemed to be some strange power inside
the woman. Surely her will guided her feet! The necessity for physical effort never once appeared. Notwithstanding the slight prejudice which he had felt against
her, it was impossible to keep his admiration altogether
in check. The fascination of her wonderful presence,

and then her glorious voice, moved him with the rest of the audience. He clapped as the others did at the end of the first act, and he leaned forward just as eagerly to catch a glimpse of her when she reappeared and stood there with that marvelous smile upon her lips, accepting with faint, deprecating gratitude the homage of the packed house.

Just before the curtain rose upon the second act, there was a knock at his box door. One of the attendants ushered in a short man of somewhat remarkable personality. He was barely five feet in height, and an extremely fat neck and a corpulent body gave him almost the appearance of a hunchback. He had black, beady eyes, a black moustache fiercely turned up, and sallow skin. His white gloves had curious stitchings on the back not common in England, and his silk hat, exceedingly glossy, had wider brims than are usually associated with Bond Street.

Laverick half rose, but the little man spread out one hand and commenced to speak. His accent was foreign, but, if not an Englishman, he at any rate spoke the language with confidence.

"My dear sir," he began, "I owe you many apologies. It was Mademoiselle Idiale's wish that I should make your acquaintance. My name is Lassen. I have the fortune to be Mademoiselle's business manager."

"I am very glad to meet you, Mr. Lassen," said Laverick. "Will you sit down?"

Mr. Lassen thereupon hung his hat upon a peg, removed his overcoat, straightened his white tie with the aid of a looking-glass, brushed back his glossy black hair with the palms of his hands, and took the seat opposite Laverick. His first question was inevitable.

"What do you think of the opera, sir?"

"It is like Mademoiselle Idiale herself," Laverick answered. "It is above criticism."

"She is," Mr. Lassen said firmly, "the loveliest woman in Europe and her voice is the most wonderful. It is a great combination, this. I myself have managed for many stars, I have brought to England most of those whose names are known during the last ten years; but there has never been another Louise Idiale, — never will be."

' I can believe it," Laverick admitted.

' She has wonderful qualities, too," continued Mr. Lassen. "Your acquaintance with her, I believe, sir, is of the shortest."

"That is so," Laverick answered, a little coldly. He was not particularly taken with his visitor.

"Mademoiselle has spoken to me of you," the latter proceeded. "She desired that I should pay my respects during the performance."

"It is very kind of you," Laverick answered. "As a matter of fact, it is exceedingly kind, also, of Mademoiselle Idiale to insist upon my coming here to-night. She did me the honor, as you may know, of paying me a visit in the city this morning."

"So she did tell me," Mr. Lassen declared. "Mademoiselle is a great woman of business. Most of her investments she controls herself. She has whims, however, and it never does to contradict her. She has also, curiously enough, a preference for the men of affairs."

Laverick had reached that stage when he felt indisposed to discuss Mademoiselle any longer with a stranger, even though that stranger should be her manager. He

nodded and took up his programme. As he did so, the
curtain rang up upon the next act. Laverick turned
deliberately towards the stage. The little man had paid
his respects, as he put it. Laverick felt disinclined for
further conversation with him. Yet, though his head
was turned, he knew very well that his companion's eyes
were fixed upon him. He had an uncomfortable sense
that he was an object of more than ordinary interest to
this visitor, that he had come for some specific object
which as yet he had not declared.

"You will like to go round and see Mademoiselle "
the latter remarked, some time afterwards.

Laverick shook his head.

"I shall find another opportunity, I hope, to congratulate her."

"But, my dear sir, she expects to see you," Mr. Lassen
protested. "You are here at her invitation. It is usual,
I can assure you."

"Mademoiselle Idiale will perhaps excuse me," Laverick said. "I have an engagement immediately after the
performance is over."

His companion muttered something which Laverick
could not catch, and made some excuse to leave the box
a few minutes later. When he returned, he carried a
little note which he presented to Laverick with an air
of triumph.

"It is as I said!" he exclaimed. "Mademoiselle
expects you."

Laverick read the few lines which she had written.

I wish to see you after the performance. If you cannot come
round or escort me yourself, will you come later to the restaurant of Luigi, where, as always, I shall sup. Do not fail.

                                         LOUISE IDIALE.

Laverick placed the note in his waistcoat pocket without immediate remark. Later on he turned to his companion.

"Will you tell Mademoiselle Idiale," he said, "that I will do myself the honor of coming to her at Luigi's Restaurant. I have an engagement after the performance which I must keep."

"You will certainly come?" Lassen asked anxiously.

"Without a doubt," Laverick promised.

Mr. Lassen took up his hat.

"I will go and tell Mademoiselle. For some reason or other she seemed particularly desirous of seeing you this evening. She has her whims, and those who have most to do with her, like myself, find it well to keep them gratified. If I do not see you again, sir, permit me to wish you good evening."

He disappeared with several bows of his pudgy little person, and Laverick was left with another puzzle to solve. He was not in the least conceited, and he did not for a moment misinterpret this woman's interest in him. Her invitation, he knew very well, was one which half London would have coveted. Yet it meant nothing personal, he was sure of that. It simply meant that for some mysterious reason, the same reason which had prompted her to visit him in the city he was of interest to her.

At a few minutes before eleven Laverick left the place and drove to the stage-door of the Universal Theatre. Zoe came out among the first and paused upon the threshold, looking up and down the street eagerly. When she recognized him, her smile was heavenly.

"Oh, how nice of you!" she exclaimed, stepping at once into his taxicab. "You don't know how different it feels to hope that there is some one waiting for you and then to find your hope come true. To-night I was not sure. You had said nothing about it, and yet I could not help believing that you would be here."

"I was hoping," he said, "that we might have another supper together. Unfortunately, I have an engagement."

"An engagement?" she repeated, her face falling.

Laverick loved the truth and he seldom hesitated to tell it.

"It is rather an odd thing," he declared. "You remember that woman at Luigi's last night — Mademoiselle Idiale?"

"Of course."

"She came to my office to-day and gave me six thousand pounds to invest for her. She made me take her out and show her where the murder was committed, and asked a great many questions about it. Then she insisted that I should go and hear her sing this evening, and I find that I was expected to take her on to supper afterwards. I excused myself for a little while, but I have promised to go to Luigi's, where she will be."

The girl was silent for a moment.

"Where are we going now, then?" she asked.

"Wherever you like. I can take you home first, or I can leave you anywhere."

She looked at him with a piteous little smile.

"The last two nights you have spoiled me," she said. "I have so many evil thoughts and I am afraid to go home."

"I am sorry. If I could think of anything or anywhere — "

"No, you must take me home, please," said she. "It was selfish of me. Only Mademoiselle Idiale is such a wonderful person. Do you think that she will want you every night?"

"Of course not," he laughed. "Come, I will make an engagement with you. We will have supper together to-morrow evening."

She brightened up at once.

"I wonder," she asked timidly, a few minutes afterwards, "have you heard anything from Arthur? He promised to send a telegram from Queenstown."

Laverick shook his head. He said nothing about the marconigram he had sent, or the answer which he had received informing him that there was no such person on board. It seemed scarcely worth while to worry her.

"I have heard nothing," he replied. "Of course, he must be half-way to America by now."

"There have been no more inquiries about him?" she asked.

"No more than the usual ones from his friends, and a few creditors. The latter I am paying as they come. But there is one thing you ought to do with me. I think we ought to go to his rooms and lock up his papers and letters. He never even went back, you know, after that night."

She nodded thoughtfully.

"When would you like to do this?"

"I am so busy just now that I am afraid I can spare no time until Monday afternoon. Would you go with me then?"

"Of course. My time is my own. We have no matinée, and I have nothing to do except in the evening."

They had reached her home. It looked very dark and very uninviting. She shivered as she took her latchkey from the bag which she was carrying.

"Come in with me, please, while I light the gas," she begged. "It looks so dreary, does n't it?"

"You ought to have some one with you," he declared, "especially in a part like this."

"Oh, I am not really afraid," she answered. "I am only lonely."

He stood in the passage while she felt for a box of matches and lit the gas jet. In the parlor there was a bowl of milk standing waiting for her, and some bread.

"Thank you so much," she said. "Now I am going to make up the fire and read for a short time. I hope that you will enjoy your supper — well, moderately," she added, with a little laugh.

"I can promise you," he answered, "that I shall enjoy it no more than last night's or to-morrow night's."

She sighed.

"Poor little me!" she exclaimed. "It is not fair to have to compete with Mademoiselle Idiale. Good night!"

Something he saw in her eyes moved him strangely as he turned away.

"Would you like me," he asked hesitatingly, "supposing I get away early — would you like me to come in and say good night to you later on?"

Her face was suddenly flushed with joy.

"Oh, do!" she begged. "Do!"

He turned away with a smile.

"Very well," he said. "Don't shut up just yet and I will try."

"I shall stay here until three o'clock," she declared, — "until four, even. You must come. Remember, you must come. See."

She held out to him her key.

"I can knock at the door," he protested. "You would hear me."

"But I might fall asleep," she answered. "I am afraid. If you have the key, I am sure that you will come."

He put it in his waistcoat pocket with a laugh.

"Very well," he said, "if it is only for five minutes, I will come."

CHAPTER XXIV

LAVERICK walked into Luigi's Restaurant at about a quarter to twelve, and found the place crowded with many little supper-parties on their way to a fancy dress ball. The demand for tables was far in excess of the supply, but he had scarcely shown himself before the head *maître d'hôtel* came hurrying up.

"Mademoiselle Idiale is waiting for you, sir," he announced at once. "Will you be so good as to come this way?"

Laverick followed him. She was sitting at the same table as last night, but she was alone, and it was laid, he noticed with surprise, only for two.

"You have treated me," she said, as she held out her fingers, "to a new sensation. I have waited for you alone here for a quarter of an hour — I! Such a thing has never happened to me before."

"You do me too much honor," Laverick declared, seating himself and taking up the carte.

"Then, too," she continued, "I sup alone with you. That is what I seldom do with any man. Not that I care for the appearance," she added, with a contemptuous wave of the hand. "Nothing troubles me less. It is simply that one man alone wearies me. Almost always he will make love, and that I do not like. You, Mr. Laverick, I am not afraid of. I do not think that you will make love to me."

"Any intentions I may have had," Laverick remarked, with a sigh, "I forthwith banish. You ask a hard task of your cavaliers, though, Mademoiselle."

She smiled and looked at him from under her eyelids.

"Not of you, I fancy, Mr. Laverick," she said. "I do not think that you are one of those who make love to every woman because she is good-looking or famous."

"To tell you the truth," Laverick admitted, "I find it hard to make love to any one. I often feel the most profound admiration for individual members of your sex, but to express one's self is difficult — sometimes it is even embarrassing. For supper?"

"It is ordered," she declared. "You are my guest."

"Impossible!" Laverick asserted firmly. "I have been your guest at the Opera. You at least owe me the honor of being mine for supper."

She frowned a little. She was obviously unused to being contradicted

"I sup with you, then, another night," she insisted. "No," she continued, "if you are going to look like that, I take it back. I sup with you to-night. This is an ill omen for our future acquaintance. I have given in to you already — I, who give in to no man. Give me some champagne, please."

Laverick took the bottle from the ice-pail by his side, but the *sommelier* darted forward and served them.

"I drink to our better understanding of one another, Mr. Laverick," she said, raising her glass, "and, if you would like a double toast, I drink also to the early gratification of the curiosity which is consuming you."

"The curiosity?"

"Yes! You are wondering all the time why it is that I chose last night to send and have you presented to me, why I came to your office in the city to-day with the excuse of investing money with you, why I invited you to the Opera to-night, why I commanded you to supper here and am supping with you alone. Now confess the truth; you are full of curiosity, is it not so?"

"Frankly, I am."

She smiled good-humoredly.

"I knew it quite well. You are not conceited. You do not believe, as so many men would, that I have fallen in love with you. You think that there must be some object, and you ask yourself all the time, 'What is it?' In your heart, Mr. Laverick, I wonder whether you have any idea."

Her voice had fallen almost to a whisper. She looked at him with a suggestion of stealthiness from under her eyelids, a look which only needed the slightest softening of her face to have made it something almost irresistible.

"I can assure you," Laverick said firmly, "that I have no idea."

"Do you remember almost my first question to you?" she asked.

"It was about the murder. You seemed interested in the fact that my office was within a few yards of the passage where it occurred."

"Quite right," she admitted. "I see that your memory is very good. There, then, Mr. Laverick, you have the secret of my desire to meet you."

Laverick drank his wine slowly. The woman knew! Impossible! Her eyes were watching his face, but he held himself bravely. What could she know? How could she guess?

"Frankly," he said, "I do not understand. Your interest in me arises from the fact that my offices are near the scene of that murder. Well, to begin with, what concern have you in that?"

"The murdered man," she declared thoughtfully, "was an acquaintance of mine."

"An acquaintance of yours!" Laverick exclaimed. "Why, he has not been identified. No one knows who he was."

, She raised her eyebrows very slightly.

"Mr. Laverick," she murmured, "the newspapers do not tell you everything. I repeat that the murdered man was an acquaintance of mine. Only three days ago I traveled part of the way from Vienna with him."

Laverick was intensely interested.

"You could, perhaps, throw some light, then, upon his death?"

"Perhaps I could," she answered. "I can tell you one thing, at any rate, Mr. Laverick, if it is news to you. At the time when he was murdered, he was carrying a very large sum of money with him. This is a fact which has not been spoken of in the Press."

Once again Laverick was thankful for those nerves of his. He sat quite still. His face exhibited nothing more than the blank amazement which he certainly felt.

"This is marvelous," he said. "Have you told the police?"

"I have not," she answered. "I wish, if I can, to avoid telling the police."

"But the money? To whom did it belong?"

"Not to the murdered man."

"To any one whom you know of?" he inquired.

"I wonder," she said, after a moment of hesitation, "whether I am telling you too much."

"You are telling me a good deal," he admitted frankly.

"I wonder how far," she asked, "you will be inclined to reciprocate?"

"I reciprocate!" he exclaimed. "But what can I do? What do I know of these things?"

She stretched out her hand lazily, and drew towards her a wonderful gold purse set with emeralds. Carefully opening it, she drew from the interior a small flat pocket-book, also of gold, with a great uncut emerald set into its centre. This, too, she opened, and drew out several sheets of foreign note-paper pinned together at the top. These she glanced through until she came to the third or fourth. Then she bent it down and passed it across the table to Laverick.

"You may read that," she said. "It is part of a report which I have had in my possession since Wednesday morning."

Laverick drew the sheet towards him and read, in thin, angular characters, very distinct and plain:

Some ten minutes after the assault, a policeman passed down the street but did not glance toward the passage. The next person to appear was a gentleman who left some offices on the same side as the passage, and walked down evidently on his homeward way. He glanced up the passage and saw the body lying there. He disappeared for a moment and struck a match. A minute afterwards he emerged from the passage, looked up and down the street, and finding it empty returned to the office from which he had issued, let himself in with his latchkey, and closed the door behind him. He was there for about ten minutes. When he reappeared, he walked quickly down the street and for obvious reasons I was unable to follow him.

The address of the offices which he left and re-entered was Messrs. Laverick & Morrison, Stockbrokers.

"That interests you, Mr. Laverick?" she asked softly.

He handed it back to her.

"It interests me very much," he answered. "Who was this unseen person who wrote from the clouds?"

"I may not tell you all my secrets, Mr. Laverick," she declared. "What have you done with that twenty thousand pounds?"

Laverick helped himself to champagne. He listened for a moment to the music, and looked into the wonderful eyes which shone from that beautiful face a few feet away. Her lips were slightly parted, her forehead wrinkled. There was nothing of the accuser in her countenance; a gentle irony was its most poignant expression.

"Is this a fairy tale, Mademoiselle Idiale?"

She shrugged her shoulders.

"It might seem so," she answered. "Sometimes I think that all the time we live two lives, — the life of which the world sees the outside, and the life inside of which no one save ourselves knows anything at all. Look, for instance, at all these people — these chorus girls and young men about town — the older ones, too — all hungry for pleasure, all drinking at the cup of life as though they had indeed but to-day and to-morrow in which to live and enjoy. Have they no shadows, too, no secrets? They seem so harmless, yet if the great white truth shone down, might one not find a murderer there, a dying man who knew his terrible secret, yonder a Croesus on the verge of bankruptcy, a strong man playing with dishonor? But those are the things of the other world which we do not see. The men look at us to-night and they envy you because you are with me. The women envy me more because I have emeralds upon my neck and shoulders for which they would give their souls, and a fame throughout Europe which would turn their foolish heads in a very few minutes. But they do not know. There are the shadows across my path, and I think that there are the shadows across yours. What do you say, Mr. Laverick?"

He looked at her, curiously moved. Now at last he began to believe that it was true what they said of her, that she was indeed a marvelous woman. She had a fame which would have contented nine hundred and ninety-nine women out of a thousand. She had beauty, and, more wonderful still, the grace, the fascination which are irresistible. She had but to lift a finger and there were few who would not kneel to do her bidding. And yet, behind it all there were other things in her life. Had she sought them, or had they come to her?

"You are one of those wise people, Mr. Laverick," she said, "who realize the danger of words. You believe in silence. Well, silence is often good. You do not choose to admit anything."

"What is there for me to admit? Do you want to know whether I am the man who left those offices, who disappeared into the passage, who reappeared again — "

"With a pocket-book containing twenty thousand pounds," she murmured across the flowers.

"At least tell me this?" he demanded. "Was the money yours?"

"I am not like you," she replied. "I have talked a great deal and I have reached the limit of the things which I may tell you."

"But where are we?" he asked. "Are you seriously accusing me of having robbed this murdered man?"

"Be thankful," she declared, "that I am not accusing you of having murdered him."

"But seriously," he insisted, "am I on my defence — have I to account for my movements that night as against the written word of your mysterious informant? Is it you who are charging me with being a thief? Is it to you I am to account for my actions, to defend myself or to plead guilty?"

She shook her head.

"No," she answered. "I have said almost my last word to you upon this subject. All that I have to ask of you is this. If that pocket-book is in your possession, empty it first of its contents, then go over it carefully with your fingers and see if there is not a secret pocket. If you discover that, I think that you will find in it a sealed document. If you find that document, you must bring it to me."

The lights went down. The voice of the waiter murmured something in his ears.

"It is after hours," Mademoiselle Idiale said, "but Luigi does not wish to disturb us. Still, perhaps we had better go."

They passed down the room. To Laverick it was all like a dream — the laughing crowd, the flushed men and bright-eyed women, the lowered lights, the air of voluptuousness which somehow seemed to have enfolded the place. In the hall her maid came up. A small motor-brougham, with two servants on the box, was standing at the doorway. Mademoiselle turned suddenly and gave him her hand.

"Our supper-party, I think, Mr. Laverick," she said, "has been quite a success. We shall before long, I hope, meet again."

He handed her into the carriage. Her maid walked with them. The footman stood erect by his side. There were no further words to be spoken. A little crowd in the doorway envied him as he stood bareheaded upon the pavement.

CHAPTER XXV

It was, in its way, a pathetic sight upon which Laverick gazed when he stole into that shabby little sitting-room. Zoe had fallen asleep in a small, uncomfortable easy-chair with its back to the window. Her supper of bread and milk was half finished, her hat lay upon the table. A book was upon her lap as though she had started to read only to find it slip through her fingers. He stood with his elbow upon the mantelpiece, looking down at her. Her eyelashes, long and silky, were more beautiful than ever now that her eyes were closed. Her complexion, pale though she was, seemed more the creamy pallor of some southern race than the whiteness of ill-health. The bodice of her dress was open a few inches at the neck, showing the faint white smoothness of her flawless skin. Not even her shabby shoes could conceal the perfect shape of her feet and ankles. Once more he remembered his first simile, his first thought of her. She seemed, indeed, like some dainty statuette, uncouthly clad, who had strayed from a world of her own upon rough days and found herself ill-equipped indeed for the struggle. His heart grew hot with anger against Morrison as he stood and watched her. Supposing she had been different! It would have been his fault, leaving her alone to battle her way through the most difficult of all lives. Brute!

He had muttered the word half aloud and she suddenly opened her eyes. At first she seemed bewildered. Then she smiled and sat up.

"I have been asleep!" she exclaimed.

"A most unnecessary statement," he answered, smiling. "I have been standing looking at you for five minutes at least."

"How fortunate that I gave you the key!" she declared. "I don't suppose I should ever have heard you. Now please stand there in the light and let me look at you."

"Why?"

"I want to look at a man who has had supper with Mademoiselle Idiale."

He shrugged his shoulders.

"Am I supposed to be a wanderer out of Paradise, then?"

She looked at him doubtfully.

"They tell strange stories about her," she said; "but oh, she is so beautiful! If I were a man, I should fall in love with her if she even looked my way."

"Then I am glad," he answered, "that I am less impressionable."

"And you are not in love with her?" she asked eagerly.

"Why should I be?" he laughed. "She is like a wonderful picture, a marvelous statue, if you will. Everything about her is faultless. But one looks at these things calmly enough, you know. It is life which stirs life."

"Do you think that there is no life in her veins, then?" Zoe asked.

"If there is," he answered, "I do not think that I am the man to stir it."

She drew a little sigh of content.

"You see," she said, "you are my first admirer, and I haven't the least desire to let you go."

"Incredible!" he declared.

"But it is true," she answered earnestly. "You would not have me talk to these boys who come and hang on at the stage-door. The men to whom I have been introduced by the other girls have been very few, and they have not been very nice, and they have not cared for me and I have not cared for them. I think," she said, disconsolately, "I am too small. Every one to-day seems to like big women. Cora Sinclair, who is just behind me in the chorus, gets bouquets every night, and simply chooses with whom she should go out to supper."

Laverick looked grave.

"You are not envying her?" he asked.

"Not in the least, as long as I too am taken out sometimes."

Laverick smiled and sat on the arm of her chair.

"Miss Zoe," he said, "I have come because you told me to, just to prove, you see, that I am not in the toils of Mademoiselle Idiale. But do you know that it is half-past one? I must not stay here any longer."

She sighed once more.

"You are right," she admitted, "but it is so lonely. I have never been here without May and her mother. I have never slept alone in the house before the other night. If I had known that they were going away, I should never have dared to come here."

"It is too bad," he declared. "Could n't you get one of the other girls to stay with you?"

She shook her head.

"There are one or two whom I would like to have," she said, "but they are all living either at home or with relatives. The others I am afraid about. They seem to like to sit up so late and — "

"You are quite right," he interrupted hastily, — "quite

right. You are better alone. But you ought to have a servant."

She laughed.

"On two pounds fifteen a week?" she asked. "You must remember that I could not even live here, only I have practically no rent to pay."

He fidgeted for a moment.

"Miss Zoe," he said, "I am perfectly serious when I tell you that I have money which should go to your brother. Why will you not let me alter your arrangements just a little? I cannot bear to think of you here all alone."

"It is very kind of you," she answered doubtfully; "but please, no. Somehow, I think that it would spoil everything if I accepted that sort of help from you. If you have any money of Arthur's, keep it for a time and I think when you write him — I do not want to seem grasping — but I think if he has any to spare you might suggest that he does give me just a little. I have never had anything from him at all. Perhaps he does not quite understand how hard it is for me."

"I will do that, of course," Laverick answered, "but I wish you would let me at least pay over a little of what I consider due to you. I will take the responsibility for it. It will come from him and not from me."

She remained unconvinced.

"I would rather wait," she said. "If you really want to give me something, I will let you — out of my brother's money, of course, I mean," she added. "I have n't anything saved at all, or I would n't have that. But one day you shall take me out and buy me a dress and hat. You can tell Arthur directly you write to him. I don't mind that, for sometimes I do feel ashamed — I did the other night to have you sit with me there, and to feel that I was dressed so very differently from all of them."

He laughed reassuringly.

"I don't think men notice those things. To me you seemed just as you should seem. I only know that I was glad enough to be there with you."

"Were you?" — rather wistfully.

"Of course I was. Now I am going, but before I go, don't forget Monday afternoon. We'll have lunch and then go to your brother's rooms."

She glanced at the clock.

"Is it really so late?" she asked.

"It is. Don't you notice how quiet it is outside?"

They stood hand in hand for a moment. A strange silence seemed to have fallen upon the streets. Laverick was suddenly conscious of something which he had never felt when Mademoiselle Idiale had smiled upon him — a quickening of the pulses, a sense of gathering excitement which almost took his breath away. His eyes were fixed upon hers, and he seemed to see the reflection of that same wave of feeling in her own expressive face. Her lips trembled, her eyes were deeper and softer than ever. They seemed to be asking him a question, asking and asking till every fibre of his body was concentrated in the desperate effort with which he kept her at arm's length.

"Is it so very late?" she whispered, coming just a little closer, so that she was indeed almost within the shelter of his arms.

He clutched her hands almost roughly and raised them to his lips.

"Much too late for me to stay here, child," he said, and his voice even to himself sounded hard and unnatural.

"Run along to bed. To-morrow night — to-morrow night, then, I will fetch you. Good-bye!"

He let himself out. He did not even look behind to the spot where he had left her. He closed the front door and walked with swift, almost savage footsteps down the quiet street, across the Square, and into New Oxford Street. Here he seemed to breathe more freely. He called a hansom and drove to his rooms.

The hall-porter had left his post in the front hall, and there was no one to inform Laverick that a visitor was awaiting him. When he entered his sitting-room, however, he gave a little start of surprise. Mr. James Shepherd was reclining in his easy-chair with his hands upon his knees — Mr. James Shepherd with his face more pasty even than usual, his eyes a trifle greener, his whole demeanor one of unconcealed and unaffected terror.

"Hullo!" Laverick exclaimed. "What the dickens — what do you want here, Shepherd?"

"Upon my word, sir, I'm not sure that I know," the man replied, "but I'm scared. I've brought you back the certificates of them shares. I want you to keep them for me. I'm terrified lest they come and search my room. I am, I tell you fair. I'm terrified to order a pint of beer for myself. They're watching me all the time."

"Who are?" Laverick demanded.

"Lord knows who," Shepherd answered, "but there's two of them at it. I told you about them as asked questions, and I thought there we'd done and finished with it. Not a bit of it! There was another one there this afternoon, said he was a journalist, making sketches of the passage and asking me no end of questions. He wasn't no journalist, I'll swear to that. I asked him about his paper. 'Half-a-dozen,' he declared. 'They're all glad

to have what I send them.' Journalist! Lord knows
who the other chap was and what he was asking questions for, but this one was a 'tec, straight. Joe Forman,
he was in to-day looking after my place, for I'd given a
month's notice, and he says to me, 'You see that big
chap?' — meaning him as had been asking me the questions — and I says 'Yes!' and he says, 'That's a 'tec.
I've seed him in a police court, giving evidence.' I went
all of a shiver so that you could have knocked me down."

"Come, come!" said Laverick. "There's no need
for you to be feeling like this about it. All that you've
done is not to have remembered those two customers who
were in your restaurant late one night. There's nothing
criminal in that."

"There's something criminal in having two hundred
and fifty pounds' worth of shares in one's pocket — something suspicious, anyway," Shepherd declared, plumping
them down on the table. "I ain't giving you these back,
mind, but you must keep 'em for me. I wish I'd never
given notice. I think I'll ask the boss to keep me on."

"Why do you suppose that this man is particularly
interested in you?" Laverick inquired.

"Ain't I told you?" Shepherd exclaimed, sitting up.
"Why, he's been to my place down in 'Ammersmith,
asking questions about me. My landlady swears he did n't
go into my room, but who can tell whether he did or not?
Those sort of chaps can get in anywhere. Then I went
out for a bit of an airing after the one o'clock rush was
over to-day, and I'm danged if he was n't at my 'eels. I
seed him coming round by Liverpool Street just as I went
in a bar to get a drop of something."

Laverick frowned.

"If there is anything in this story, Shepherd," he said,

210 HAVOC

"if you are really being followed, what a thundering fool you were to come here! All the world knows that Arthur Morrison was my partner."

"I could n't help it, sir," the man declared. "I could n't, indeed. I was so scared, I felt I must speak about it to some one. And then there were these shares. There was nowhere I could keep 'em safe."

"Look here," Laverick went on, "you're alarming yourself about nothing. In any case, there is only one thing for you to do. Pull yourself together and put a bold face upon it. I'll keep these certificates for you, and when you want some money you can come to me for it. Go back to your place, and if your master is willing to keep you on perhaps it would be a good thing to stay there for another month or so. But don't let any one see that you're frightened. Remember, there's nothing that you can get into trouble for. No one's obliged to answer such questions as you've been asked, except in a court and under oath. Stick to your story, and if you take my advice," Laverick added, glancing at his visitor's shaking fingers, "you will keep away from the drink."

"It's little enough I've had, sir," Shepherd assured him. "A drop now and then just to keep up one's spirits — nothing that amounts to anything."

"Make it as little as possible," Laverick said. "Remember, I'm back of you, I'll see that you get into no trouble. And don't come here again. Come to my office, if you like — there's nothing in that — but don't come here, you understand?"

Shepherd took up his hat.

"I understand, sir. I'm sorry to have troubled you, but the sight of that man following me about fairly gave me the shivers."

"Come into the office as often as you like, in reason," Laverick said, showing him out, "but not here again. Keep your eyes open, and let me know if you think you've been followed here."

"There's no more news in the papers, sir? Nothing turned up?"

"Nothing," replied Laverick. "If the police have found out anything at all, they will keep it until after the inquest."

"And you've heard nothing, sir," Shepherd asked, speaking in a hoarse whisper, "of Mr. Morrison?"

"Nothing," Laverick answered. "Mr. Morrison is abroad."

The man wiped his forehead with his hand.

"Of course!" he muttered. "A good job, too, for him!"

CHAPTER XXVI

THE DOCUMENT DISCOVERED

On the following morning, Laverick surprised his office cleaner and one errand-boy by appearing at about a quarter to nine. He found a woman busy brushing out his room and a man cleaning the windows. They stared at him in amazement. His arrival at such an hour was absolutely unprecedented.

"You can leave the office just as it is, if you please," he told them. "I have a few things to attend to at once."

He was accordingly left alone. He had reckoned upon this as being the one period during the day when he could rely upon not being disturbed. Nevertheless, he locked the door so as to be secure against any possible intruder. Then he went to his safe, unlocked it, and drew from its secret drawer the worn brown-leather pocket-book.

First of all he took out the notes and laid them upon the table. Then he felt the pocket-book all over and his heart gave a little leap. It was true what Mademoiselle Idiale had told him. On one side there was distinctly a rustling as of paper. He opened the case quite flat and passed his fingers carefully over the lining. Very soon he found the opening — it was simply a matter of drawing down the stiff silk lining from underneath the overlapping edge. Thrusting in his fingers, he drew out a long foreign envelope, securely sealed. Scarcely stopping to glance at it, he rearranged the pocket-book, replaced the notes, and locked it up again. Then he unbolted his door and sat down at his desk, with the document which he had discovered, on the pad in front of him.

There was not much to be made of it. There was no address, but the black seal at the end bore the impression of a foreign coat of arms, and a motto which to him was indecipherable. He held it up to the light, but the outside sheet had not been written on, and he gained no idea as to its contents. He leaned back in his chair for a moment, and looked at it. So this was the document which would probably reveal the secret of the murder in Crooked Friars' Alley! This was the document which Mademoiselle Idiale considered of so much more importance than the fortune represented by that packet of bank-notes! What did it all mean? Was this man, who had either expiated a crime or been the victim of a terrible vengeance, — was he a politician, a dealer in trade secrets, a member of a secret society, an informer? Or was he one of the underground criminals of the world, one of those who crawl beneath the surface of known things — a creature of the dark places? Perhaps during those few minutes, when his brain was cool and active, with the great city awakening all around him, Laverick realized more completely than ever before exactly how he stood. Without doubt he was walking on the brink of a precipice. Four days ago there had been nothing for him but ruin. The means of salvation had suddenly presented themselves in this startling and dramatic manner, and without hesitation he had embraced them. What did it all amount to? How far was he guilty, and of what? Was he a thief? The law would probably call him so. The law might have even more to say. It would say that by keeping his mouth closed as to his adventure on that night he had ranged himself on the side of the criminals, — he was

guilty not only of technical theft, but of a criminal knowledge of this terrible crime. Events had followed upon
one another so rapidly during these last few days that he
had little enough time for reflection, little time to realize exactly how he stood. The long-expected boom in " Unions,"
the coming of Zoe, the strange advances made to him by
Mademoiselle Idiale, her incomprehensible connection
with this tragedy across which he had stumbled, and her
apparent knowledge of his share in it, — these things were
sufficient, indeed, to give him food for thought. Laverick
was not by nature a pessimist. Other things being equal,
he would have made, without doubt, a magnificent soldier,
for he had courage of a rare and high order. It never
occurred to him to sit and brood upon his own danger.
He rather welcomed the opportunity of occupying his
mind with other thoughts. Yet in those few minutes,
while he waited for the business of the day to commence,
he looked his exact position in the face and he realized
more thoroughly how grave it really was. How was he
to find a way out — to set himself right with the law?
What could he do with those notes? They were there
untouched. He had only made use of them in an indirect
way. They were there intact, as he had picked them up
upon that fateful night. Was there any possible chance
by means of which he might discover the owner and
restore them in such a way that his name might never be
mentioned? His eyes repeatedly sought that envelope
which lay before him. Inside it must lie the secret of the
whole tragedy. Should he risk everything and break the
seal, or should he risk perhaps as much and tell the whole
truth to Mademoiselle Idiale? It was a strange dilemma
for a man to find himself in.

Then, as he sat there, the business of the day commenced.

A pile of letters was brought in, the telephones in the outer office began to ring. He thrust the sealed envelope into the breast-pocket of his coat and buttoned it up. There, for the present, it must remain. He owed it to himself to devote every energy he possessed to make the most of this great tide of business. With set face he closed the doors upon the unreal world, and took hold of the levers which were to guide his passage through the one in which he was an actual figure.

Her visit was not altogether unexpected, and yet, when they told him that Mademoiselle Idiale was outside, he hesitated.

"It is the lady who was here the other day," his head-clerk reminded him. "We made a remarkably good choice of stocks for her. They must be showing nearly sixteen hundred pounds profit. Perhaps she wants to realize."

"In any case, you had better show her in," said Laverick.

She came, bringing with her, notwithstanding her black clothes and heavy veil, the atmosphere of a strange world into his somewhat severely furnished office. Her skirts swept his carpet with a musical swirl. She carried with her a faint, indefinable perfume of violets, — a perfume altogether peculiar, dedicated to her by a famous chemist in the Rue Royale, and supplied to no other person upon earth. Who else was there, indeed, who could have walked those few yards as she walked?

He rose to his feet and pointed to a chair.

"You have come to ask about your shares?" he asked politely. "So far, we have nothing but good news for you."

She recognized that he spoke to her in the presence of his clerk, and she waved her hand.

"Women who will come themselves to look after their poor investments are a nuisance, I suppose," she said. "But indeed I will not keep you long. A few minutes are all that I shall ask of you. I am beginning to find city affairs so interesting."

They were alone by now and Louise raised her veil, raised it so high that he could see her eyes. She leaned back in her chair, supporting her chin with the long, exquisite fingers of her right hand. She looked at him thoughtfully.

"You have examined the pocket-book?" she asked.

"I have."

"And the document was there?"

"The document was there," he admitted. "Perhaps you can tell me how it would be addressed?"

Looking at her closely, it came to him that her indifference was assumed. She was shivering slightly, as though with cold.

"I imagine that there would be no address," she said.

"You are right. That document is in my pocket."

"What are you going to do with it?" she asked.

"What do you advise me to do with it?"

"Give it to me."

"Have you any claim?"

She leaned a little nearer to him.

"At least I have more claim to it," she whispered, "than you to that twenty thousand pounds."

"I do not claim them," he replied. "They are in my safe at this moment, untouched. They are there ready to be returned to their proper owner."

"Why do you not find him?" — with a note of incredulity in her tone.

"How am I to do that?" Laverick demanded.

"We waste words," she continued coldly. "I think that if I leave you with the contents of your safe, it will be wise for you to hand me that document."

"I am inclined to do so," Laverick admitted. "The very fact that you knew of its existence would seem to give you a sort of claim to it. But, Mademoiselle Idiale, will you answer me a few questions?"

"I think," she said, "that it would be better if you asked me none."

"But listen," he begged. "You are the only person with whom I have come into touch who seems to know anything about this affair. I should rather like to tell you exactly how I stumbled in upon it. Why can we not exchange confidence for confidence? I want neither the twenty thousand pounds nor the document. I want, to be frank with you, nothing but to escape from the position I am now in of being half a thief and half a criminal. Show me some claim to that document and you shall have it. Tell me to whom that money belongs, and it shall be restored."

"You are incomprehensible," she declared. "Are you, by any chance, playing a part with me? Do you think that it is worth while?"

"Mademoiselle Idiale," Laverick protested earnestly, "nothing in the world is further from my thoughts. There is very little of the conspirator about me. I am a plain man of business who stumbled in upon this affair at a critical moment and dared to make temporary use of his discovery. You can put it, if you like, that I am afraid. I want to get out. Nothing would give me greater pleasure, if such a thing were possible, than to send this pocket-book and its contents anonymously to Scotland Yard, and never hear about them again."

She listened to him with unchanged face. Yet for some moments after he had finished speaking she was thoughtful.

"You may be speaking the truth," she said. "If so, I have been deceived. You are not quite the sort of man I did believe you were. What you tell me is amazing, but it may be true."

"It is the truth," Laverick repeated calmly.

"Listen," she said, after a brief pause. "You were at school, were you not, with Mr. David Bellamy? You know well who he is?"

"Perfectly well," Laverick admitted.

"You would consider him a person to be trusted?"

"Absolutely."

"Very well, then," she declared. "You shall come to my flat at five o'clock this afternoon and bring that document. If it is possible, David Bellamy shall be there himself. We will try then and prove to you that you do no harm in parting with that document to us."

"I will come," Laverick promised, "at five o'clock; but you must tell me where."

"You will put it down, please," she said. "There must not be any mistake. You must come, and you must come to-day. I am staying at number 15, Dover Street. I will leave orders that you are shown in at once."

She rose to her feet and he walked to the door with her. On the way she hesitated.

"Take care of yourself to-day, Mr. Laverick," she begged. "There are others beside myself who are interested in that packet you carry with you. You represent to them things beside which life and death are trivial happenings."

Laverick laughed shortly. He was a matter-of-fact man, and there seemed something a little absurd in such a warning.

"I do not think," he declared, "that you need have any fear. London is, as you doubtless find it, a dull old city, but it is a remarkably safe one to live in."

"Nevertheless, Mr. Laverick," she repeated earnestly, "be on your guard to-day, for all our sakes."

He bowed and changed the subject.

"Your investments," he remarked, "you will be content, perhaps, to leave as they are. It is, no doubt, of some interest to you to know that they are showing already a profit of considerably over a thousand pounds."

She shrugged her shoulders.

"It was an excuse — that investment," she declared. "Yet money is always good. Keep it for me, Mr. Laverick, and do what you will. I will trust your judgment. Buy or sell as you please. You will let nothing prevent your coming this afternoon?"

"Nothing," he promised her.

From the window of her beautifully appointed little electric brougham she held out her hand in farewell.

"You think me foolish, I know, that I persist," she said, "but I do beg that you will remember what I say. Do not be alone to-day more than you can help. Suspect every one who comes near to you. There may be a trap before your feet at any moment. Be wary always and do not forget — at five o'clock I expect you."

Laverick smiled as he bowed his adieux.

"It is a promise, Mademoiselle," he assured her.

CHAPTER XXVII

ABOUT an hour after Mademoiselle Idiale's departure a note marked "Urgent" was brought in and handed to Laverick. He tore it open. It was dated from the address of a firm of stockbrokers, with two of the partners of which he was on friendly terms. It ran thus:

> MY DEAR LAVERICK, — I want a chat with you, if you can spare five minutes at lunch time. Come to Lyons' a little earlier than usual, if you don't mind, — say at a quarter to one.
>
> J. HENSHAW.

Laverick read the typewritten note carelessly enough at first. He had even laid it down and glanced at the clock, with the intention of starting out, when a thought struck him. He took it up and read it through again. Then he turned to the telephone.

"Put me on to the office of Henshaw & Allen. I want to speak to Mr. Henshaw particularly."

Two minutes passed. Laverick, meanwhile, had been washing his hands ready to go out. Then the telephone bell rang. He took up the receiver.

"Hullo! Is that Henshaw?"

"I'm Henshaw," was the answer. "That's Laverick, is n't it? How are you, old fellow?"

"I'm all right," Laverick replied. "What is it that you want to see me about?"

"Nothing particular that I know of. Who told you that I wanted to?"

Laverick, who had been standing with the instrument in his hand, sat down in his chair.

"Look here," he said, "did n't you send me a note a few minutes ago, asking me to come out to lunch at a quarter to one and meet you at Lyons'?"

Henshaw's laugh was sufficient response.

"Delighted to lunch with you there or anywhere, old chap, — you know that," was the answer, "but some one 's been putting up a practical joke on you."

"You did not send me a note round this morning, then?" Laverick insisted.

"I'll swear I did n't," came the reply. "Do you seriously mean that you've had one purporting to come from me?"

Laverick pulled himself together.

"Well, the signature 's such a scrawl," he said, "that no one could tell what the name really was. I guessed at you but I seem to have guessed wrong. Good-bye!"

He set down the receiver and rang off to escape further questioning. Now indeed the plot was commencing to thicken. This was a deliberate effort on the part of some one to secure his absence from his offices at a quarter to one.

With the document in his pocket and the safe securely locked, Laverick felt at ease as to the result of any attempted burglary of his premises. At the same time his curiosity was excited. Here, perhaps, was a chance of finding some clue to this impenetrable mystery.

There were three clerks in the outer office. He put on his hat and despatched two of them on errands in different directions. The last he was obliged to take into his confidence.

"Halsey," he said, "I am going out to lunch. At least,

I wish it to be thought that I am going out to lunch. As a matter of fact, I shall return in about ten minutes by the back way. I do not wish you, however, to know this. I want you to have it in your mind that I have gone to lunch and shall not be back until a quarter past two. If there are visitors for me — inquirers of any sort — act exactly as you would have done if you really believed that I was not in the building."

Halsey appeared a good deal mystified. Laverick took him even further into his confidence.

"To tell you the truth, Halsey," he said, "I have just received a bogus letter from Mr. Henshaw, asking me to lunch with him. Some one was evidently anxious to get me out of my office for an hour or so. I want to find out for myself what this means, if possible. You understand?"

"I think so, sir," the man replied doubtfully. "I am not to be aware that you have returned, then?"

"Certainly not," Laverick answered. "Please be quite clear about that. If you hear any commotion in the office, you can come in, but do not send for the police unless I tell you to. I wish to look into this affair for myself."

Halsey, who had started life as a lawyer's clerk, and was distinctly formal in his ideas, was a little shocked.

"Would it not be better, sir," he suggested, "for me to communicate with the police in the first case? If this should really turn out to be an attempt at burglary, it would surely be best to leave the matter to them."

Laverick frowned.

"For certain reasons, Halsey, which I do not think it necessary to tell you, I have a strong desire to investigate this matter personally. Please do exactly as I say."

He left the office and strolled up the street in the direction of the restaurant which he chiefly frequented. He reached it in a moment or two, but left it at once by another entrance. Within ten minutes he was back at his office.

"Has any one been, Halsey?"

"No one, sir," the clerk answered.

"You will be so good," Laverick continued, "as to forget that I have returned."

He passed on quickly into his own room and made his way into the small closet where he kept his coat and washed his hands. He had scarcely been there a minute when he heard voices in the outside hall. The door of his office was opened.

"Mr. Laverick said nothing about an appointment at this hour," he heard Halsey protest in a somewhat deprecating tone.

"He had, perhaps, forgotten," was the answer, in a totally unfamiliar voice. "At any rate, I am not in a great hurry. The matter is of some importance, however, and I will wait for Mr. Laverick."

The visitor was shown in. Laverick investigated his appearance through a crack in the door. He was a man of medium height, well-dressed, clean-shaven, and wore gold-rimmed spectacles. He made himself comfortable in Laverick's easy-chair, and accepted the paper which Halsey offered him.

"I shall be quite glad of a rest," he remarked genially. "I have been running about all the morning."

"Mr. Laverick is never very long out for lunch, sir," Halsey said. "I daresay he will not keep you more than a quarter of an hour or twenty minutes."

The clerk withdrew and closed the door. The man in

the chair waited for a moment. Then he laid down his
newspaper and looked cautiously around the room. Satisfied apparently that he was alone, he rose to his feet and
walked swiftly to Laverick's writing-table. With fingers
which seemed gifted with a lightning-like capacity for
movement, he swung open the drawers, one by one, and
turned over the papers. His eyes were everywhere. Every
document seemed to be scanned and as rapidly discarded.
At last he found something which interested him. He
held it up and paused in his search. Laverick heard a
little breath come through his teeth, and with a thrill he
recognized the paper as one which he had torn from a
memorandum tablet and upon which he had written
down the address which Mademoiselle Idiale had given
him. The man with the gold-rimmed glasses replaced
the paper where he had found it. Evidently he had
done with the writing-table. He moved swiftly over to
the safe and stood there listening for a few seconds. Then
from his pocket he drew a bunch of keys. To Laverick's
surprise, at the stranger's first effort the great door of the
safe swung open. He saw the man lean forward, saw his
hand reappear almost directly with the pocket-book
clenched in his fingers. Then he stood once more quite
still, listening. Satisfied that no one was disturbed, he
closed the door of the safe softly and moved once more
to the writing-table. With marvelous swiftness the notes
were laid upon the table, the pocket-book was turned
upside down, the secret place disclosed — the secret place
which was empty. It seemed to Laverick that from his
hiding-place he could hear the little oath of disappointment which broke from the thin red lips. The man replaced the notes and, with the pocket-book in his hand,
hesitated. Laverick, who thought that things had gone

far enough, stepped lightly out from his hiding-place and stood between his unbidden visitor and the door.

"You had better put down that pocket-book," he ordered quietly.

The man was upon him with a single spring, but Laverick, without the slightest hesitation, knocked him prone upon the floor, where he lay, for a moment, motionless. Then he slowly picked himself up. His spectacles were broken — he blinked as he stood there.

"Sorry to be so rough," Laverick said. "Perhaps if you will kindly realize that of the two I am much the stronger man, you will be so good as to sit in that chair and tell me the meaning of your intrusion."

The man obeyed. He covered his eyes with his hand, for a moment, as though in pain.

"I imagine," he said — and it seemed to Laverick that his voice had a slight foreign accent — "I imagine that the motive for my paying you this visit is fairly clear to you. People who have compromising possessions may always expect visits of this sort. You see, one runs so little risk."

"So little risk!" Laverick repeated.

"Exactly," the other answered. "Confess that you are not in the least inclined to ring your bell and send for a constable to give me in charge for being in possession of a pocket-book abstracted from your safe, containing twenty thousand pounds in Bank of England notes."

"It wouldn't do at all," Laverick admitted.

"You are a man of common sense," declared the other. "It would *not* do. Now comes the time when I have a question to ask you. There was a sealed document in this pocket-book. Where is it? What have you done with it?"

"Can you tell me," Laverick asked, "why I should answer questions from a person whom I discover apparently engaged in a nefarious attempt at burglary?"

The man's hand shot out from his trouser-pocket, and Laverick looked into the gleaming muzzle of a revolver.

"Because if you don't, you die," was the quick reply. "Whether you've read that document or not, I want it. If you've read it, you know the sort of men you've got to deal with. If you haven't, take my word for it that we waste no time. The document! Will you give it me?"

"Do I understand that you are threatening me?" Laverick asked, retreating a few steps.

"You may understand that this is a repeating revolver, and that I seldom miss a half-crown at twenty paces," his visitor answered. "If you put out your hand toward that bell, it will be the last movement you'll ever make on earth."

"London isn't really the place for this sort of thing," Laverick said. "If you discharge that revolver, you haven't a dog's chance of getting clear of the building. My clerks would rush out after you into the street. You'd find yourself surrounded by a crowd of business men. You couldn't make your way through anywhere. You'd be held up before you'd gone a dozen yards. Put down your revolver. We can perhaps settle this little matter without it."

"The document!" the man ordered. "You've got it! You must have it! You took that pocket-book from a dead man, and in that pocket-book was the document. We must have it. We intend to have it."

"And who, may I ask, are we?" Laverick inquired.

"If you do not know, what does it matter? Will you give it to me?"

Laverick shook his head.

"I have no document."

The man in the chair leaned forward. The muzzle of his revolver was very bright, and he held it in fingers which were firm as a rock.

"Give it to me!" he repeated. "You ought to know that you are not dealing with men who are unaccustomed to death. You have it about you. Produce it, and I've done with you. Deny me, and you have not time to say your prayers!"

Laverick was leaning against a small table which stood near the door. His fingers suddenly gripped the ledger which lay upon it. He held it in front of his face for a single moment, and then dashed it at his visitor. He followed behind with one desperate spring. Once, twice, the revolver barked out. Laverick felt the skin of his temple burn and a flick on the ear which reminded him of his school-days. Then his hand was upon the other man's throat and the revolver lay upon the carpet.

"We'll see about that. By the Lord, I've a good mind to wring the life out of you. That bullet of yours might have been in my temple."

"It was meant to be there," the man gasped. "Hand over the document, you pig-headed fool! It'll cost you your life — if not to-day, to-morrow."

"I'll be hanged if you get it, anyway!" Laverick answered fiercely. "You assassin! Scoundrel! To come here and make a cold-blooded effort at murder! You shall see what you think of the inside of an English prison."

The man laughed contemptuously.

"And what about the pocket-book?" he asked.

Laverick was silent. His assailant smiled and shrugged his shoulders.

"Come," he said, "I have made my effort and failed. You have twenty thousand pounds. That's a fair price, but I'll add another twenty thousand for that document unopened."

"It is possible that we might deal," Laverick remarked, kicking the revolver a little further away. "Unfortunately, I am too much in the dark. Tell me the real position of the murdered man? Tell me why he was murdered? Tell me the contents of this document and why it was in his possession? Perhaps I may then be inclined to treat with you."

"You are either an astonishingly ingenuous person, Mr. Laverick," his visitor declared, "or you're too subtle for me. You do not expect me to believe that you are in this with your eyes blindfolded? You do not expect me to believe that you do not know what is in that sealed envelope? Bah! It is a child's game, that, and we play as men with men."

Laverick shook his head.

"Your offer," he asked, "what is it exactly?"

"Twenty thousand pounds," the man answered. "The document is worth no more than that to you. How you came into this thing is a mystery, but you are in and, what is more, you have possession. Twenty thousand pounds, Mr. Laverick. It is a large sum of money. You find it interesting?"

"I find it interesting," Laverick answered dryly, "but I am not a seller."

The intruder moved his hand away from his eyes. His expression was full of wonder.

"Consider for a moment," he said. "While that document remains in your possession, you walk the narrow way, your life hangs upon a thread. Better surrender it and attend to your stocks and shares. Heaven knows how you first came into our affairs, but the sooner you are out of them the better. What do you say now to my offer?"

"It is refused," Laverick declared. "I regret to add," he continued, "that I have already spared you all the time I have at my disposal. Forgive me."

He pressed a button with his finger. His visitor rose up in anger.

"You are not such a fool!" he exclaimed. "You are not going to send me away without it? Why, I tell you that there won't be a safe corner in the world for you!"

Halsey opened the door. Laverick nodded toward his visitor.

"Show this gentleman out, Halsey," he ordered.

Halsey started. The noise of the revolver shot had evidently been muffled by the heavy connecting doors, but there was a smell of gunpowder in the room, and a little wreath of smoke. The man rose slowly to his feet, still blinking.

"It must be as you will, of course. I wonder if you would be so good as to let your clerk direct me to an oculist? I am, unfortunately, a helpless man in this condition."

"There is one a few yards off," Laverick answered. "Put on your hat, Halsey, and show this gentleman where he can get some glasses."

His visitor leaned towards Laverick.

"It is your life which is in question, not my eyesight,"

he muttered. "Do you accept my offer? Will you give me the document?"

"I do not and I will not," Laverick replied. "I shall not part with anything until I know more than I know at present."

The man stood motionless for a moment. His fingers seemed to be twitching. Laverick had a fancy that he was about to spring, but if ever he had had any thoughts of the kind, Halsey's reappearance checked them.

"I am much obliged to you, Mr. Laverick," he said quietly. "We shall, perhaps, resume this discussion at some future date."

With that he turned and followed Halsey out of the room. Laverick went to the window and threw it wide open. The smoke floated out, the smell of gunpowder was gradually dispersed. Then he walked back to his seat. Once more he locked up the notes. The document was safe in his pocket. There was a slight mark by the side of his temple, and his ear, he discovered, was bleeding. He rang the bell and Halsey entered.

"Has our friend gone, Halsey?"

"I left him in the optician's, sir," the clerk answered. "He was buying some spectacles."

Laverick glanced at the floor, where the remains of those gold-rimmed glasses were scattered.

"You had better send for a locksmith at once," he said. "The gentleman who has been here had a skeleton key to my safe. We'll have a combination put on."

"Very good, sir," Halsey answered.

"And, Halsey," his master continued, "be careful about one thing, for your own sake as well as mine. If that man presents himself again, don't let him come into my room unannounced. If you can help it, don't let him come in at all. I have an idea that he might be dangerous."

The clerk's face was a study.

"If he presents himself here, sir," he announced stiffly, "I shall take the liberty of sending for the police."

Laverick made no reply.

CHAPTER XXVIII

LAVERICK'S NARROW ESCAPE

AT precisely a quarter past four, nothing having happened in the meantime but a steady rush of business, Laverick ordered a taxicab to be summoned. He then unlocked his safe, placed the pocket-book securely in his breast pocket, walked through the office, and directed the man to drive to Chancery Lane. Here at the headquarters of the Safe Deposit Company he engaged a compartment, and down in the strong-room locked up the pocket-book. There was only now the document left. Stepping once more into the street, he found that his taxicab had vanished. He looked up and down in vain. The man had not been paid and there seemed to be no reason for his departure. A policeman who was standing by touched his hat and addressed him.

"Were you looking for that taxi you stepped out of a few minutes ago, sir?" he asked.

"I was," Laverick answered. "I had n't paid him and I told him to wait."

"I thought there was something queer about it," the policeman remarked. "Soon after you had gone inside, two gentlemen drove up in a hansom. They got out here and one of them spoke to your driver, who shook his head and pointed to his flag. The gent then said something else to him — can't say as I heard what it was, but it was probably offering him double fare. Anyway, they both got in and off went your taxi, sir."

"Thank you," Laverick said thoughtfully. "It sounds a little perplexing."

He hesitated for a moment.

"Constable," he continued, "I have just made a very valuable deposit in there, and I had an idea that I might be followed. I have still in my pocket a document of great importance. I have no doubt whatever but that the object of the men who have taken my taxicab is to leave me in the street here alone under circumstances which will render a quick attack upon me likely to be successful."

The policeman turned his head and looked at Laverick incredulously. He was more than half inclined to believe that this was a practical joke. Were they not standing on the pavement in Chancery Lane, and was not he an able-bodied policeman of great bulk and immense muscle! Yet his companion did not look by any means a man of the nervous order. Laverick was broad-shouldered, his skin was tanned a wholesome color, his bearing was the bearing of a man prepared to defend himself at any time. The constable smiled in a non-committal manner.

"If you'll excuse my saying so, sir," he remarked, "I don't think this is exactly the spot any one would choose for an assault."

"I agree with you," Laverick answered, "but, on the other hand, you must remember that these gentlemen have had no choice. I stepped from my office direct into the taxi, and I proposed to drive straight from here to the place where I shall probably leave the other document I am carrying with me. Why I have taken you into my confidence is to ask you this. Can you walk with me to the corner of the street, or until we meet a taxicab? It sounds cowardly, but, as a matter of fact, I am not afraid. I simply want to make sure of delivering this document to the person to whom it belongs."

The constable stood still, a little perplexed.

"My beat, sir," he said, "only goes about twenty-five yards further on. I will walk to the corner of Holborn with you, if you desire it. At the same time, I may say that I am breaking regulations. How do I know that it is not your scheme to get me away from this neighborhood for some purpose of your own?"

"You don't believe anything of the sort," Laverick declared, with a smile.

"I do not, sir," the policeman admitted. "Keep by my side, and I think that nothing will happen to you before we reach Holborn."

Laverick was a man of more than medium height, but by the side of the policeman he seemed short. Both scanned the faces of the passers-by closely — the policeman with mild interest, Laverick with almost feverish anxiety. It was a gray afternoon, pleasant but close. There seemed to be nothing whatever to account for the feeling of nervousness which had suddenly come over Laverick. He felt himself in danger — he had no idea how, or in what way — but the conviction was there. He took every step fully alert, absolutely on his guard.

They were almost within sight of Holborn when a cry from the bystanders caused them to look away into the middle of the road. Laverick only cast one glance there and abandoned every instinct of curiosity, thinking once more only of himself and his own position. With the constable, however, it was naturally different. He saw something which called at once for his intervention, and he immediately forgot the somewhat singular task upon which he was engaged. A man had fallen in the middle

of the street, either knocked down by the shaft of a passing
vehicle or in some sort of fit. There was a tangle of
rearing horses, an omnibus was making desperate efforts
to avoid the prostrate body. The constable sprang to
the rescue. Laverick, instantly suspicious and realizing
that there was no one in front of him, turned swiftly around.
He was just in time to receive upon his left arm the blow
which had been meant for the back of his head. He was
confronted by a man dressed exactly as he himself was,
in morning coat and silk hat, a man with long, lean face
and legal appearance, such a person as would have passed
anywhere without attracting a moment's suspicion. Yet,
in the space of a few seconds he had whipped out from
one pocket, with the skill almost of a juggler, a vicious-
looking life-preserver, and from the other a pocket-hand-
kerchief soaked with chloroform. Laverick, quick and
resourceful, feeling his left arm sink helpless, struck at
the man with his right and sent him staggering against
the wall. The handkerchief, with its load of sickening
odor, fell to the pavement. The man was obviously
worsted. Laverick sprang at him. They were almost
unobserved, for the crowd was all intent upon the accident in the roadway. With wonderful skill, his assailant
eluded his attempt to close, and tore at his coat. Laverick
struck at him again but met only the air. The man's
fingers now were upon his pocket, but this time Laverick
made no mistake. He struck downward so hard that
with a fierce cry of pain the man relaxed his hold. Before
he could recover, Laverick had struck him again. He
reeled into the crowd that was fast gathering around them,
attracted by what seemed to be a fight between two men
of unexceptionable appearance. But there was to be no
more fight. Through the people, swift-footed, cunning,

resourceful, his assailant seemed to find some hidden
way. Laverick glared fiercely around him, but the man
had gone. His left hand crept to his chest. The victory
was with him; the document was still there.

At the outside of the double crowd he perceived a taxi.
Ignoring the storm of questions with which he was assailed,
and the advancing helmet of his friend the policeman at
the back of the crowd, Laverick hailed it and stepped
quickly inside.

"Back out of this and drive to Dover Street," he directed.

The man obeyed him. People raced to look through
the window at him. The other commotion had died away,
— the man in the road had got up and walked off. A
policeman came hurrying along but he was just too late.
Very soon they were on their way down Holborn. Once
more Laverick had escaped.

A French man-servant, with the sad face and immacu-
late dress of a High-Church cleric, took possession of him
as soon as he had asked for Mademoiselle Idiale. He
was shown into one of the most delightful little rooms he
had ever even dreamed of. The walls were hung with that
peculiar shade of blue satin which Mademoiselle so often
affected in her clothes. Laverick, who was something
of a connoisseur, saw nowhere any object which was not,
of its sort, priceless, — French furniture of the best and
choicest period, a statuette which made him, for a moment, almost forget the scene from which he had just
arrived. The air in the room seemed as though it had
passed through a grove of lemon trees, — it was fresh
and sweet yet curiously fragrant. Laverick sank down
into one of the luxurious blue-brocaded chairs, conscious
for the first time that he was out of breath. Then the

door opened silently and there entered not the woman whom he had been expecting, but Mr. Lassen. Laverick rose to his feet half doubtfully. Lassen's small, queerly-shaped face seemed to have become one huge ingratiating smile.

"I am very glad to see you, Mr. Laverick," he said, — "very glad indeed."

"I have come to call upon Mademoiselle Idiale," Laverick answered, somewhat curtly. He had disliked this man from the first moment he had seen him, and he saw no particular reason why he should conceal his feelings.

"I am here to explain," Mr. Lassen continued, seating himself opposite to Laverick. "Mademoiselle Idiale is unfortunately prevented from seeing you. She has a severe nervous headache, and her only chance of appearing to-night is to remain perfectly undisturbed. Women of her position, as you may understand, have to be exceptionally careful. It would be a very serious matter indeed if she were unable to sing to-night."

"I am exceedingly sorry to hear it," Laverick answered. "In that case, I will call again when Mademoiselle Idiale has recovered."

"By all means, my dear sir!" Mr. Lassen exclaimed. "Many times, let us hope. But in the meantime, there is a little affair of a document which you were going to deliver to Mademoiselle. She is most anxious that you should hand it to me — most anxious. She will tender you her thanks personally, to-morrow or the next day, if she is well enough to receive."

Laverick shook his head firmly.

"Under no circumstances," he declared, "should I think of delivering the document into any other hands save those of Mademoiselle Idiale. To tell you the truth, I had not fully decided whether to part with it even to her. I was simply prepared to hear what she had to say. But it may save time if I assure you, Mr. Lassen, that nothing would induce me to part with it to any one else."

There was no trace left of that ingratiating smile upon Mr. Lassen's face. He had the appearance now of an ugly animal about to show its teeth. Laverick was suddenly on his guard. More adventures, he thought, casting a somewhat contemptuous glance at the physique of the other man. He laid his fingers as though carelessly upon a small bronze ornament which reposed amongst others on a table by his side. If Mr. Lassen's fat and ugly hand should steal toward his pocket, Laverick was prepared to hurl the ornament at his head.

"I am very sorry to hear you say that, Mr. Laverick," Lassen said slowly. "I hope very much that you will see your way clear to change your mind. I can assure you that I have as much right to the document as Mademoiselle Idiale, and that it is her earnest wish that you should hand it over to me. Further, I may inform you that the document itself is a most incriminating one. Its possession upon your person, or upon the person of any one who was not upon his guard, might be a very serious matter indeed."

Laverick shrugged his shoulders.

"As a matter of fact," he declared, "I certainly have no idea of carrying it about with me. On the other hand, I shall part with it to no one. I might discuss the matter with Mademoiselle Idiale as soon as she is recovered. I am not disposed — I mean no offence, sir — but I may say frankly that I am not disposed even to do as much with you."

Laverick rose to his feet with the obvious intention of leaving. Lassen followed his example and confronted him.

"Mr. Laverick," he said, "in your own interests you must not talk like that, — in your own interests, I say."

"At any rate," Laverick remarked, "my interests are better looked after by myself than by strangers. You must forgive my adding, Mr. Lassen, that you are a stranger to me."

"No more so than Mademoiselle Idiale!" the little man exclaimed.

"Mademoiselle Idiale has given me certain proof that she knew at least of the existence of this document," Laverick answered. "She has established, therefore, a certain claim to my consideration. You announce yourself as Mademoiselle Idiale's deputy, but you bring me no proof of the fact, nor, in any case, am I disposed to treat with you. You must allow me to wish you good afternoon."

Lassen shook his head.

"Mr. Laverick," he declared, "you are too impetuous. You force me to remind you that your own position as holder of that document is not a very secure one. All the police in this capital are searching to-day for the man who killed that unfortunate creature who was found murdered in Crooked Friars' Alley. If they could find the man who was in possession of his pocket-book, who was in possession of twenty thousand pounds taken from the dead man's body and with it had saved his business and his credit, how then, do you think? I say nothing of the document."

Laverick was silent for a moment. He realized, however, that to make terms with this man was impossible.

Besides, he did not trust him. He did not even trust him so far as to believe him the accredited envoy of Mademoiselle.

"My unfortunate position," Laverick said, "has nothing whatever to do with the matter. Where you got your information from I cannot say. I neither accept nor deny it. But I can assure you that I am not to be intimidated. This document will remain in my possession until some one can show me a very good reason for parting with it."

Lassen beat the back of the chair against which he was standing with his clenched fist.

"A reason why you should part with it!" he exclaimed fiercely. "Man, it stares you there in the face! If you do not part with it, you will be arrested within twenty-four hours for the murder or complicity in the murder of Rudolph Von Behrling! That I swear! That I shall see to myself!"

"In which case," Laverick remarked, "the document will fall into the hands of the English police."

The shot told. Laverick could have laughed as he watched its effect upon his listener. Mr. Lassen's face was black with unuttered curses. He looked as though he would have fallen upon Laverick bodily.

"What do you know about its contents?" he hissed. "Why do you suppose it would not suit my purpose to have it fall into the hands of the English police?"

"I can see no reason whatever," Laverick answered, "why I should take you into my confidence as to how much I know and how much I do not know. I wish you good afternoon, Mr. Lassen! I shall be ready to wait upon Mademoiselle Idiale at any time she sends for me. But in case it should interest you to be made aware of the fact," he added, with a little bow, "I am not going round with this terrible document in my possession."

He moved to the door. Already his hand was upon the knob when he saw the movement for which he had watched. Laverick, with a single bound, was upon his would-be assailant. The hand which had already closed upon the butt of the small revolver was gripped as though in a vice. With a scream of pain Lassen dropped the weapon upon the floor. Laverick picked it up, thrust it into his coat pocket and, taking the man's collar with both hands, he shook him till the eyes seemed starting from his head and his shrieks of fear were changed into moans. Then he flung him into a corner of the room.

"You cowardly brute!" he exclaimed. "You come of the breed of men who shoot from behind. If ever I lay my hands upon you again, you'll be lucky if you live to whimper about it."

He left the room and rang for the lift. He saw no trace of any servants in the hall, nor heard any sound of any one moving. From Dover Street he drove straight to Zoe's house. Keeping the cab waiting, he knocked at the door. She opened it herself at once, and her eyes glowed with pleasure.

"How delightful!" she cried. "Please come in. Have you come to take me to the theatre?"

He followed her into the parlor and closed the door behind them.

"Zoe," he said, "I am going to ask you a favor."

"Me a favor?" she repeated. "I think you know how happy it will make me if there is anything — anything at all in the world that I could do."

"A week ago," Laverick continued, "I was an honest but not very successful stockbroker, with a natural longing for adventures which never came my way. Since then things have altered. I have stumbled in upon the most curious little chain of happenings which ever became entwined with the life of a commonplace being like myself. The net result, for the moment, is this. Every one is trying to steal from me a certain document which I have in my pocket. I want to hide it for the night. I cannot go to the police, it is too late to go back to Chancery Lane, and I have an instinctive feeling that my flat is absolutely at the mercy of my enemies. May I hide my document in your room? I do not believe for a moment that any one would think of searching here."

"Of course you may," she answered. "But listen. Can you see out into the street without moving very much?"

He turned his head. He had been standing with his back to the window, and Zoe had been facing it.

"Yes, I can see into the street," he assented.

"Tell me — you see that taxi on the other side of the way?" she asked.

He nodded.

"It wasn't there when I drove up," he remarked.

"I was at the window, looking out, when you came," she said. "It followed you out from the Square into this street. Directly you stopped, I saw the man put on the brake and pull up his cab. It seemed to me so strange, just as though some one were watching you all the time."

Laverick stood still, looking out of the window.

"Who lives in the house opposite?" he asked.

"I am afraid," she answered, "that there are no very nice people who live round here. The people whom I see coming in and out of that house are not nice people at all."

"I understand," he said. "Thank you, Zoe. You are right. Whatever I do with my precious document, I will not leave it here. To tell you the truth, I thought, for certain reasons, that after I had paid my last call this afternoon I should not be followed any more. Come back with me and I will give you some dinner before you go to the theatre."

She clapped her hands.

"I shall love it," she declared. "But what shall you do with the document?"

"I shall take a room at the Milan Hotel," he said, "and give it to the cashier. They have a wonderful safe there. It is the best thing I can think of. Can you suggest anything?"

She considered for a moment.

"Do you know what is inside?" she asked.

He shook his head.

"I have no idea. It is the most mysterious document in the world, so far as I am concerned."

"Why not open it and read it?" she suggested; "then you will know exactly what it is all about. You can learn it by heart and tear it up."

"I must think that over," he said. "One second before we go out."

He took from his pocket the revolver which Lassen had dropped. It was a perfect little weapon, and fully charged. He replaced it in his pocket, keeping his finger upon the trigger.

"Now, Zoe, if you are ready," he said, "come along."

They stepped out and entered the taxi, unmolested, and Laverick ordered:

"To the Milan Hotel."

CHAPTER XXIX

LASSEN'S TREACHERY DISCOVERED

ABOUT twenty minutes past six on the same evening, Bellamy, his clothes thick with dust, his face dark with anger, jumped lightly from a sixty horse-power car and rang the bell of the lift at number 15, Dover Street. Arrived on the first floor, he was confronted almost immediately by the sad-faced man-servant of Mademoiselle Idiale.

"Mademoiselle is in?" Bellamy asked quickly.

The man's expression was one of sombre regret.

"Mademoiselle is spending the day in the country, sir."

Bellamy took him by the shoulders and flung him against the wall.

"Thank you," he said, "I've heard that before."

He walked down the passage and knocked softly at the door of Louise's sleeping apartment. There was no answer. He knocked again and listened at the key-hole. There was some movement inside but no one spoke.

"Louise," he cried softly, "let me in. It is I — David."

Again the only reply was the strangest of sounds. Almost it seemed as though a woman were trying to speak with a hand over her mouth. Then Bellamy suddenly stiffened into rigid attention. There were voices in the small reception room, — the voice of Henri, the butler, and another. Reluctantly he turned away from the closed door and walked swiftly down the passage. He entered the reception room and looked around him in amazement. It was still in disorder. Lassen sat in an easy-chair with a tumbler of brandy by his side. Henri was tying a bandage around his head, his collar was torn, there were marks of blood about his shirt. Bellamy's eyes sparkled. He closed the door behind him.

"Come," he exclaimed, "after all, I fancy that my arrival is somewhat opportune!"

Henri turned towards him with a reproachful gesture.

"Monsieur Lassen has been unwell, Monsieur," he said. "He has had a fit and fallen down."

Bellamy laughed contemptuously.

"I think I can reconstruct the scene a little better than that," he declared. "What do you say, Mr. Lassen?"

The man glared at him viciously.

"I do not know what you are talking about," he said. "I do not wish to speak to you. I am ill. You had better go and persuade Mademoiselle to return. She is at Dover, waiting."

"You are a liar!" Bellamy answered. "She is in her room now, locked up — guarded, perhaps, by one of your creatures. I have been half-way to Dover, but I tumbled to your scheme in time, Mr. Lassen. You found our friend Laverick a trifle awkward, I fancy."

Lassen swore through his teeth but said nothing.

"From your somewhat dishevelled appearance," Bellamy continued, "I think I may conclude that you were not able to come to any amicable arrangement with Mademoiselle's visitor. He declined to accept you as her proxy, I imagine. Still, one must make sure."

He advanced quickly. Lassen shrank back in his chair.

"What do you mean?" he asked gruffly. "Keep him away from me, Henri. Ring the bell for your other man. This fellow will do me a mischief."

"Not I," Bellamy answered scornfully. "Stay where

you are, Henri. To your other accomplishments I have no doubt you include that of valeting. Take off his coat."

"But, Monsieur!" Henri protested.

"I'm d—d if he shall!" the man in the chair snarled.

Bellamy turned to the door, locked it, and put the key in his pocket.

"Look here," he said, "I do not for one moment believe that Laverick handed over to you the document you were so anxious to obtain. On the other hand, I imagine that your somewhat battered appearance is the result of fruitless argument on your part with a view to inducing him to do so. Nevertheless, I can afford to run no risks. The coat first, please, Henri. It is necessary that I search it thoroughly."

There was a brief hesitation. Bellamy's hand went reluctantly into his pocket.

"I hate to seem melodramatic," he declared, "and I never carry firearms, but I have a little life-preserver here which I have learned how to use pretty effectively. Come, you know, it is n't a fair fight. You 've had all you want, Lassen, and Henri there has n't the muscle of a chicken."

Lassen rose, groaning, to his feet and allowed his coat to be removed. Bellamy glanced through the pockets, holding one letter for a moment in his hands as he glanced at the address.

"The writing of our friend Streuss," he remarked, with a smile. "No, you need not fear, Lassen! I am not going to read it. There is plenty of proof of your treachery without this."

Lassen's face was livid and his eyes seemed like beads. Bellamy handed back the coat.

"That's all right," he said. "Nothing there, I am glad to see — or in the waistcoat," he added, passing his hands over it. "I'll trouble you to stand up for a moment, Mr. Lassen."

The man did as he was bid and Bellamy felt him all over. When he had finished, he held in his hand a key.

"The key of Mademoiselle's chamber, I have no doubt," he announced, "I will leave you, then, while I see what deviltry you have been up to."

He walked calmly to the table which stood by the window and deliberately cut the telephone wire. With the instrument under his arm, he left the room. Lassen blundered to his feet as though to intercept him, but Bellamy's eyes suddenly flashed red fury, and the life-preserver of which he had spoken glittered above his head. Lassen staggered away.

"I'm a long-suffering man," Bellamy said, "and if you don't remember now that you're the beaten dog, I may lose my temper."

He locked them in, walked down the passage and opened the door of Louise's bedchamber with fingers that trembled a little. With a smothered oath he cut the cord from the arms of the maid and the gag from her mouth. Louise, clad in a loose afternoon gown, was lying upon the bed, as though asleep. Bellamy saw with an impulse of relief that she was breathing regularly.

"This is Lassen's work, of course!" he exclaimed. "What have they done to her?"

The maid spoke thickly. She was very pale, and unsteady upon her feet.

"It was something they put in her wine," she faltered. "I heard Mr. Lassen say that it would keep her quiet for three or four hours. I think — I think that she is waking now."

Louise opened her eyes and looked at them with amazement. Bellamy sat by the side of the bed and supported her with his arm.

"It is only a skirmish, dear," he whispered, "and it is a drawn battle, although you got the worst of it."

She put her hand to her head, struggling to remember.

"Mr. Laverick has been here?" she asked.

"He has. Your friend Lassen has been taking a hand in the game. I came here to find you like this and Annette tied up. Henri is in with him. What has become of your other servants I don't know."

"Henri asked for a holiday for them," she said, the color slowly returning to her cheeks. "I begin to understand. But tell me, what happened when Mr. Laverick came?"

"I can only guess," Bellamy answered, "but it seems that Lassen must have received him as though with your authority."

"And what then?" she asked quickly.

"I am almost certain," Bellamy declared, "that Laverick refused to have anything to do with him. I received a wire from Dover to say that you were on your way home, and asking me to meet you at the Lord Warden Hotel. I borrowed Montresor's racing-car, but I sent telegrams, and I was pretty soon on my way back. When I arrived here, I found Lassen in your little room with a broken head. Evidently Laverick and he had a scrimmage and he got the worst of it. I have searched him to his bones and he has no paper. Laverick brought it here, without a doubt, and has taken it away again."

She rose to her feet.

"Go and let Lassen out," she said. "Tell him he must never come here again. I will see him at the Opera House to-night or to-morrow night — that is, if I can get there. I do not know whether I shall feel fit to sing."

"I shall take the liberty, also," remarked Bellamy, "of kicking Henri out."

Louise sighed.

"He was such a good servant. I think it must have cost our friend Streuss a good deal to buy Henri. You will come back to me when you have finished with them?"

Bellamy made short work of his discomfited prisoners. Lassen was surly but only eager to depart; Henri was resigned but tearful. Almost as they went the other servants began to return from their various missions. Bellamy went back to Louise, who was lying down again and drinking some tea. She motioned Bellamy to come over to her side.

"Tell me," she asked, "what are you going to do now?"

"I am going to do what I ought to have done before," Bellamy answered. "Laverick's connection with this affair is suspicious enough, but after all he is a sportsman and an Englishman. I am going to tell him what that envelope contains — tell him the truth."

"You are right!" she exclaimed. "Whatever he may have done, if you tell him the truth he will give you that document. I am sure of it. Do you know where to find him?"

"I shall go to his rooms," Bellamy declared. "I must be quick, too, for Lassen is free — they will know that he has failed."

"Come back to me, David," she begged, and he kissed her fingers and hurried out.

CHAPTER XXX

LAVERICK, sitting with Zoe at dinner, caught his companion looking around the restaurant with an expression in her face which he did not wholly understand.

"Something is the matter with you this evening, Zoe," he said anxiously. "Tell me what it is. You don't like this place, perhaps?"

"Of course I do."

"It is your dinner, then, or me?" he persisted. "Come, out with it. Have n't we promised to tell each other the truth always?"

The pink color came slowly into her cheeks. Her eyes, raised for a moment to his, were almost reproachful.

"You know very well that it is not anything to do with you," she whispered. "You are too kind to me all the time. Only," she went on, a little hesitatingly, "don't you realize — can't you see how differently most of the girls here are dressed? I don't mind so much for myself — but you — you have so many friends. You keep on seeing people whom you know. I am afraid they will think that I ought not to be here."

He looked at her in surprise, mingled, perhaps, with compunction. For the first time he appreciated the actual shabbiness of her clothes. Everything about her was so neat — pathetically neat, as it seemed to him in one illuminating moment of realization. The white linen collar, notwithstanding its frayed edges, was spotlessly clean.

The black bow was carefully tied to conceal its worn parts. Her gloves had been stitched a good many times. Her gown, although it was tidy, was old-fashioned and had distinctly seen its best days. He suddenly recognized the effort — the almost despairing effort — which her toilette had cost her.

"I don't think that men notice these things," he said simply. "To me you look just as you should look — and I would n't change places with any other man in the room for a great deal."

Her eyes were soft — perilously soft — as she looked at him with uplifted eyebrows and a faint smile struggling at the corners of her lips. A wave of tenderness crept into his heart. What a brave little child she was!

"You will quite spoil me if you make such nice speeches," she murmured.

"Anyhow," he went on, speaking with decision, "so long as you feel like that, you are going to have a new gown — or two — and a new hat, and you are going to have them at once. They are going to be bought with your brother's money, mind. Shall I come shopping with you?"

She shook her head.

"Mind, it is partly for your sake that I give in," she said. "It would be lovely to have you come, but you would spend far too much money. You really mean it all?"

"Absolutely," he answered. "I insist upon it."

She leaned towards him with dancing eyes. After all, she was very much of a child. The prospect of a new gown, now that she permitted herself to think of it, was enthralling.

"I might get a coat and skirt," she remarked thoughtfully, "and a simple white dress. A black hat would do for both of them, then."

"Don't you study your brother too much," Laverick declared. "His stock is going up all the time."

"Tell me your favorite color," she begged confidentially.

"I can't conceive your looking nicer than you do in black," he replied.

She made a wry face.

"I suppose it must be black," she murmured doubtfully. "It is much more economical than anything——"

She broke off to bow to a stout, red-faced man who, after a rude stare, had greeted her with a patronizing nod.

Laverick frowned.

"Who is that fellow?" he asked.

"Mr. Heepman, our stage-manager," Zoe answered, a little timidly.

"Is there any particular reason why he should behave like a boor?" Laverick continued, raising his voice a little.

She caught at his arm in terror. The man was sitting at the next table.

"Don't, please!" she implored. "He might hear you. He is just behind there."

Laverick half turned in his chair. She guessed what he was about to say, and went on rapidly.

"He has been so foolish," she whispered. "He has asked me so often to go out with him. And he could get me sent away, if he wanted, any time. He almost threatened it, the last time I refused. Now that he has seen me with you, he will be worse than ever."

Laverick's face darkened, and there was a peculiar flash in his eyes. The man was certainly looking at them in a rude manner.

"There are so many of the girls who would only be too pleased to go with him," Zoe continued, in a terrified undertone. "I can't think why he bothers me."

"I can," Laverick muttered. "Let's forget about the brute."

But the dinner was already spoiled for Zoe, so Laverick paid the bill a few minutes later, and walked across to the stage-door of the theatre with her. Her little hand, when she gave it to him at parting, was quite cold.

"I'm as nervous as I can be," she confessed. "Mr. Heepman will be watching all the night for something to find fault with me about."

"Don't you let him bully you," Laverick begged.

"I won't," she promised. "Good-bye! Thanks so much for my dinner."

She turned away with a brave attempt at a smile, but it was only an attempt. Laverick walked on to his club. There was no one in the dining-room whom he knew, and the card-room was empty. He played one game of billiards, but he played badly. He was upset. His nerves were wrong he told himself, and little wonder. There seemed to be no chance of a rubber at bridge, so he sallied out again and walked aimlessly towards Covent Garden. Outside the Opera House he hesitated and finally entered, yielding to an impulse the nature of which he scarcely recognized. While he was inquiring about a stall, a small printed notice was thrust into his hand. He read it with a slight start.

> We regret to announce that owing to indisposition Mademoiselle Idiale will not be able to appear this evening. The part of Delilah will be taken by Mademoiselle Blanche Temoigne, late of the Royal Opera House, St. Petersburg.

Ten minutes later, Laverick rang the bell of her flat in Dover Street. A strange man-servant answered him.

"I came to inquire after Mademoiselle Idiale," Laverick said.

The man held out a tray on which was already a small heap of cards. Laverick, however, retained his.

"I should be glad if you would take mine in to her," he said. "I think it is just likely that she may see me for a moment."

The servant's attitude was one of civil but unconcealed hostility. He would have closed the door had not Laverick already passed over the threshold.

"Madame is not well enough to receive visitors, sir," the man declared. "She shall have your card as soon as possible."

"I should like her to have it now," Laverick persisted, drawing a five-pound note from his pocket.

The man looked at the note longingly.

"It would be only waste of time, sir," he declared. "Mademoiselle is confined to her bedroom and my orders are absolute."

"You are not the man who was here earlier in the day," Laverick remarked. "I wonder," he continued, with a sudden inspiration, "whether you are not Mr. Bellamy's servant?"

"That is so, sir. Mr. Bellamy has sent me here to see that no one has access to Mademoiselle Idiale."

"Then there is no harm whatever in taking in my card," Laverick declared convincingly. "You can put that note in your pocket. I am perfectly certain that Mademoiselle Idiale will see me, and that your master would wish her to do so."

"I will take the risk, sir," the man decided, "but the orders I have received were stringent."

He disappeared and was gone for several moments. When he came back he was accompanied by a pale-faced woman dressed in black, obviously a maid.

"Monsieur Laverick," she said, "Mademoiselle Idiale will receive you. If you will come this way?"

She opened the door of the little reception-room, and Laverick followed her. The man returned to his place in the hall.

"Madame will be here in a moment," the maid said. "She will be glad to see you, but she has been very badly frightened."

Laverick bowed sympathetically. The woman herself was gray-faced, terror-stricken.

"It is Monsieur Lassen, the manager of Madame, who has caused a great deal of trouble here," she said. "Madame never trusted him and now we have discovered that he is a spy."

The woman seemed to fade away. The door of the inner room was opened and Louise came out. She was still exceedingly pale, and there were dark rims under her eyes. She came across the room with outstretched hands. There was no doubt whatever as to her pleasure.

"You have seen Mr. Bellamy?" she asked.

Laverick shook his head.

"No, I have seen nothing of Bellamy to-day. I came to call upon you this afternoon."

She wrung her hands.

"You understand, of course!" she exclaimed. "I did not trust Lassen, but I never imagined anything like this. He is an Austrian. Only a few hours ago I learned that he is one of their most heavily paid spies. Streuss got hold of him. But there, I forgot — you do not understand this. It is enough that he laid a plot to get that document from you. Where is it, Mr. Laverick? You have brought it now?"

"Why, no," Laverick answered, "I have not."

Her eyes were round with terror. She held out her hands as though to keep away some tormenting thought.

"Where is it?" she cried. "You have not parted with it?"

"I have not," Laverick replied gravely. "It is in the safe deposit of a hotel to which I have moved."

She closed her eyes and drew a long breath of relief.

"You are not well," Laverick said. "Let me help you to a chair."

She sat down wearily.

"Why have you moved to a hotel?" she asked.

"To tell you the truth," Laverick answered, "I seem to have wandered into a sort of modern Arabian Nights. Three times to-day attempts have been made to get that document from me by force. I have been followed wherever I went. I felt that it was not safe in my chambers, so I moved to a hotel and deposited it in their strong-room. I have come to the conclusion that the best thing I can do is to open it to-morrow morning, and decide for myself as to its destination."

Louise sat quite still for several moments. Then she opened her eyes.

"What you say is an immense relief to me, Mr. Laverick," she declared. "I perceive now that we have made a mistake. We should have told you the whole truth from the first. This afternoon when Mr. Bellamy left me, it was to come to you and tell you everything."

Laverick listened gravely.

"Really," he said, "it seems to me the wisest course. I have n't the least desire to keep the document. I cannot think why Bellamy did not treat me with confidence from the first — "

He stopped short. Suddenly he understood. Something in Louise's face gave him the hint.

"Of course!" he murmured to himself.

"Mr. Laverick," Louise said quietly, "in this matter I am no man's judge, yet, as you and I know well, that paper could have come into your hands in one way, and one way only. There may be some explanation. If so, it is for you to offer it or not, as you think best. Mr. Bellamy and I are allies in this matter. It is not our business to interfere with the course of justice. You will run no risk in parting with that paper."

"Where can I see Bellamy?" Laverick inquired, rising and taking up his hat.

"He would go straight to your rooms," she answered. "Did you leave word there where you had gone?"

"Purposely I did not," Laverick replied. "I had better try and find him, perhaps."

"It is not necessary," she announced. "No wonder that you feel yourself to have wandered into the Arabian Nights, Mr. Laverick. There are two sets of spies who follow you everywhere — two sets that I know of. There may be another."

"You think that Bellamy will find me?" he asked.

"I am sure of it."

"Then I'll go back to the hotel and wait."

She hurried him away, but at the door she detained him for a moment.

"Mr. Laverick," she said, looking at him earnestly, "somehow or other I cannot help believing that you are an honest man."

Laverick sighed. He opened his lips but closed them again.

"You are very kind, Mademoiselle," he declared simply.

Laverick, as he entered the reception hall at the Milan Hotel, noticed a man leaning over the cashier's desk talking confidentially to the clerk in charge. The latter recognized Laverick with obvious relief, and at once directed his questioner's attention to him. Kahn turned swiftly around and without a moment's hesitation came smiling towards Laverick with the apparent intention of accosting him. He was correctly garbed, tall and fair, with every appearance of being a man of breeding. He glanced at Laverick carelessly as he passed, but, as though changing his original purpose, made no attempt to address him. The cashier, who had been watching, gave vent to a little exclamation of surprise and sprang over the counter. He approached Laverick hastily.

"Do you know that gentleman just going out, sir?" he asked.

"I never saw him before in my life," Laverick answered. "Why?"

"Is this your handwriting, sir?" the man inquired, touching with his forefinger the half sheet of note-paper which he had been carrying.

Laverick read quickly, —

To the Cashier at the Milan Hotel, — Deliver to bearer document deposited with you.   STEPHEN LAVERICK.

"It is not," he declared promptly. "It is an impudent forgery. Good God! You don't mean to say that you parted with my property to — "

The cashier stopped his breathless question.

"I have n't parted with anything, sir," he said. "I was just wondering what to do when you came in. I'd no reason to believe that the signature was a forgery, but I did n't like the look of it, somehow. We'd better be after him. Come along, sir."

They hurried outside. The man was nowhere in sight. The cashier summoned the head porter.

"A gentleman has just come out," he exclaimed, — "tall and fair, very carefully dressed, with a single eyeglass! Which way did he go?"

"He's just driven off in a big Daimler car, sir," the porter answered. "I noticed him particularly. He spoke to the chauffeur in Austrian."

Laverick looked out into the Strand.

"Can't we stop him?" he asked rapidly.

The porter smiled as he shook his head.

"Not the ghost of a chance, sir. He shot round the corner there as though he were in a desperate hurry, and went the wrong side of the island. I heard the police calling to him. I hope there's nothing wrong, Mr. Dean?"

The cashier hesitated and glanced at Laverick.

"Nothing much," Laverick answered. "We should have liked to have asked him a question — that is all."

Bellamy came out from the hotel and paused to light a cigarette.

"How are you, Laverick?" he said quietly. "Nothing the matter, I hope?"

"Nothing worth mentioning," Laverick replied.

The cashier returned to his duties. The two men were alone. Bellamy, most carefully dressed, with his silverheaded cane under his arm, and his silk hat at precisely the correct angle, seemed very far removed from the world

of intrigue into which Laverick felt himself to have
blundered. He looked down for a moment at the tips of
his patent shoes and up again at the sky, as though anxious
about the weather.

"What about a drink, Laverick?" he asked non-
chalantly.

"Delighted!" Laverick assented.

CHAPTER XXXI

THE two men stepped back into the hotel. The cashier had returned to his desk, and the incident which had just transpired seemed to have passed unnoticed. Nevertheless, Laverick felt that the studied indifference of his companion's manner had its significance, and he endeavored to imitate it.

"Shall we go through into the bar?" he asked. "There's very seldom any one there at this time."

"Anywhere you say," Bellamy answered. "It's years since we had a drink together."

They passed into the inner room and, finding it empty, drew two chairs into the further corner. Bellamy summoned the waiter.

"Two whiskies and sodas quick, Tim," he ordered. "Now, Laverick, listen to me," he added, as the waiter turned away. "We are alone for the moment but it won't be for long. You know very well that it wasn't to renew our schoolboy acquaintance that I've asked you to come in here with me."

Laverick drew a little breath.

"Please go on," he said. "I am as anxious as you can be to grasp this affair properly."

"When we left school," Bellamy remarked, "you were destined for the Stock Exchange. I went first to Magdalen. Did you ever hear what became of me afterwards?"

"I always understood," Laverick answered, "that you went into one of the Government offices."

"Quite right," Bellamy assented. "I did. At this moment I have the honor to serve His Majesty."

"Two thousand a year and two hours work a day." Laverick laughed. "I know the sort of thing."

"You evidently don't," Bellamy answered. "I often work twenty hours a day, I don't get half two thousand a year, and most of the time I carry my life in my hands. When I am working — and I am working now — I am never sure of the morrow."

Laverick looked at him incredulously.

"You're not joking, Bellamy?" he asked.

"Not by any manner of means. I have the honor to be a humble member of His Majesty's Secret Service."

Laverick glanced at his companion wonderingly.

"I really did n't know," he said, "that such a service had any actual existence except in novels."

"I am a proof to the contrary," Bellamy declared grimly. "Abroad, I run always the risk of being dubbed a spy and treated like one. At home, I am simply the head of the A2 Branch of the Secret Service. Here come our drinks."

Laverick raised his whiskey and soda to his lips mechanically.

"Here's luck!" he exclaimed. "Now go on, Bellamy," he continued. "The waiter can't overhear."

Bellamy smiled.

"Tim is one of the few persons in the place," he said, "whom one can trust. As a matter of fact, he has been very useful to me more than once. Now listen to me attentively, Laverick. I am going to speak to you as one man to another."

Laverick nodded.

"I am ready," he said.

"Last Monday," Bellamy went on, leaning forward and speaking in a soft but very distinct undertone, "a man was murdered late at night in the heart of the city — within one hundred yards of the Stock Exchange. The papers called it a mysterious murder. No one knows who the man was, or who committed the crime, or why. You and I, Laverick, both know a little more than the rest of the world."

"Well?"

"The murder," Bellamy continued, with a strange light in his eyes, "was accomplished only a stone's throw from your office."

Laverick lit a cigarette and threw the match away.

"Horrible affair it was," he remarked.

Bellamy glanced toward the door, — a man had looked in and departed.

"Enough of this fencing, Laverick," he said. "A theft was committed from the person of that murdered man, of which the general public knows nothing. A pocket-book was stolen from him containing twenty thousand pounds and a sealed document. As to who murdered the man, I want you to understand that that is not my affair. As to what has become of that twenty thousand pounds, I have not the slightest curiosity. I want the document."

"What claim have you to it?" Laverick asked quickly.

"I might retort, but I will not," Bellamy replied. "Time is too short. I will answer you by explaining who the man was and what that document consists of. The man's name was Von Behrling, and he was a trusted agent of the Austrian Secret Service. The document of which he was robbed contains a verbatim report of the conference which recently took place at Vienna between the Emperor of Germany, the Emperor of Austria, and the Czar of Russia. It contains the details of a plot against this country and the undertakings entered into by those several Powers. I want that document, Laverick. Have I established my claim?"

"You have," Laverick answered. "Why on earth did n't you come to me before? Don't you believe that I should have listened to you as readily as to Mademoiselle Idiale?"

"I wish that I had come," Bellamy admitted, "and yet, here is the truth, Laverick, because the truth is best. Twenty-two years lie between us and the time when we knew anything of one another. To me, therefore, you are a stranger. I had my spies following Von Behrling that night. I know that you took the pocket-book from his dead body. If you did not murder him yourself, the deed was done by an accomplice of yours. How was I to trust you? We are speaking naked words, my friend. We are dealing with naked truths. To me you were a murderer and a thief. A word from me and you would have realized the value of that document. I tell you frankly that Austria would give you almost any sum for it to-day."

Laverick, strong man though he was, was conscious of a sudden weakness. He raised his hand to his forehead and drew it away — wet. He struggled desperately for self-control.

"Bellamy," he said, "here's truth for truth. I am not on my trial before you. Believe me, man, for God's sake!"

"I'll try," Bellamy promised. "Go on."

"That night I stayed at my office late because I saw

ruin before me on the morrow. I left it meaning to go
straight home. I lit a cigarette near that entry, and by
the light of a match, as I was throwing it away, I saw the
murdered man. I think for a time I was paralyzed. The
pocket-book was half dragged out from his pocket. Why
I looked inside it I don't know. I had some sort of wild
idea that I must find out who he was. Mind you, though,
I should have given the alarm at once, but there was n't a
soul in the street. There was a man lurking in the entry
and I chased him, unsuccessfully. When I came back,
the body was still there and the street empty. I looked
inside that pocket-book, which would have been in the
possession of his murderer but for my unexpected appearance. I saw the notes there. Once more I went out into
the street. I gave no alarm, — I am not attempting to
explain why. I was like a man made suddenly mad. I
went back to my office and shut myself in."

Bellamy pointed to the glasses silently. The waiter
came forward and refilled them.

"Bellamy," Laverick continued, "your career and
mine lie far apart, and yet, at their backbone, as there is
at the backbone of every man's life, there must be something of the same sort of ambition. My grandfather lived
and died a member of the Stock Exchange, honored and
well thought of. My father followed in his footsteps. I,
too, was there. Without becoming wealthy, the name I
bear has become known and respected. Failure, whatever one may say, means a broken life and a broken
honor. I sat in my office and I knew that the use of those
notes for a few days might save me from disgrace, might
keep the name, which my father and grandfather had
guarded so jealously, free from shame. I would have
paid any price for the use of them. I would have paid

with my life, if that had been possible. Think of the risk
I ran — the danger I am now in. I deposited those notes
on the morrow as security at my bank, and I met all my
engagements. The crisis is over! Those notes are in a
safe deposit vault in Chancery Lane! I only wish to
Heaven that I could find the owner!"

"And the document?" Bellamy asked. "The document?"

"It is in the hotel safe," Laverick answered.

Bellamy drew a long sigh of relief. Then he emptied
his tumbler and lit a cigarette.

"Laverick," he declared, "I believe you."

"Thank God!" Laverick muttered.

"I am no crime investigator," Bellamy went on thoughtfully. "As to who killed Von Behrling, or why, I cannot now form the slightest idea. That twenty thousand
pounds, Laverick, is Secret Service money, paid by me
to Von Behrling only half-an-hour before he was murdered, in a small restaurant there, for what I supposed to
be the document. He deceived me by making up a false
packet. The real one he kept. He deserved to die, and
I am glad he is dead."

Laverick's face was suddenly hopeful.

"Then you can take these notes!" he exclaimed.

Bellamy nodded.

"In a few days," he said, "I shall take you with me to
a friend of mine — a Cabinet Minister. You shall tell
him the story exactly as you've told it to me, and restore
the money."

Laverick laughed like a child.

"Don't think I'm mad," he apologized, "but I am not
a person like you, Bellamy, — used to adventures and
this sort of wild happenings. I'm a steady-going, matter-

of-fact Englishman, and this thing has been like a hateful nightmare to me. I can't believe that I'm going to get rid of it."

Bellamy smiled.

"It's a great adventure," he declared, "to come to any one like you. To tell you the truth, I can't imagine how you had the pluck — don't misunderstand me, I mean the moral pluck — to run such a risk. Why, at the moment you used those notes," Bellamy continued, "the odds must have been about twenty to one against your not being found out."

"One does n't stop to count the odds," Laverick said grimly. "I saw a chance of salvation and I went for it. And now about this letter."

Bellamy rose to his feet.

"On the King's service!" he whispered softly.

They walked once more to the cashier's desk. A stranger greeted them. Laverick produced his receipt.

"I should like the packet I deposited here this evening," he said. "I am sorry to trouble you, but I find that I require it unexpectedly."

The clerk glanced at the receipt and up at the clock.

"I am afraid, sir," he answered, "that we cannot get at it before the morning."

"Why not?" Laverick demanded, frowning.

"Mr. Dean has just gone home," the man declared, "and he is the only one who knows the combination on the 'L' safe. You see, sir," he continued, "we keep this particular safe for documents, and we did not expect that anything would be required from it to-night."

Bellamy drew Laverick away.

"After all," he said, "perhaps to-morrow morning would be better. There's no need to get shirty with these fellows. As a matter of fact, I don't think that I should have dared to receive it without making some special preparations. I can get some plain clothes men here upon whom I can rely, at nine o'clock."

They strolled back into the hall.

"Tell me," Laverick asked, "do you know who the man was who forged my name to the order a few hours ago?"

Bellamy nodded.

"It was Adolf Kahn, an Austrian spy. I have been watching him for days. If they'd given him the paper I had four men at the door, but it would have been touch and go. He is a very prince of conspirators, that fellow. To tell you the truth, I think I might as well go home."

Bellamy was drawing on his gloves when the hall-porter brought a note to Laverick.

"A messenger has just left this for you, sir," he explained.

Laverick tore open the envelope. The contents consisted of a few words only, written on plain note-paper and in a handwriting which was strange to him.

"Ring up 1232 Gerrard."

Laverick frowned, turned over the half sheet of paper and looked once more at the envelope. Then he passed it on to his companion.

"What do you make of that, Bellamy?" he asked.

Bellamy smiled as he perused and returned it.

"What could any one make of it?" he remarked, laconically. "Do you know the handwriting?"

"Never saw it before, to my knowledge," Laverick answered. "What should you do about it?"

"I think," Bellamy suggested, "that I should ring up number 1232 Gerrard."

They crossed the hall and Laverick entered one of the telephone booths.

"1232 Gerrard," he said.

The connection was made almost at once.

"Who are you?" Laverick asked.

"I am speaking for Miss Zoe Leneveu," was the reply. "Are you Mr. Laverick?"

"I am," Laverick answered. "Is Miss Leneveu there? Can she speak to me herself?"

"She is not here," the voice continued. "She was fetched away in a hurry from the theatre — we understood by her brother. She left two and sixpence with the doorkeeper here to ring you up and explain that she had been summoned to her brother's rooms, 25, Jermyn Street, and would you kindly go on there."

"Who are you?" Laverick demanded.

There was no reply. Laverick remained speechless, listening intently. He stood still with the receiver pressed to his ear. Was it his fancy, or was that really Zoe's protesting voice which he heard in the background? It was a woman or a child who was speaking — he was almost sure that it was Zoe.

"Who are you?" he asked fiercely. "Miss Leneveu is there with you. Why does she not speak for herself?"

"Miss Leneveu is not here," was the answer. "I have done what she desired. You can please yourself whether you go or not. The address is 25, Jermyn Street. Ring off."

The connection was gone. Laverick laid down the receiver and stepped out of the booth.

"I must be off at once," he said to Bellamy. "You'll be round in the morning?"

Bellamy smiled.

"After all," he remarked, "I have changed my plans. I shall not leave the hotel. I am going to telephone round to my man to bring me some clothes. By the bye, do you mind telling me whether this message which you have just received had anything to do with the little affair in which we are interested?"

"Not directly," Laverick answered, after a moment's hesitation. "The message was from a young lady. I have to go and meet her."

"A young lady whom you can trust?" Bellamy inquired quietly.

"Implicitly," Laverick assured him.

"She spoke herself?"

"No, she sent a message. Excuse me, Bellamy, won't you, but I must really go."

"By all means," Bellamy answered.

They stood at the entrance to the hotel together while a taxicab was summoned. Laverick stepped quickly in.

"25, Jermyn Street," he ordered.

Bellamy watched him drive off. Then he sighed.

"I think, my friend Laverick," he said softly, "that you will need some one to look after you to-night."

CHAPTER XXXII

CERTAINLY it was a strange little gathering that waited in Morrison's room for the coming of Laverick. There was Lassen — flushed, ugly, breathing heavily, and watching the door with fixed, beady eyes. There was Adolf Kahn, the man who had strolled out from the Milan Hotel as Láverick had entered it, leaving the forged order behind him. There was Streuss — stern, and desperate with anxiety. There was Morrison himself, in the clothes of a workman, worn to a shadow, with the furtive gleam of terrified guilt shining in his sunken eyes, and the slouched shoulders and broken mien of the habitual criminal. There was Zoe, around whom they were all standing, with anger burning in her cheeks and gleaming out of her passion-filled eyes. She, too, like the others, watched the door. So they waited.

Streuss, not for the first time, moved to the window and drawing aside the curtains looked down into the street.

"Will he come — this Englishman?" he muttered. "Has he courage?"

"More courage than you who keep a girl here against her will!" Zoe panted, looking at him defiantly. "More courage than my poor brother, who stands there like a coward!"

"Shut up, Zoe!" Morrison exclaimed harshly. "There

is nothing for you to be furious about or frightened. No one wants to ill-treat you. These gentlemen all want to behave kindly to us. It is Laverick they want."

"And you," she cried, "are content to stand by and let him walk into a trap — you let them even use my name to bring him here! Arthur, be a man! Have nothing more to do with them. Help me to get away from this place. Call out. Do something instead of standing there and wasting the precious minutes."

He came towards her — ugly and threatening.

"I'll do something in a minute," he declared savagely, — "something you won't like, either. Keep your mouth shut, I tell you. It's me or him, and, by Heavens, he deserves what he'll get!"

Streuss turned away from the window and looked towards Zoe.

"Young lady," he said quietly, "let me beg you not to distress yourself so. I sincerely trust that nothing unpleasant will happen. If it does, I promise you that we will arrange for your temporary absence. You shall not be disturbed in any way."

"And as regards your brother, have a care, young lady," Lassen growled. "If any one's in danger, it's he. He'll be lucky if he saves his own skin."

The young man glowered at her.

"You hear that, you little fool!" he muttered. "Keep still, can't you?"

Her face was full of defiance. He came nearer to her and changed his tone.

"Zoe," he whispered hoarsely, "don't you understand? If they can't get what they want from Laverick, they'll visit it upon me. They're desperate, I tell you. They mean mischief all the time."

"Yet you let him be brought here, your partner who looked after you when you were ill, and who helped you to get away!" she cried indignantly.

He laughed unpleasantly.

"When it comes to a matter of life or death, it's every man for himself. Besides, if I'd known as much about Laverick as I know now, I'm not sure that I should have been so ready to go — not empty-handed, by any manner of means."

"What have you done that you should be so much in the power of these people?" she demanded, fixing her dark eyes upon him searchingly.

The terror whitened his face once more. The perspiration stood out in beads upon his forehead.

"Don't dare to ask me questions!" he exclaimed nervously. "I should like to know what Laverick is to you, eh, that you take so much interest in him? Listen here, my fine young lady. If I've been mug enough to do the dirty work, he hasn't made any bones about taking advantage of it. He's a nice sort of sportsman, I can tell you."

The man at the window suddenly dropped the curtain and spoke across the room to them all.

"He is here," he announced.

"Alone?" Lassen asked thickly.

"Alone," Streuss echoed.

A little thrill seemed to pass through the room. Zoe made no attempt to cry out. Instead she leaned forward towards the door, as though listening. Her attitude seemed harmless enough. No one took any more notice of her. They all watched the entrance to the apartment. Zoe remembered the two flights of stairs. She was absorbed in a breathless calculation. Now — now he should be coming quite close. Her whole being was concentrated upon one effort of listening. At last she raised her head. The room resounded with her cries.

"Don't come in! Don't come in here!" she shrieked. "Mr. Laverick, do you hear? Go away! Don't come in here alone!"

Her brother was the first to reach her, his hand fell upon her mouth brutally. Her little effort was naturally a failure — defeating, in fact, its own object. Laverick, hearing her cries, simply hastened his coming, threw open the door without waiting to knock, and stepped quickly across the threshold. He saw a man dressed in shabby workman's clothes, unshaven, dishevelled, holding Zoe in a rough grasp, and with a single well-directed blow he sent him reeling across the room. Then something in the man's cry, a momentary glimpse of his white face, revealed his identity.

"Morrison!" he cried. "Good God, it's Morrison!"

Arthur Morrison was crouching in a corner of the room, his evil face turned upon his aggressor. Laverick took quick stock of his surroundings. There was the tall, fair young man — Adolf Kahn — whom he had seen at the Milan a few hours ago — the man who had unsuccessfully forged his name. There was Lassen, the man who, under pretence of being her manager, had been a spy upon Louise. There was Streuss, with blanched face and hard features, standing with his back to the door. There was Zoe, and, behind, her brother. She held out her hands timidly towards him, and her eyes were soft with pleading.

"I did not want you to come here, Mr. Laverick," she cried softly. "I tried so hard to stop you. It was not I who sent that message."

He took her cold little fingers and raised them to his lips.

"I know it, dear," he murmured.

Then a movement in the room warned him, and he was suddenly on guard. Lassen was close to his side, some evil purpose plainly enough written in his pasty face and unwholesome eyes. Laverick gave him his left shoulder and sent him staggering across the floor. He was angry at having been outwitted and his eyes gleamed ominously.

"Well, gentlemen," he exclaimed, "you seem to have taken unusual pains to secure my presence here! Tell me now, what can I do for you?"

It was Streuss who became spokesman. He addressed Laverick with the consideration of one gentleman addressing another. His voice had many agreeable qualities. His demeanor was entirely amicable.

"Mr. Laverick," he answered, "let us first apologize if we used a little subterfuge to procure for us the pleasure of your visit. We are men who are in earnest, and across whose path you have either wilfully or accidentally strayed. An understanding between us has become a necessity."

"Go on," Laverick interrupted. "Tell me exactly who you are and what you want."

"As to who we are," Streuss answered, "does that really matter? I repeat that we are men who are in earnest — let that be enough. As to what we want, it is a certain document to which we have every claim, and which has come into your possession — I flatter you somewhat, Mr. Laverick, if I say by chance."

Laverick shrugged his shoulders.

"Let that go," he said. "I know all about the document you refer to, and the notes. They were contained

in a pocket-book which it is perfectly true has come into
my possession. Prove your claim to both and you shall
have them."

Streuss smiled.

"You will admit that our claim, since we know of its
existence," he asked suavely, "is equal to yours?"

"Certainly," Laverick answered, "but then I never
had any idea of keeping either the document or the
money. That your claim is better than mine is no guarantee that there is not some one else whose title is better
still."

Streuss frowned.

"Be reasonable, Mr. Laverick," he begged. "We are
men of peace — when peace is possible. The money
of which you spoke you can consider as treasure trove,
if you will, but it is our intention to possess ourselves of
the document. It is for that reason that we are here in
London. I, personally, am committed to the extent of
my life and my honor to its recovery."

A declaration of war, courteously veiled but decisive.
Laverick looked around him a little defiantly, and shrugged
his shoulders.

"You know very well that I do not carry it about with
me," he said. "The gentleman on my left," he added,
pointing to Kahn, "can tell you where it is kept."

"Quite so," Streuss admitted. "We are not doing you
the injustice to suppose that you would be so foolhardy
as to trust yourself anywhere with that document upon
your person. It is in the safe at the Milan Hotel. I may
add that probably, if it had not occurred to you to change
your quarters, it would have been in our possession before now. We are hoping to persuade you to return to
the hotel with one of our friends here, and procure it."

"As it happens," Laverick remarked, "that is impossible. The man who set the combination for that particular safe has gone off duty, and will not be back again at the hotel till to-morrow morning."

"But he is to be found," Streuss answered easily. "His present whereabouts and his address are known to us. He lives with his family at Harvard Court, Hampstead. We shall assist you in making it worth his while to return to the hotel or to give you the combination word for the safe."

"You are rather great on detail!" Laverick exclaimed.

"It is our business. The question for you to decide, and to decide immediately, is whether you are ready to end this, in some respects, constrained situation, and give your word to place that document in our hands."

"You are ready to accept my word, then?" Laverick asked.

"We have a certain hold upon you," Streuss continued slowly. "Your partner Mr. Morrison's position in connection with the murder in Crooked Friars' Alley is, as you may have surmised, a somewhat unfortunate one. Your own I will not allude to. I will simply suggest that for both your sakes publicity — any measure of publicity, in fact, as regards this little affair — would not be desirable."

Laverick hesitated. He understood all that was implied. Morrison's eyes were fixed upon him — the eyes of a craven coward. He felt the intensity of the moment. Then Zoe turned suddenly towards him.

"You are not to give it up!" she cried, with trembling lips. "They cannot hurt you, and it is not true — about Arthur."

Kahn, who was nearest, clapped his hand over her

mouth and Laverick knocked him down. Instantly the
pacific atmosphere of the room was changed. Lassen
and Morrison closed swiftly upon Laverick from different
sides. Streuss covered him with the shining barrel of a
revolver.

"Mr. Laverick," he said, "we are not here to be trifled
with. Keep your sister quiet, Morrison, or, by God,
you'll swing!"

Laverick looked at the revolver — fascinated, for an
instant, by its unexpected appearance. The face of the
man who held it had changed. There was lightning playing about the room.

"It's the dock for you both!" Streuss exclaimed
fiercely, — "for you, Laverick, and you, Morrison, too,
if you play with us any longer! One of you's a murderer and the other receives the booty. Who are you
to have scruples — criminals, both of you? Your place is
in the dock, and you shall be there within twenty-four
hours if there are any more evasions. Now, Laverick,
will you fetch that document? It is your last chance."

Upon the breathless silence that followed a quiet voice
intervened — a voice calm and emotionless, tinged with
a measure of polite inquiry. Yet its level utterance fell
like a bomb among the little company. The curtain
separating this from the inner room had been drawn a
few feet back, and Bellamy was standing there, in black
overcoat and white muffler, his silk hat on the back of
his head, his left hand, carefully gloved, resting still upon
the curtain which he had drawn aside.

"I hope I am not disturbing you at all?" he murmured softly.

For a moment the development of the situation remained uncertain. The gleaming barrel of Streuss's

revolver changed its destination. Bellamy glanced at it with the pleased curiosity of a child.

"I really ought not to have intruded," he continued amiably. "I happened to hear the address my friend Laverick gave to the taxicab driver, and I was particularly anxious to have a word or two with him before I left for the Continent."

Streuss was surely something of a charlatan! His revolver had disappeared. The smile upon his lips was both gracious and unembarrassed.

"One is always only too pleased to welcome Mr. Bellamy anywhere — anyhow," he declared. "If apologies are needed at all," he continued, "it is to our friend and host — Mr. Morrison here. Permit me — Mr. Arthur Morrison — the Honorable David Bellamy! These are Mr. Morrison's rooms."

Morrison could do no more than stare. Bellamy, on the contrary, with a little bow came further into the apartment, removing his hat from his head. Lassen glided round behind him, remaining between Bellamy and the heavy curtains. Adolf Kahn moved as though unconsciously in front of the door of the room in which they were.

Bellamy smiled courteously.

"I am afraid," he said, "that I must not stay for more than a moment. I have a car full of friends below — we are on our way, in fact, to the Covent Garden Ball — and one or two of them, I fear," he added indulgently, "have already reached that stage of exhilaration which such an entertainment in England seems to demand. They will certainly come and rout me out if I am here much longer. There!" he exclaimed, "you hear that?"

There was the sound of a motor horn from the street

below. Streuss, with an oath trembling upon his lips, lifted the blind. There were two motor-cars waiting there — large cars with Limousine bodies, and apparently full of men. After all, it was to be expected. Bellamy was no fool!

"Since we are to lose you, then Mr. Laverick," Streuss remarked with a gesture of farewell, "let us say good night. The little matter of business which we were discussing can be concluded with your partner."

Laverick turned toward Zoe. Their eyes met and he read their message of terror.

"You are coming back to your own rooms, Miss Leneveu," he said. "You must let me offer you my escort."

She half rose, but in obedience to a gesture from Streuss Morrison moved near to them.

"If you leave me here, Laverick," he muttered beneath his breath, — "if you leave me to these hounds, do you know what they will do? They will hand me over to the police — they have sworn it!"

"Why did you come back?" Laverick asked quickly.

"They stopped me as I was boarding the steamer," Morrison declared. "I tell you they have eyes everywhere. You cannot move without their knowledge. I had to come. Now that I am here they have told me plainly the price of my freedom. It is that document. Laverick, it is my life! You must give in — you must, indeed! Remember you're in it, too."

"Am I?" Laverick asked quietly.

"You fool, of course you are!" Morrison whispered hoarsely. "Didn't you come into the entry and take the pocket-book? Heaven knows what possessed you to do it! Heaven knows how you found the pluck to use the money!

But you did it, and you are a criminal — a criminal as I am. Don't be a fool, Laverick. Make terms with these people. They want the document — the document — nothing but the document! They will let us keep the money."

"And you?" Laverick asked, turning suddenly to Zoe. "What do you say about all this?"

She looked at him fearlessly.

"I trust you," she said. "I trust you to do what is right."

CHAPTER XXXIII

"At last, David!"

Louise welcomed her visitor eagerly with outstretched hands, which Bellamy raised for a moment to his lips. Then she turned toward the third person, who had also risen at the opening of the door — a short, somewhat thick-set man, with swarthy complexion, close-cropped black hair, and upturned black moustache.

"You remember Prince Rosmaran?" she said to Bellamy. "He left Servia only the day before yesterday. He has come to England on a special mission to the King."

Bellamy shook hands.

"I think," he remarked, "I had the honor of meeting you once before, Prince, at the opening of the Servian Parliament two years ago. It was just then, I believe, that you were elected to lead the patriotic party."

The Prince bowed sadly.

"My leadership, I fear," he declared, "has brought little good to my unhappy country."

"It is a terrible crisis through which your nation is passing," Bel'amy reminded him sympathetically. "At the same time, we must not despair. Austria holds out her clenched hands, but as yet she has not dared to strike."

The face of the Prince was dark with passion.

"As yet, no!" he answered. "But how long — how long, I wonder — before the blow falls? We in Servia

have been blamed for arming ourselves, but I tell you
that to-day the Austrian troops are being secretly concentrated on the frontier. Their arsenals are working night
and day. Her soldiers are manœuvering almost within
sight of Belgrade. We have hoped against hope, yet in
our hearts we know that our fate was sealed when the
Czar of Russia left Vienna last week."

"Nothing is certain," Bellamy declared restlessly.
"England has been ill-governed for a great many years,
but we are not yet a negligible Power."

Louise leaned a little towards him.

"David," she whispered, "the compact!"

He answered her unspoken question.

"It is arranged," he said, — "finished. To-morrow
morning at nine o'clock I receive it."

"You are sure?" she begged. "Why need there be any
delay?"

"It is locked up in a powerful safe," he explained, "and
the clerk who has the combination will not be on duty
again till nine. Laverick is there simply waiting for the
hour. You were right, Louise, as usual. I should have
trusted him from the first."

The Prince had been listening to their conversation
with undisguised interest.

"There is a rumor," he said, "that some secret information concerning the compact of Vienna has found its
way to this country."

Bellamy smiled.

"Hence, I presume, your mission, Prince."

"We three have no secrets from one another," the
Prince declared. "Our interests in this matter are absolutely identical. What you suggest, Mr. Bellamy, is the
truth. There is a rumor that the Chancellor, in the first

few moments of his illness, gave valuable information to
some one who is likely to have communicated it to the
Government here. To be forewarned is to be forearmed.
That, I know, is one of your own mottoes. So I am here
to know if there is anything to be learned."

Bellamy nodded.

"Your arrival is not inopportune, Prince. When did
you come?"

"I reached Charing Cross at midnight," the Prince
answered. "Our train was an hour late. I am presenting my credentials early this morning, and I am hoping
for an interview during the afternoon."

Bellamy considered for a moment.

"It is true!" he said. "Between us three there is
indeed no need for secrecy. The information you speak
of will be in our hands within a few hours. I have no
doubt whatever but that your Minister will share in it."

"You know of what it consists?" the Prince inquired
curiously.

"I think so," Bellamy answered, glancing at the clock.
"For my own part, although the information itself is in-
valuable, I see another and a profounder source of interest in that document. If, indeed, it is what we believe it
to be, it amounts to a *casus belli*."

"You mean that you would provoke war?" Prince
Rosmaran asked.

Bellamy shrugged his shoulders.

"I," said he, — "I am not even a politician. But, you
know, the lookers-on see a good deal of the game, and in
my opinion there is only one course open for this country,
— to work upon Russia so that she withdraws from any
compact she may have entered into with Austria and
Germany, to accept Germany's co-operation with Austria

in the despoilment of your country as a *casus belli*, and to declare war at once while our fleet is invincible and our Colonies free from danger."

The Prince nodded.

"It is good," he admitted, "to hear man's talk once more. Wherever one moves, people bow the head before the might of Germany and Austria. Let them alone but a little longer, and they will indeed rule Europe."

Three o'clock struck. The Prince rose.

"I go," he announced.

"And I," Bellamy declared. "Come to my rooms at ten o'clock to-morrow morning, Prince, and you shall hear the news."

Bellamy lingered behind. For a moment he held Louise in his arms and gazed sorrowfully into her weary face.

"Is it worth while, I wonder?" he asked bitterly.

"Worth while," she answered, opening her eyes and looking at him, "to feel the mother love? Who can help it who would not be ignoble?"

"But yours, dear," he murmured, "is all grief. Even now I am afraid."

"We can do no more than toil to the end," she said. "David, you are sure this time?"

"I am sure," he replied. "I am going back now to the hotel where Laverick is staying. We are going to sit together and smoke until the morning. Nothing short of an army could storm the hotel. I was with them all only an hour ago, — Streuss, that blackguard Lassen, and Adolf Kahn, the police spy. They are beaten men and they know it. They had Laverick, had him by a trick, but I made a dramatic entrance and the game was up."

"Telephone me directly you have taken it safely to Downing Street," she begged.

"I will," he promised.

Bellamy walked from Dover Street to the Strand. The streets were almost brilliant with the cold, hard moonlight. The air seemed curiously keen. Once or twice the fall of his feet upon the pavement was so clear and distinct that he fancied he was being followed and glanced sharply around. He reached the Milan Hotel, however, without adventure, and looked towards the little open space in the hall where he had expected to find Laverick. There was no one there! He stood still for a moment, troubled with a sudden sense of apprehension. The place was deserted except for a couple of sleepy-looking clerks and a small army of cleaners busy with their machines down in the restaurant, moving about like mysterious figures in the dim light.

Bellamy turned back to the hall-porter who had admitted him.

"Do you happen to know what has become of the gentleman whom I was with about an hour ago?" he asked, — "a tall, fair gentleman — Mr. Laverick his name was?"

The hall-porter recognized Bellamy and touched his hat.

"Why, yes, sir!" he answered with a somewhat mysterious air. "Mr. Laverick was sitting over there in an easy-chair until about half-an-hour ago. Then two gentlemen arrived in a taxicab and inquired for him. They talked for a little time, and finally Mr. Laverick went away with them."

Bellamy was puzzled.

"Went away with them?" he repeated. "I don't

understand that, Reynolds. He was to have waited here till I returned."

The man hesitated.

"It did n't strike me, sir," he said, "that Mr. Laverick was very wishful to go. It seemed as though he had n't much choice about the matter."

Bellamy looked at him keenly.

"Tell me what is in your mind?" he asked.

"Mr. Bellamy, sir," the hall-porter replied, "I knew one of those gentlemen by sight. He was a detective from Scotland Yard, and the one who was with him was a policeman in plain clothes."

"Good God!" Bellamy exclaimed. "You think, then, — "

"I am afraid there was no doubt about it, sir," the man answered. "Mr. Laverick was arrested on some charge or another."

CHAPTER XXXIV

INTO New Oxford Street, one of the ceaseless streams of polyglot humanity, came Zoe from her cheerless day bound for the theatre. She was a little whiter, a little more tired than usual. All day long she had heard nothing of Laverick. All day long she had sat in her tiny room with the memory of that horrible night before her. She had tried in vain to sleep, — she had made no effort whatever to eat. She knew now why Arthur Morrison had fled away. She knew the cause of that paroxysm of fear in which he had sought her out. The horror of the whole thing had crept into her blood like poison. Life was once more a dreary, profitless struggle. All the wonderful dreams, which had made existence seem almost like a fairy-tale for this last week, had faded away. She was once more a mournful little waif among the pitiless crowds.

She turned to the left and past the Holborn Tube. Boys were shouting everywhere the contents of the evening papers. Nearly every one seemed to be carrying one of the pink sheets. She herself passed on with unseeing eyes. News was nothing to her. Governments might rise and fall, war might come and go, — she had still life to support, a friendless little life, too, on two pounds fifteen shillings a week. The news they shouted fell upon deaf ears, but one boy unfurled almost before her eyes the headlines of his sheet.

SENSATIONAL ARREST OF A WELL–KNOWN STOCKBROKER. CHARGE OF MURDER.

She came to a sudden stop and pulled out her purse. Her
fingers trembled so that the penny fell on to the pavement. The boy picked it up willingly enough, however,
and she passed on with the paper in her hand. There it
was on the front page — staring her in the face:

> Early yesterday morning Mr. Stephen Laverick,
> of the firm of Laverick & Morrison, Stockbrokers,
> Old Broad Street, was arrested at the Milan Hotel
> on the charge of being concerned in the murder of a
> person unknown, in Crooked Friars' Alley, on Mon-
> day last. The accused, who made no reply to the
> charge, was removed to Bow Street Police-Station.
> Particulars of his examination before the magis-
> trates will be found on page 4.

There was a dull singing in her ears. An electric tram,
coming up from the underground passage, seemed to
bring with it some sort of thunder from an unknown world.
She staggered on, unseeing, gasping for breath. If she
could find somewhere to sit down! If she could only
rest for a moment! Then a sudden wave of strength came
to her, the blood flowed once more in her veins — blood
that was hot with anger, that stained her cheeks with a
spot of red. It was the man she loved, this, being made
to suffer falsely. It was the fulfilment of their threat —
a deliberate plot against him. The murderer of Crooked
Friars' Alley — she knew who that was! — she knew!
Perhaps she might help!
She had not the slightest recollection of the remainder
of that walk, but she found herself presently sitting in a
quiet corner of the theatre with the paper spread out
before her. She read that Stephen Laverick had been
brought before Mr. Rawson, the magistrate of Bow Street

Police Court, on a warrant charging him with having been concerned with the murder of a person unknown, and that he had pleaded " Not Guilty ! " Her eyes glittered as she read that the first witness called was Mr. Arthur Morrison, late partner of the accused. She read his deposition — that he had left Laverick at their offices at eleven o'clock on the night in question, that they were at that time absolutely without means, and had no prospect of meeting their engagements on the morrow. She read the evidence of Mr. Fenwick, bank manager, to the effect that Mr. Laverick had, on the following morning, deposited with him the sum of twenty thousand pounds in Bank of England notes, by means of which the engagements of the firm were duly met, that those notes had since been redeemed, and that he had no idea of their present whereabouts. She read, too, the evidence of Adolf Kahn, an Austrian visiting this country upon private business, who deposed that he was in the vicinity just before midnight, that he saw a person, whom he identified as the accused, walking down the street and, after disappearing for a few minutes down the entry, return and re-enter the offices from which he had issued. He explained his presence there by the fact that he was waiting for a clerk employed by the Goldfields' Corporation, Limited, whose offices were close by. Further formal evidence was given, and a remand asked for. The accused's solicitor was on the point of addressing the court when Mr. Rawson was unfortunately taken ill. After waiting for some time, the case was adjourned until the next day, and the accused man was removed in custody.

Zoe laid down the paper and rose to her feet. She made her way to where the stage-manager was superintending the erection of some new scenery.

"Mr. Heepman," she exclaimed, "I cannot stay to rehearsal! I have to go out."

He turned heavily round and looked at her.

"Rehearsal postponed," he declared solemnly. "Shall you be back for the evening performance, or shall we close the theatre?"

His clumsy irony missed its mark. Her thoughts were too intensely focussed upon one thing.

"I am sorry," she replied, turning away. "I will come back as soon as I can."

He called out after her and she paused.

"Look here," he said, "you were absent from the performance the other evening, and now you are skipping rehearsal without even waiting for permission. It can't be done, young lady. You must do your playing around some other time. If you're not here when you're called, you needn't trouble to turn up again. Do you understand?"

Her lips quivered and the sense of impending disaster which seemed to be brooding over her life became almost overwhelming.

"I'll come back as soon as I can," she promised, with a little break in her voice, — "as soon as ever I can, Mr. Heepman."

She hurried out of the theatre and took her place once more among the hurrying throng of pedestrians. Several people turned round to look at her. Her white face, tight-drawn mouth, and eyes almost unnaturally large, seemed to have become the abiding-place for tragedy. She herself saw no one. She would have taken a cab, but a glimpse at the contents of her purse dissuaded her. She walked steadily on to Jermyn Street, walked up the stairs to the third floor, and knocked at her brother's door. No one answered her at first. She turned the handle and entered to find the room empty. There were sounds, however, in the further apartment, and she called out to him.

"Arthur," she cried, "are you there?"

"Who is it?" he demanded.

"It is I — Zoe!" she exclaimed.

"What do you want?"

"I want to speak to you, Arthur. I must speak to you. Please come as quickly as you can."

He growled something and in a few moments he appeared. He was wearing the morning clothes in which he had attended court earlier in the day, but the change in him was perhaps all the more marked by reason of this resumption of his old attire. His cheeks were hollow, his eyes scarcely for an instant seemed to lose that feverish gleam of terror with which he had returned from Liverpool. He knew very well what she had come about, and he began nervously to try and bully her.

"I wish you would n't come to these rooms, Zoe," he said. "I've told you before they're bachelors' apartments, and they don't like women about the place. What is it? What do you want?"

"I was brought here last time without any particular desire on my part," she answered, looking him in the face. "I've come now to ask you what accursed plot this is against Stephen Laverick? What were you doing in the court this morning, lying? What is the meaning of it, Arthur?"

"If you've come to talk rubbish like that," he declared roughly, "you'd better be off."

"No, it is not rubbish!" she went on fearlessly. "I think I can understand what it is that has happened. They have terrified you and bribed you until you are willing to do any despicable thing — even this. Your father was good to my mother, Arthur, and I have tried to feel towards you as though you were indeed a relation. But nothing of that counts. I want you to realize that I know the truth, and that I will not see an innocent man convicted while the guilty go free."

He moved a step towards her. They were on opposite sides of the small round table which stood in the centre of the apartment.

"What do you mean?" he demanded hoarsely.

"Isn't it plain enough?" she exclaimed. "You came to my rooms a week or so ago, a terrified, broken-down man. If ever there was guilt in a man's face, it was in yours. You sent for Laverick. He pitied you and helped you away. At Liverpool they would not let you embark — these men. They have brought you back here. You are their tool. But you know very well, Arthur, that it was not Stephen Laverick who killed the man in Crooked Friars' Alley! You know very well that it was not Stephen Laverick!"

"Why the devil should I know anything about it?" he asked fiercely.

A note of passion suddenly crept into her voice. Her little white hand, with its accusing forefinger, shot out towards him.

"Because it was you, Arthur Morrison, who committed that crime," she cried, "and sooner than another man should suffer for it, I shall go to court myself and tell the truth."

He was, for the moment, absolutely speechless, pale as death, with nervously twitching lips and fingers. But there was murder in his eyes.

"What do you know about this?" he muttered.

"Never mind," she answered. "I know and I guess quite enough to convince me — and I think anybody else — that you are the guilty man. I would have helped you and shielded you, whatever it cost me, but I will not do so at Stephen Laverick's expense."

"What is Laverick to you?" he growled.

"He is nothing to me," she replied, "but the best of friends. Even were he less than that, do you suppose that I would let an innocent man suffer?"

He moistened his dry lips rapidly.

"You are talking nonsense, Zoe," he said, — "nonsense! Even if there has been some little mistake, what could I do now? I have given my evidence. So far as I am concerned, the case is finished. I shall not be called again until the trial."

"Then you had better go to the magistrates to-morrow morning and take back your evidence," she declared boldly, "for if you do not, I shall be there and I shall tell the truth."

"Zoe," he gasped, "don't try me too high. This thing has upset me. I'm ill. Can't you see it, Zoe? Look at me. I have n't slept for weeks. Night and day I've had the fear — the fear always with me. You don't know what it is — you can't imagine. It's like a terrible ghost, keeping pace with you wherever you go, laying his icy finger upon you whenever you would rest, mocking at you when you try to drown thought even for a moment. Don't you try me too far, Zoe. I'm not responsible. Laverick is n't the man you think him to be. He is n't the man I believed. He did have that money — he did, indeed."

"That," she said, "is to be explained. But he is not a murderer."

"Listen to me, Zoe," Morrison continued, leaning

across the table. "Come and stay with me for a time and we will go away for a week — somewhere to the seaside. We will talk about this and think it over. I want to get away from London. We will go to Brighton, if you like. I must do something for you, Zoe. I'm afraid I've neglected you a good deal. Perhaps I could get you a better part at one of the theatres. I must make you an allowance. You ought to be wearing better clothes."

She drew a little away.

"I want nothing from you, Arthur," she said, "except this — that you speak the truth."

He wiped his forehead and struck the table before her.

"But, good God, Zoe!" he exclaimed, "do you know what it is that you are asking me? Do you want me to go into court and say —'That is n't the man. It is I who am the murderer'? Do you want me to feel their hands upon my shoulder, to be put there in the dock and have all the people staring at me curiously because they know that before very long I am to stand upon the scaffold and have that rope around my neck and —"

He broke off with a low cry, wringing his hands like a child in a fit of impotent terror. But the girl in front of him never flinched.

"Arthur," she said, "crime is a terrible thing, but nothing in the world can alter its punishment. If it is frightful for you to think of this, what must it be for him? And you are guilty and he is not."

"I was mad!" Morrison went on, now almost beside himself. "Zoe, I was mad! I called there to have a drink. We were broke, — the firm was broke. I'd a hundred or so in my pocket and I was going to bolt the next day. And there, within a few yards of me, was that man, with such a roll of notes as I had never seen in my life. Five hundred pounds, every one of them, and a wad as thick as my fist. Zoe, they fascinated me. I had two drinks quickly and I followed him out. Somehow or other, I found that I'd caught up a knife that was on the counter. I never meant to hurt him seriously, but I wanted some of those notes! I was leaving the next day for Africa and I had n't enough money to make a fair start. I wanted it — my God, how I wanted money!"

"It could n't have been worth — that!" she cried, looking at him wonderingly.

"I was mad," he continued. "I saw the notes and they went to my head. Men do wild things sometimes when they are drunk, or for love. I don't drink much, and I'm not over fond of women, but, my God, money is like the blood of my body to me! I saw it, and I wanted it and I wanted it, and I went mad! Zoe, you won't give me away? Say you won't!"

"But what am I to do?" she protested. "He must not suffer."

"He'll get off," Morrison assured her thickly. "I tell you he'll get off. He's only to part with the document, which never belonged to him, and the charge will be withdrawn. They know who the murdered man was. They know where the money came from which he was carrying. I tell you he can save himself. You would n't dream of sending me to the gallows, Zoe!"

"Stephen Laverick will never give up that document to those people," she declared. "I am sure of that."

"It's his own lookout," Morrison muttered. "He has the chance, anyway."

She turned toward the door.

"I must go away," she said. "I must go away and think. It is all too horrible."

He came round the table swiftly and caught at her wrists.

"Listen," he said, "I can't let you go like this. You must tell me that you are not going to give me up. Do you hear?"

"I can make no promises, Arthur," she answered sadly, "only this — I shall not let Stephen Laverick suffer in your stead."

He opened his hand and she shrank back, terrified, when she saw what it was that he was holding. Then he struck her down and without a backward glance fled out of the place.

CHAPTER XXXV

LATE that afternoon the hall-porter at the Milan Hotel, the *commissionaire*, and the chief *maître d'hôtel* from the Café, who happened to be in the hall, together with several others around the place who knew Stephen Laverick by sight, were treated to an unexpected surprise. A large closed motor-car drove up to the front entrance and several men descended, among whom was Laverick himself. He nodded to the hall-porter, whose salute was purely mechanical, and making his way without hesitation to the interior of the hotel, presented his receipt at the cashier's desk and asked for his packet. The clerk looked up at him in amazement. He did not, for the moment, notice that the two men standing immediately behind bore the stamp of plain-clothes policemen. He had only a few minutes ago finished reading the report of Laverick's examination before the magistrates and his remand until the morrow, upon the charge of murder. His knowledge of English law was by no means perfect, but he was at least aware that Laverick's appearance outside the purlieus of the prison was an unusual happening.

"Your packet, sir!" he repeated, in amazement. "Why, this is Mr. Laverick himself, is it not?"

"Certainly," was the quiet reply. "I am Stephen Laverick."

The clerk called the head cashier, who also stared at

Laverick as though he were a ghost. They whispered
together in the background for a moment, and their
faces were a study in perplexity. Of Laverick's identity,
however, there was no manner of doubt. Besides, the
presence of what was obviously a very ample escort
somewhat reassured them. The cashier himself came
forward.

"We shall be exceedingly glad, Mr. Laverick," he
said dryly, "to get rid of your packet. Your instructions
were that we should disregard all orders to hand it over
to any person whatsoever, and I may say that they have
been strictly adhered to. We have, however, had two
applications in your name this morning."

"They were both forgeries," Laverick declared.

The cashier hesitated. Then he leaned across the
broad mahogany counter towards Laverick. One of the
men who appeared to form part of the escort detached
himself from them and approached a few steps nearer.

"This gentleman is your friend, sir?" the cashier
asked, glancing towards him.

"He is my solicitor," Laverick answered, "and is entirely in my confidence. If you have anything to tell me,
I should like Mr. Bellamy also to hear."

Bellamy, who was standing a little in the background,
took his place by Laverick's side. The cashier, who
knew him by sight, bowed.

"Beside these two forged orders, sir," he said, turning
again to Laverick, "we have had a man who took a room
in the hotel leave a small black bag here, which he insisted upon having deposited in our document safe. My
assistant had accepted it and was actually locking it up
when he noticed a faint sound inside which he could not
understand. The bag was opened and found to contain

an infernal machine which would have exploded in a quarter of an hour."

Bellamy drew his breath sharply between his teeth.

"We should have thought of that!" he exclaimed softly. "That's Kahn's work!"

"I seem to have given you a great deal of trouble," Laverick remarked quietly. "I gather, however, from what you say, that my packet is still in your possession?"

"It is, sir," the man assented. "We have two detectives from Scotland Yard here at the present moment, though, and we had almost decided to place it in their charge for greater security."

"It will be well taken care of from now, I promise you," Laverick declared.

The cashier and his clerk led the way into the inner office. At their invitation Laverick and his solicitor followed, and a few yards behind came the two plain-clothes policemen, Bellamy, and the superintendent. The safe was opened and the packet placed in Laverick's hands. He passed it on at once to Bellamy, and immediately afterwards the doorway behind was thronged with men, apparently ordinary loiterers around the hotel. They made a slow and exceedingly cautious exit. Once outside, Bellamy turned to Laverick with outstretched hand.

"Au revoir and good luck, old chap!" he said heartily. "I think you'll find things go your way all right to-morrow morning."

He departed, forming one of a somewhat singular cavalcade — two of his friends on either side, two in front, and two behind. It had almost the appearance of a procession. The whole party stepped into a closed motor-car. Three or four men were lounging on the

pavement and there was some excited whispering, but no
one actually interfered. As soon as they had left the
courtyard, Laverick and his solicitor, with his own guard,
re-entered the motor-car in which they had arrived, and
drove back to Bow Street. Very few words were exchanged during the short journey. His solicitor, however,
bade him good-night cheerfully, and Laverick's bearing
was by no means the bearing of a man in despair.

In Downing Street, within the next half-an-hour, a
somewhat remarkable little gathering took place. The
two men chiefly responsible for the destinies of the nation
— the Prime Minister and the Secretary of State for
Foreign Affairs — sat side by side before a small table.
Facing them was Bellamy, and spread out in front were
those few pages of foolscap, released from their envelope
a few minutes ago for the first time since the hand of
the great Chancellor himself had pressed down the seal.
The Foreign Minister had just finished a translation for
the benefit of his colleague, and the two men were silent,
as men are in the presence of big events.

"Bellamy," the Prime Minister said slowly, "you are
willing to stake, I presume, your reputation upon the
authenticity of this document?"

"My honor and my life, if you will," Bellamy answered
earnestly. "That is no copy which you have there. On
the contrary, the handwriting is the handwriting of the
Chancellor himself."

The Prime Minister turned silently towards his colleague. The latter, whose eyes still seemed glued to those
fateful words, looked up.

"All I can say is this," he remarked impressively,
"that never in my time have I seen written words pos-

sessed of so much significance. One moment, if you please."

He touched the bell, and his private secretary entered at once from an adjoining room.

"Anthony," he said, "telephone to the Great Western Railway Company at Paddington. Ask for the station-master in my name, and see that a special train is held ready to depart for Windsor in half-an-hour. Tell the station-master that all ordinary traffic must be held up, but that the destination of the special is not to be divulged."

The young man bowed and withdrew.

"The more I consider this matter," the Foreign Minister went on, "the more miraculous does the appearance of this document seem. We know now why the Czar is struggling so frantically to curtail his visit — why he came, as it were, under protest, and seeks everywhere for an opportunity to leave before the appointed time. His health is all right. He has had a hint from Vienna that there has been a leakage. His special mission only reached Paris this morning. The President is in the country and their audience is not fixed until to-morrow. Rawson will go over with a copy of these papers and a dispatch from His Majesty by the nine o'clock train. It is not often that we have had the chance of such a 'coup' as this."

He drew his chief a few steps away. They whispered together for several moments. When they returned, the Foreign Minister rang the bell again for his secretary.

"Anthony," he said, "Sir James and I will be leaving in a few minutes for Windsor. Go round yourself to General Hamilton, telephone to Aldershot for Lord Neville, and call round at the Admiralty Board for Sir John Harrison. Tell them all to be here at ten o'clock to-night. If I am not back, they must wait. If either of them have royal commands, you need only repeat the word 'Finisterre.' They will understand."

The young man once more withdrew. The Prime Minister turned back to the papers.

"It will be worth a great deal," he remarked, with a grim smile, "to see His Majesty's face when he reads this."

"It would be worth a great deal more," his fellow statesman answered dryly, "to be with his august cousin at the interview which will follow. A month ago, the thought that war might come under our administration was a continual terror to me. To-day things are entirely different. To-day it really seems that if war does come, it may be the most glorious happening for England of this century. You saw the last report from Kiel?"

Sir James nodded.

"There is n't a battleship or a cruiser worth a snap of the fingers south of the German Ocean," his colleague continued earnestly. "They are cooped up — safe enough, they think — under the shelter of their fortifications. Hamilton has another idea. Between you and me, Sir James, so have I. I tell you," he went on, in a deeper and more passionate tone, "it's like the passing of a terrible nightmare — this. We have had ten years of panic, of nervous fears of a German invasion, and no one knows more than you and I, Sir James, how much cause we have had for those fears. It will seem strange if, after all, history has to write that chapter differently."

The secretary re-entered and announced the result of his telephone interview with the superintendent at Paddington. The two great men rose. The Prime Minister held out his hand to Bellamy.

"Bellamy," he declared, "you've done us one more

important service. There may be work for you within
the next few weeks, but you've earned a rest for a day or
two, at any rate. There is nothing more we can do?"

"Nothing except a letter to the Home Secretary, Sir
James," Bellamy answered. "Remember, sir, that although I have worked hard, the man to whom we really
owe those papers is Stephen Laverick."

The Prime Minister frowned thoughtfully.

"It's a difficult situation, Bellamy," he said. "You
are asking a great deal when you suggest that we should
interfere in the slightest manner with the course of justice. You are absolutely convinced, I suppose, that this
man Laverick had nothing to do with the murder?"

"Absolutely and entirely, sir," Bellamy replied.

"The murdered man has never been identified by the
police," Sir James remarked. "Who was he?"

"His name was Rudolph Von Behrling," Bellamy announced, "and he was actually the Chancellor's nephew,
also his private secretary. I have told you the history,
sir, of those papers. It was Von Behrling who, without a
doubt, murdered the American journalist and secured
them. It was he who insisted upon coming to London
instead of returning with them to Vienna, which would have
been the most obvious course for him to have adopted. He
was a pauper, and desperately in love with a certain lady
who has helped me throughout this matter. He agreed
to part with the papers for twenty thousand pounds, and
the lady incidentally promised to elope with him the same
night. I met him by appointment at that little restaurant
in the city, paid him the twenty thousand pounds, and
received the false packet which you remember I brought
to you, sir. As a matter of fact, Von Behrling, either by
accident or design, and no man now will ever know which,

left me with those papers which I was supposed to have bought in his possession, and also the money. Within five minutes he was murdered. Doubtless we shall know sometime by whom, but it was not by Stephen Laverick. Laverick's share in the whole thing was nothing but this — that he found the pocket-book, and that he made use of the notes in his business for twenty-four hours to save himself from ruin. That was unjustifiable, of course. He has made atonement. The notes at this minute are in a safe deposit vault and will be returned intact to the fund from which they came. I want, also, to impress upon you, Sir James, the fact that Baron de Streuss offered one hundred thousand pounds for that letter."

Sir James nodded thoughtfully. He stooped down and scrawled a few lines on half a sheet of note-paper.

"You must take this to Lord Estcourt at once," he said, "and tell him the whole affair, omitting all specific information as to the nature of the papers. The thing must be arranged, of course."

Half-a-dozen reporters, who had somehow got hold of the fact that the Prime Minister and his colleague from the Foreign Office were going down to Windsor on a special mission, followed them, but even they remained altogether in the dark as to the events which were really transpiring. They knew nothing of the interview between the Czar and his august host — an interview which in itself was a chapter in the history of these times. They knew nothing of the reason of their royal visitor's decision to prolong his visit instead of shortening it, or of his autograph letter to the President of the French Republic, which reached Paris even before the special mission from St. Petersburg had presented themselves. The one thing which they did know, and that alone was significant enough, was that the Czar's Foreign Minister was cabled for that night to come to his master by special train from St. Petersburg. At the Austrian and German Embassies, forewarned by a report from Baron de Streuss, something like consternation reigned. The Russian Ambassador, heckled to death, took refuge at Windsor under pretence of a command from his royal master. The happiest man in London was Prince Rosmaran.

CHAPTER XXXVI

LAVERICK ACQUITTED

At mid-day on the following morning Laverick stepped down from the dock at Bow Street and, as the evening papers put it, " in company with his friends left the court." The proceedings altogether took scarcely more than half-an-hour. Laverick's solicitor first put Shepherd in the box, who gave his account of Morrison's visit to the restaurant, spoke of his hurried exit, and identified the knife which he had seen him snatch up. Cross-examined as to why he had kept silent, he explained that Mr. Morrison had been a good customer and he saw no reason why he should give unsolicited evidence which would cost a man his life. Directly, however, another man had been accused, the matter appeared to him to be altogether different. He had come forward the moment he had heard of Laverick's arrest, to offer his evidence.

While the opinion of the court was still undecided, Laverick's solicitor called Miss Zoe Leneveu. A little murmur of interest ran through the court. Laverick himself started. Zoe stepped into the witness-box, looking exceedingly pale, and with a bandage over the upper part of her head. She admitted that she was the half-sister of Arthur Morrison, although there was no blood relationship. She described his sudden visit to her rooms on the night of the murder, and his state of great alarm. She declared that he had confessed to her on the previous afternoon that he had been guilty of the murder in question.

Her place in the witness-box was taken by the Honorable

David Bellamy. He declared that the prisoner was an old friend of his, and that the twenty thousand pounds of which he had been recently possessed, had come from him for investment in Laverick's business. The circumstances, he admitted, were somewhat peculiar, and until negotiations had been concluded Mr. Laverick had doubtless felt uncertain how to make use of the money. But he assured the court that there was no person who had any claim to the sum of money in question save himself, and that he was perfectly aware of the use to which Laverick had put it.

Laverick was discharged within a very few minutes, and a warrant was issued for the apprehension of Morrison. Laverick found Bellamy waiting for him, and was hurried into his motor.

"Well, you see," the latter exclaimed, "we kept our word! That dear plucky little friend of yours turned the scale, but in any case I think that there would not have been much trouble about the matter. The magistrate had received a communication direct from the Home Secretary concerning your case."

"I am very grateful indeed," Laverick declared. "I tell you I think I am very lucky. I wish I knew what had become of Miss Leneveu. The usher told me she left the court before we came out."

"I asked her to go straight back to her rooms," Bellamy said. "You must excuse me for interfering, Laverick, but I found her almost in a state of collapse last night in Jermyn Street. I was having Morrison watched, and my man reported to me that he had left his rooms in a state of great excitement, and that a young lady was there who appeared to be seriously injured."

"D—d scamp!" Laverick muttered.

"I did everything I could," Bellamy continued. "I fetched her at once and sent her back to her house with a hospital nurse and some one to look after her. The wound was n't serious, but the fellow must have been a brute indeed to have lifted his hand against such a child. I wonder whether he 'll get away."

"I should doubt it," Laverick remarked. "He has n't the nerve. He 'll probably get drunk and blow his brains out. He 's a broken-spirited cur, after all."

"You 'll have some lunch?" Bellamy asked.

Laverick shook his head.

"If you don't mind, I 'd like to go on and see Miss Leneveu."

"Put me down at the club, then, and take my car on, if you will."

Laverick walked up and down the pavement outside Zoe's little house for nearly half-an-hour. He had found the door closed and locked, and a neighbor had informed him that Miss Leneveu had gone out in a cab with the nurse, some time ago, and had not returned. Laverick sent Bellamy's car back and waited. Presently a four-wheel cab came round the corner and stopped in front of her house. Laverick opened the door and helped Zoe out. She was as white as death, and the nurse who was with her was looking anxious.

"You are safe, then?" she murmured, holding out her hands.

"Quite," he answered. "You dear little girl!"

Zoe had fainted, however, and Laverick hurried out for the doctor. Curiously enough, it was the same man who only a week or so ago had come to see Arthur Morrison.

"She has had a bad scalp wound," he declared, "and her nervous system is very much run down. There is nothing serious. She seems to have just escaped concussion. The nurse had better stay with her for another day, at any rate."

"You are sure that it is n't serious?" Laverick asked eagerly.

"Not in the least," the doctor answered dryly. "I see worse wounds every day of my life. I'll come again to-morrow, if you like, but it really is n't necessary with the nurse on the spot."

His natural pessimism was for a moment lightened by the fee which Laverick pressed upon him, and he departed with a few more encouraging words. Laverick stayed and talked for a short time with the nurse.

"She has gone off to sleep now, sir," the latter announced. "There is n't anything to worry about. She seems as though she had been having a hard time, though. There was scarcely a thing in the house but half a packet of tea — and these."

She held up a packet of pawn tickets.

"I found these in a drawer when I came," she said. "I had to look round, because there was no money and nothing whatever in the house."

Laverick was suddenly conscious of an absurd mistiness before his eyes.

"Poor little woman!" he murmured. "I think she'd sooner have starved than ask for help."

The nurse smiled.

"I thought at first that she was rather a vain young lady," she remarked. "An empty larder and a pile of pawn tickets, and a new hat with a receipted bill for thirty shillings," she added, pointing to the sofa.

Laverick placed some notes in her hands.

"Please keep these," he begged, "and see that she has everything she wants. I shall be here again later in the day. There is not the slightest need for all this. She will be quite well off for the rest of her life. Will you try and engage some one for a day or two to come in until she is able to be moved?"

"I'll look after her," the nurse promised.

Laverick went reluctantly away. The events of the last few days were becoming more and more like a dream to him. He went to his club almost from habit. Presently the excitement which all London seemed to be sharing drove his own personal feelings a little into the background. The air was full of rumors. The Prime Minister and the Foreign Secretary were spoken of as one speaks of heroes. Nothing was definitely known, but there was a splendid feeling of confidence that for once in her history England was preparing to justify her existence as a great Power.

CHAPTER XXXVII

THE PLOT THAT FAILED

THE progress of the Czar from Buckingham Palace to the Mansion House, where he had, after all, consented to lunch with the Lord Mayor, witnessed a popular outburst of enthusiasm absolutely inexplicable to the general public. It was known that affairs in Central Europe were in a dangerously precarious state, and it was felt that the Czar's visit here, and the urgent summons which had brought from St. Petersburg his Foreign Minister, were indications that the long wished-for *entente* between Russia and this country was now actually at hand. There was in the Press a curious reticence with regard to the development of the political situation. One felt everywhere that it was the calm before the storm — that at any moment the great black headlines might tell of some startling stroke of diplomacy, some dangerous peril averted or defied. The circumstances themselves of the Czar's visit had been a little peculiar. On his arrival it was announced that, for reasons of health, the original period of his stay, namely a week, was to be cut down to two days. No sooner had he arrived at Windsor, however, than a change was announced. The Czar had so far recovered as to be able even to extend the period at first fixed for his visit. Simultaneously with this, the German and Austrian Press were full of bitter and barely veiled articles, whose meaning was unmistakable. The Czar had thrown in his lot at first with Austria and Germany. That he was going deliberately to break away from that arrangement there seemed now scarcely any manner of doubt.

Bellamy and Louise, from a window in Fleet Street, watched him go by. Prince Rosmaran had been specially bidden to the luncheon, but he, too, had been with them earlier in the morning. Afterwards they turned their backs upon the city, and as soon as the crowd had thinned made their way to one of the west-end restaurants.

"It seems too good to be true," declared Louise.

Bellamy nodded.

"Nevertheless I am convinced that it is true. The humor of the whole thing is that it was our friends in Germany themselves who pressed the Czar not to altogether cancel his visit for fear of exciting suspicion. That, of course, was when there seemed to be no question of the news of the Vienna compact leaking out. They would never have dared to expose a man to such a trial as the Czar must have faced when the résumé of the Vienna proceedings, in the Chancellor's own handwriting, was read to him at Windsor."

"You saw the telegram from Paris?" Louise interposed. "The special mission from St. Petersburg has been recalled."

Bellamy smiled.

"It all goes to prove what I say," he went on. "Any morning you may expect to hear that Austria and Germany have received an ultimatum."

"I wonder," she remarked, "what became of Streuss."

"He is hiding somewhere in London, without a doubt," Bellamy answered. "There's always plenty of work for spies."

"Don't use that word," she begged.

He made a little grimace.

"You are thinking of my own connection with the profession, are you not?" he asked. "Well, that counts for
nothing now. I hope I may still serve my country for
many years, but it must be in a different way."

"What do you mean?" she demanded.

"I heard from my uncle's solicitors this morning,"
Bellamy continued, "that he is very feeble and cannot
live more than a few months. When he dies, of course, I
must take my place in the House of Lords. It is his wish
that I should not leave England again now, so I suppose
there is nothing left for me but to give it up. I have done
my share of traveling and work, after all," he concluded,
thoughtfully.

"Your share, indeed," she murmured. "Remember
that but for that document which was read to the Czar
at Windsor, Servia must have gone down, and England
would have had to take a place among the second-class
Powers. There may be war now, it is true, but it will be
a glorious war."

"Louise, very soon we shall know. Until then I will
say nothing. But I do not want you altogether to forget
that there has been something in my life dearer to me
even than my career for these last few years."

Her blue eyes were suddenly soft. She looked across
towards him wistfully.

"Dear," she whispered, "things will be altered with
you now. I am not fit to be the wife of an English peer —
I am not noble."

He laughed.

"I am afraid," he assured her, "that I am democrat
enough to think you one of the noblest women on earth.
Why should I not? Your life itself has been a study in
devotion. The modern virtues seem almost to ignore

patriotism, yet the love of one's country is a splendid thing. But don't you think, Louise, that we have done our work — that it is time to think of ourselves?"

She gave him her hand.

"Let us see," she said. "Let us wait for a little time and see what comes."

That night another proof of the popular feeling, absolutely spontaneous, broke out in one of the least expected places. Louise was encored for her wonderful solo in a modern opera of bellicose trend, and instead of repeating it she came alone on the stage after a few minutes' absence, dressed in Servian national dress. For a short time the costume was not recognized. Then the music — the national hymn of Servia, and the recollection of her parentage, brought the thing home to the audience. They did not even wait for her to finish. In the middle of her song the applause broke like a crash of thunder. From the packed gallery to the stalls they cheered her wildly, madly. A dozen times she came before the curtain. It seemed impossible that they would ever let her go. Directly she turned to leave the stage, the uproar broke out again. The manager at last insisted upon it that she should speak a few words. She stood in the centre of the stage amid a silence as complete as the previous applause had been unanimous. Her voice reached easily to every place in the House.

"I thank you all very much," she said. "I am very happy indeed to be in London, because it is the capital city of the most generous country in the world — the country that is always ready to protect and help her weaker neighbors. I am a Servian, and I love my country, and therefore," she added, with a little break in her voice, — "therefore I love you all."

It was nearly midnight before the audience was got rid of, and the streets of London had not been so impassable for years. Crowds made their way to the front of Buckingham Palace and on to the War Office, where men were working late. Everything seemed to denote that the spirit of the country was roused. The papers next morning made immense capital of the incident, and for the following twenty-four hours suspense throughout the country was almost at fever height. It was known that the Cabinet Council had been sitting for six hours. It was known, too, that without the least commotion, with scarcely any movements of ships that could be called directly threatening, the greatest naval force which the world had ever known was assembling off Dover. The stock markets were wildly excited. Laverick, back again in his office, found that his return to his accustomed haunts occasioned scarcely any comment. More startling events were shaping themselves. His own remarkable adventure remained, curiously enough, almost undiscussed.

He left the office shortly before his usual time, notwithstanding the rush of business, and drove at once to the little house in Theobald Square. Zoe was lying on the sofa, still white, but eager to declare that the pain had gone and that she was no longer suffering.

"It is too absurd," she declared, smiling, "my having this nurse here. Really, there is nothing whatever the matter with me. I should have gone to the theatre, but you see it is no use."

She passed him the letter which she had been reading, and which contained her somewhat curt dismissal. He laughed as he tore it into pieces.

"Are you so sorry, Zoe? Is the stage so wonderful a place that you could not bear to think of leaving it?"

She shook her head.

"It is not that," she whispered. "You know that it is not that."

He smiled as he took her confidently into his arms.

"There is a much more arduous life in front of you, dear," he said. "You have to come and look after me for the rest of your days. A bachelor who marries as late in life as I do, you know, is a trying sort of person."

She shrank away a little.

"You don't mean it," she murmured.

"You know very well that I mean it," he answered, kissing her. "I think you knew from the very first that sooner or later you were doomed to become my wife."

She sighed faintly and half-closed her eyes. For the moment she had forgotten everything. She was absolutely and completely happy.

Later on he made her dress and come out to dinner, and afterwards, as they sat talking, he laid an evening paper before her.

"Zoe," he declared, "the best thing that could has happened. You will not be foolish, dear, about it, I know. Remember the alternative — and read that."

She glanced at the few lines which announced the finding of Arthur Morrison in a house in Bloomsbury Square. The police had apparently tracked him down, and he had shot himself at the final moment. The details of his last few hours were indescribable. Zoe shuddered, and her eyes filled with tears. She smiled bravely in his face, however.

"It is terrible," she whispered simply, "but, after all, he was no relation of mine, and he tried to do you a frightful injury. When I think of that, I find it hard even to be sorry."

There was indeed almost a pitiless look in her face as she folded up the paper, as though she felt something of that common instinct of her sex which transforms a gentle woman so quickly into a hard, merciless creature when the being whom she loves is threatened.

Laverick smiled.

"Let us go out into the streets," he said, "and hear what all this excitement is about."

They bought a late edition, and there it was at last in black and white. An ultimatum had been presented at Berlin and Vienna. Certain treaty rights which had been broken with regard to Austria's action in the East were insisted upon by Great Britain. It was demanded that Austria should cease the mobilization of her troops upon the Servian frontier, and renounce all rights to a protectorate over that country, whose independence Great Britain felt called upon, from that time forward, to guarantee. It was further announced that England, France, and Russia were acting in this matter in complete concert, and that the neutrality of Italy was assured. Further, it was known that the great English fleet had left for the North Sea with sealed orders.

Laverick took Zoe home early and called later at Bellamy's rooms. Bellamy greeted him heartily. He was on the point of going out, and the two men drove off together in the latter's car.

"See, my dear friend," Bellamy exclaimed, "what great things come from small means! The document which you preserved for us, and for which we had to fight so hard, has done all this."

"It is marvelous!" Laverick murmured.

"It is very simple," Bellamy declared. "That meeting in Vienna was meant to force our hands. It is all a

question of the balance of strength. Germany and Austria
together, with Russia friendly, — even with Russia neu-
tral, — could have defied Europe. Germany could have
spread out her army westwards while Austria seized upon
her prey. It was a splendid plot, and it was going very
well until the Czar himself was suddenly confronted by
our King and his Ministers with a revelation of the whole
affair. At Windsor the thing seemed different to him.
The French Government behaved splendidly, and the
Czar behaved like a man. Germany and Austria are
left *planté la.* If they fight, well, it will be no one-sided
affair. They have no fleet, or rather they will have none
in a fortnight's time. They have no means of landing
an army here. Austria, perhaps, can hold Russia, but
with a French army in better shape than it has been for
years, and the English landing as many men as they care
to do, with ease, anywhere on the north coast of Germany,
the entire scheme proved abortive. Come into the club
and have a drink, Laverick. To-day great things have
happened to me."

"And to me," Laverick interposed.

"You can guess my news, perhaps," Bellamy said,
as they seated themselves in easy-chairs. "Mademoiselle
Idiale has promised to be my wife."

Laverick held out his hand.

"I congratulate you heartily!" he exclaimed. "I have
been an engaged man myself for something like half-
an-hour."

CHAPTER XXXVIII

"ONE thing, at least, these recent adventures should teach whoever may be responsible for the government of this country," Bellamy remarked to his wife, as he laid down the morning paper. "For the first time in many years we have taken the aggressive against Powers of equal standing. We were always rather good at bullying smaller countries, but the bare idea of an ultimatum to Germany would have made our late Premier go light-headed."

"And yet it succeeded," Louise reminded him.

"Absolutely," he affirmed. "To-day's news makes peace a certainty. If your country knew everything, Louise, they'd give us a royal welcome next month."

"You really mean that we are to go there, then?" she asked.

"It isn't exactly one of my privileges," he declared, "to fix upon the spot where we shall take our belated honeymoon, but I haven't been in Belgrade for years, and I know you'd like to see your people."

"It will be more happiness than I ever dreamed of," she murmured. "Do you think we shall be safe in passing through Vienna?"

Bellamy laughed.

"Remember," he said, "that I am no longer David Bellamy, with a silver greyhound attached to my watch-chain and an obnoxious reputation in foreign countries.

I am Lord Denchester of Denchester, a harmless English peer traveling on his honeymoon. By the way, I hope you like the title."

"I shall love it when I get used to it," she declared. "To be an English Countess is dazzling, but I do think that I ought not to go on singing at Covent Garden."

"To-morrow will be your last night," he reminded her. "I have asked Laverick and the dear little girl he is going to marry to come with me. Afterwards we must all have supper together."

"How nice of you!" she exclaimed.

"I don't know about that," Bellamy said, smiling. "I really like Laverick. He is a decent fellow and a good sort. Incidentally, he was thundering useful to us, and pretty plucky about it. He interests me, too, in another way. He is a man who, face to face with a moral problem, acted exactly as I should have done myself!"

"You mean about the twenty thousand pounds?" she asked.

Bellamy assented.

"He was practically dishonest," he pointed out. "He had no right to use that money and he ought to have taken the pocket-book to the police-station. If he had done so — that is to say, if he had waited there for the police, if he had been seen to hold out that pocket-book, to have discussed it with any one, it is ten to one that there would have been another tragedy that night. At any rate, the document would never have come to us."

She smiled.

"My moral judgment is warped," she asserted, "from the fact that Laverick's decision brought us the document."

He nodded.

"Perhaps so," he agreed, "and yet, there was the man

face to face with ruin. The use of that money for a few hours did no one any harm, and saved him. I say that such a deed is always a matter of calculation, and in this case that he was justified."

"I wonder what he really thinks about it himself," she remarked.

"Perhaps I'll ask him."

But when the time came, and he sat in the box with Laverick and Zoe, he forgot everything else in the joy of watching the woman whom he had loved so long. She moved about the stage that night as though her feet indeed fell upon the air. She appeared to be singing always with restraint, yet with some new power in her voice, a quality which even in her simpler notes left the great audience thrilled. Already there was a rumor that it was her last appearance. Her marriage to Bellamy had been that day announced in the *Morning Post*. When, in the last act, she sang alone on the stage the famous love song, it seemed to them all that although her voice trembled more than once, it was a new thing to which they listened. Zoe found herself clasping Laverick's hand in tremulous excitement. Bellamy sat like a statue, a little back in the box, his clean-cut face thrown into powerful relief by the shadows beyond. Yet, as he listened, his eyes, too, were marvelously soft. The song grew and grew till, with the last notes, the whole story of an exquisite and expectant passion seemed trembling in her voice. The last note came from her lips almost as though unwillingly, and was prolonged for an extraordinary period. When it died away, its passing seemed something almost unrealizable. It quivered away into a silence which lasted for many seconds before the gathering roar of applause swept the house. And in those last few seconds she had turned and faced Bellamy. Their eyes met, and the light which flashed from his seemed answered by the quivering of her throat. It was her good-bye. She was singing a new love-song, singing her way into the life of the man whom she loved, singing her way into love itself. Once more the great house, packed to the ceiling, was worked up to a state of frenzied excitement. Bellamy was recognized, and the significance of her song sent a wave of sentiment through the house whose only possible form of expression took to itself shape in the frantic greetings which called her to the front again and again. But the three in the box were silent. Bellamy stood back in the shadows. Laverick and Zoe seemed suddenly to become immersed in themselves. Bellamy threw open the door of the box and pointed outside.

"At Luigi's in half-an-hour," said he softly. "You will excuse me for a few minutes? I am going to Louise."

THE END